Whispers

Saving Grace Series, Volume 2

Landon Prosser

Published by Landon Prosser, 2026.

While every precaution has been taken in the preparation of this book, the publisher assumes no responsibility for errors or omissions, or for damages resulting from the use of the information contained herein.

WHISPERS

First edition. January 26, 2026.

Copyright © 2026 Landon Prosser.

ISBN: 979-8992553208

Written by Landon Prosser.

Also by Landon Prosser

Saving Grace Series
Mind Games
Whispers

Table of Contents

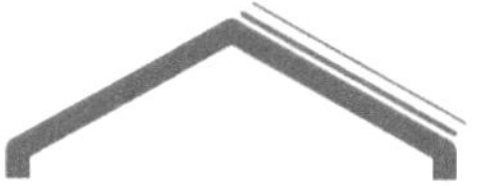

Chapter 1: Fault Lines in the Mind

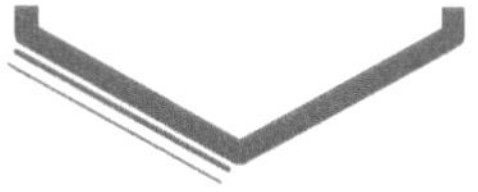

Keesha Marshall had been awake for hours before the sun finally scorched the horizon, though she couldn't remember the precise moment her eyes had snapped open. All night, she'd drifted between a restless dozing and a jolting, heart-pounding alertness, her mind a hive of buzzing worries. Now she sat upright on the edge of the living room couch, arms wrapped tightly around her ribs, surveying the remnants of a battle that felt both like a nightmare from a previous century and a wound that had happened seconds ago. Rough-hewn wooden boards still covered the front door, the plywood grain standing out in the dim light where a lock had once promised sanctuary. A bullet hole marred the plaster—a dark, airless puncture that had turned her home into a museum of the unthinkable.

The early light filtering through the gaps cast long, distorted shadows across the floorboards. Keesha tried to conjure the memory of how the house used to look—warm and welcoming, a place where Grace would do her homework while the kitchen smelled of simmering sauce. That version of her life felt like a postcard from a country she'd been exiled from. These days, the entire structure felt uneasy, as if even its walls were on edge, anticipating another intrusion, another splintering of its skin.

Her eyes settled on Grace, sprawled across the other end of the couch in a body that did not belong to her. A quiver of raw pain tightened Keesha's chest. Beneath the angular jawline and the heavy, broad shoulders of a grown man, she could still see the ghost of her ten-year-old daughter—the gentle curl of her lashes, the rhythmic twitch of her lips whenever she dreamed. It was a masterpiece hidden behind a vandal's canvas, heartbreakingly familiar and profoundly unsettling. Keesha's mind flickered to nights spent tucking a small, slender girl into bed, brushing back curly hair to kiss a forehead that was now hidden behind a mask of stubble and bone. Grace was still here, trapped in the body of the man who had tried to destroy them.

She forced herself to stand, movement being her only defense against paralysis. Quietly, she rose, wishing she could leave her anguish behind. She peered through a gap in the plywood at the front door. Quincy stood outside in the cool mist, his broad shoulders forming a stone wall against the gray dawn. He carried the same watchful air he always did: a man trying to hold the world at bay with sheer military will. She knew how heavily the last few days weighed on him—sleep-deprived and tense—but it was in his nature to stand guard.

The hallway still smelled faintly of sawdust from Quincy's hurried repairs. Keesha caught sight of her phone glowing on a console table. The screen displayed a new message:

> Rodriguez (5:12 AM): Heading to juvenile ward. D. tried to cause a disturbance overnight. More details soon.

Keesha's stomach turned. D.—her daughter's ten-year-old body, currently piloted by the shark-mind of Darius King. The thought of him prowling around in Grace's flesh made her breath catch. She typed a terse reply—I'm up. Call me ASAP—and leaned her forehead against the cool drywall, dreading the next vibration.

She glanced once more at the bullet hole. If she tilted her head just right, she could see clean through to the insulation. The day she'd first seen that bullet rip the air felt like a fever dream. She remembered the gunshot's roar, how she'd screamed Grace's name, Quincy's thunderous footsteps as he ran to protect them, and the echo of Darius's mocking laughter. Shaking herself out of the memory, she steeled her shoulders. The past would not define her, nor would it define Grace, regardless of which body she currently inhabited.

Keesha lingered by the hole, letting her hand rest lightly on the wall. This gap in the plaster was a fault line, pulling her into a memory she tried to keep as a shield:

Just a few months ago, the house had been alive with the sounds of an ordinary evening. Grace—her ten-year-old self, in her ten-year-old body—sat at the dining table, brow furrowed as she color-coded a homework worksheet. Keesha stood in the kitchen, the aroma of garlic and onions sizzling as she prepared spaghetti, Grace's favorite. The TV mumbled in the background with some game show Keesha half-listened to while stirring the gravy.

Every so often, Grace would call out, "Mom, can you help me with this?" and Keesha would turn off the burner, drying her hands on a dish towel. Sometimes it was a math problem—fractions that Grace found tricky. Sometimes it was a question about the solar system. Each time, Keesha would lean down, her hand gently on Grace's back, guiding her daughter through the puzzle. The glow of the overhead lamp turned Grace's curly hair into a halo, and Keesha couldn't help but smile at how absorbed her child became whenever she learned something new.

Then the routine would wrap up with bowls of spaghetti and a playful argument over whether to have extra cheese. Grace always tried to sneak another sprinkle of Parmesan, insisting it made the noodles taste better, while Keesha threatened to hide the shaker if her daughter didn't eat some vegetables, too. They'd dissolve into giggles, and Quincy—often passing by on his way home—would tap on the window and make a silly face, prompting even more laughter.

It was nothing special, Keesha thought in the moment: just a slice of quiet, daily life. But now, in this battered living room marred by bullet holes and boarded-up windows, that memory felt impossibly precious. A life measured by simple joys: homework at the table, dinner sizzling on the stove, Grace's giggles echoing off the walls.

Slowly, Keesha's mind returned to the present. She took in the musty air and the ragged boards. The hush felt haunted. Even so, the memory steadied her—reminding her why she fought. She fought for the chance to cook dinner in peace again, for afternoons spent arguing about fractions and too much Parmesan.

Barely fifteen minutes later, a gentle knock against the plywood made Keesha's heart lurch. She hurried to unlatch the barricade, letting Detective Rodriguez step inside. A fresh drizzle had dampened Rodriguez's hair, and the detective wasted no time scanning the room for Grace.

"You two all right?" Rodriguez asked in a low, urgent voice. Her eyes flicked over Keesha, then to the bullet hole, and finally to Grace's large, sleeping form.

Keesha offered a small nod. "We're holding on," she replied, voice tight. "But what happened?"

Rodriguez took a step closer, her expression grim. "Darius—still in Grace's body—caused a scene around three in the morning, threatening the night staff. He claimed he still had his powers, that he could manifest their worst nightmares, and insisted his 'people' from Redwood Ridge surrounded the building. One of the newer officers panicked."

At the detective's words, a tremor of ice rippled along Keesha's arms. She'd already endured enough illusions courtesy of Darius to last a lifetime. "Did he actually... manipulate anyone's mind?"

The detective shook her head, relief softening her features for an instant. "Doesn't look like it. If his power still exists, it's weak or dormant. He tried to bluff his way out, but the staff sedated him before he could escalate things. But Keesha, the headlines are already a nightmare. The press is calling her the 'Psychic Seed.' They're sensationalizing a ten-year-old girl as a monster."

Keesha let out a breath she hadn't realized she was holding. "Thank God. But word's going to spread, isn't it?"

Rodriguez's grim nod confirmed Keesha's fears. "Rumors are already circulating. Some of the DA's office think we might actually have the real Darius King on this couch—that he's just a manipulative criminal faking a swap to avoid an adult sentence. They don't believe in mind-swaps; they believe in forensics, and the fingerprints in that ward belong to a minor."

A soft groan drifted from the couch, and Grace stirred, letting out a low, resonant sound that belonged to Darius's adult throat. The incongruity made Keesha flinch. She crossed the room in quick strides, kneeling beside Grace. The moment Grace opened her eyes—still hazy with sleep and confusion—Keesha touched her hand gently.

"It's all right," she murmured. "Detective Rodriguez is here."

Grace propped herself up on the couch, looking disoriented. Dark stubble shadowed her jaw, and her shoulders bunched in tension that no ten-year-old's face should carry. Seeing her child like this always triggered a near-physical ache.

Rodriguez moved to an armchair, leaning in. "Darius tried to scare the guards," she explained quietly, her gaze flicking to Grace's large hands. "How are you feeling?"

Grace dragged a hand over her short-cropped hair—his hair—and let out a slow, shuddering breath. "I'm okay, I guess. I haven't felt him trying to swap or anything, but it's like... a buzzing in the back of my mind. Like he's pulling at a tether whenever I slip into sleep."

The detective shot Keesha a worried glance. Keesha could sense the question in Rodriguez's eyes: How much can Grace take? She only knew that Grace was enduring something no child should ever have to endure.

Grace's words clung to the space between them, heavy with implications. Finally, Rodriguez cleared her throat. "We'll keep an eye on him. If he tries anything else, they'll notify us immediately."

Keesha nodded, the tremor of her own heartbeat echoing in her ears. "Thank you," she whispered. Nothing about this is natural. I wish I could tear that tether out of you, baby, she thought fiercely, her gaze drifting to Grace's borrowed body, helpless rage coiling in her gut.

The day slogged forward, weighed down by a flurry of phone calls and legal back-and-forth. Quincy did his best to repair the shattered door, his hammer strikes echoing through the house like a grim metronome. Every so often, he'd pause and glance out into the yard, as though expecting Darius to appear from behind a tree. The tension wore on him, lines etching themselves around his eyes. Yet he didn't complain—he just kept working, trying to restore security to a place that felt beyond saving.

Meanwhile, Grace retreated to her old bedroom, seeking solace in the little comforts she remembered: a stack of drawing pads, charcoal pencils, and colored markers. But the moment she picked up a pencil, frustration flashed across her face. Her hands—bigger, rougher—trembled over those delicate tools. The mismatch of thick adult fingers and fragile pencils made her brow furrow in anger, and Keesha felt a renewed surge of fury toward Darius. He had stolen yet another simple pleasure from Grace—her ability to create art with a child's abandon.

Keesha stood in the doorway, unsure whether to offer support or space. Grace stared at a blank page for nearly a minute before clenching her teeth, setting the pencil down, and burying her face in her palms. Without a word, Keesha crossed the room and placed a gentle hand on Grace's shoulder. In that quiet gesture, she tried to convey everything: I'm with you. We will find a way to fix this.

Around midday, Dr. Miriam Flores arrived, towing a suitcase of medical gear and wearing an apologetic smile. She was a short woman in her fifties, hair neatly pinned back and eyes creased with concern. She'd been working with them ever since Grace's first symptoms appeared—back when they thought it was some neurological anomaly.

"I wish this wasn't happening to you," she said softly to Grace, eyeing her stubbled jaw and tense shoulders. "But we need more imaging to prove in court that you're... well, you."

Grace managed a tight laugh that sounded jarringly low. "Nothing about my life is normal anymore. Just tell me what to do."

They set up the equipment in the living room, moving aside a coffee table that still bore scratches from some previous scuffle. Quincy hovered near the doorway, arms folded protectively, his gaze never straying far from Keesha or Grace. Keesha didn't blame him. She felt like they were constantly on the verge of a new catastrophe.

"Relax," Dr. Flores urged, her voice gentle as she attached electrodes to Grace's scalp. The machine hummed and clicked, reading neural activity and logging it for analysis. Every beep made Keesha's nerves twinge. For a few minutes, the only sounds were the whir of machinery, the faint hiss of the air conditioning, and the rustle of cables against the worn couch. Grace's eyes fluttered closed, her chest rising and falling in even breaths. Keesha prayed for calm, for any sign that this test could confirm Grace's mind didn't belong in this body.

Then Grace's breath hitched. "I feel him again," she whispered, her voice taut with anxiety. "He's... twisting at that tether between us."

Keesha clenched Grace's wrist, offering whatever comfort she could. "Breathe, sweetie. I'm right here." She felt helpless, remembering how unstoppable Darius's powers had once seemed. If he still had a fraction of that strength, could he yank Grace's mind out again?

"He's furious. And hurting, too," Grace said, her eyes still shut tight. "They sedated him, but it's wearing off. It's like his anger is ricocheting back into me."

Dr. Flores's gaze flicked to the screen. The lines of data spiked erratically. "I'm seeing unusual activity in your temporal lobe. This is definitely not normal neural function." Suddenly, a jolt coursed through Grace, her muscles tensing. A low groan tore from her throat.

Keesha almost pulled her hand away in alarm but held on tighter instead. "Mom, it hurts..." Grace gasped.

Flores powered down the machine, gently removing the electrodes. "I've got enough data for now," she said, looking shaken. "I just hope we haven't done any harm."

Grace fell back against the couch, chest heaving. "It's not your fault," she murmured. "Nothing compared to what Darius could do if he stays in my body."

Flores nodded somberly. "We'll keep testing. These scans might help your case—they show something is very off—but we're walking a tightrope. The courts might not welcome a story about psychic powers."

At this, Quincy cleared his throat from near the door, his fingers drumming an anxious rhythm on the frame. "What about the old scans? The ones showing Grace's surgeries in this body?"

Flores carefully packed her equipment. "They're under review. Detective Rodriguez is pressing for an official hearing to prove the man in custody isn't who everyone thinks he is. But we still have no clear plan for returning Grace to her rightful self."

A hush fell over the living room, interrupted only by the hum of the scanner's cooling fan. Keesha closed her eyes. She felt the echoes of too many sleepless nights pounding at her temples. She would burn down every court in the country if that's what it took to get Grace back. One battle at a time, she told herself. One more fight for my child.

Night had long fallen by the time Rodriguez reappeared, tension etched in the rigid lines of her posture. Keesha recognized the detective's faint limp—an old knee injury aggravated by stressful days and endless hours on her feet. She carried an expression that was equal parts urgency and dread, and Keesha's pulse kicked up in response.

"Darius wants to speak with you personally," Rodriguez said, voice taut. "He says he has information that could help Grace."

Those words hammered at Keesha's frayed nerves. Instantly, her mind filled with visions of Darius's manipulative grin, the nightmares he had orchestrated. She swallowed hard, teeth gritting. "No," she said, fighting the panic that threatened to swallow her. "He's not getting another chance to crawl inside my head."

Rodriguez's face softened, but her voice remained grim. "He's threatening to cause more stunts at the juvenile ward. If he pulls another scene, the public might see a frightened 'child' rather than a dangerous criminal. That could give him leverage."

A cold wave of memory swept over Keesha: how easily Darius had twisted situations to appear vulnerable or misunderstood—while behind that mask, he was a predator. He'd fooled more than one person in their neighborhood back then. Some people had even blamed Keesha for overreacting, until the truth finally unraveled. "He knows exactly how to corner us," she said bitterly. And that's what he does best—finds your weakest spot and digs in until you have no choice but to give.

"We won't leave you unprotected," Rodriguez continued. "We'll wire you up, keep you under constant watch. The moment he steps out of line, we move in."

Keesha's gaze turned to the hallway where Grace lay, an ice pack on her forehead to ease the splitting headache left by the scans. That was her child in a stranger's body, her mind battered by a madman's power. The only path to saving Grace might be walking right into Darius's trap.

"Fine," she said at last, her throat tight. "Let's do it."

Relief flickered in Rodriguez's eyes. "Tomorrow morning, then. I'll arrange everything." But the detective didn't look happy about it, just resigned—like someone running out of time and options.

The rest of the evening brought little comfort. Only one lamp remained on, its flickering bulb casting jittery shadows on the walls. Keesha, Quincy, and Grace tried to share a meal at the dining table, a half-hearted attempt at normalcy. The plates held simple fare—roasted chicken, mashed potatoes, and green beans—but the tension made every bite feel tasteless and forced.

Keesha stole glances at Grace, who was hunched over her plate as if it might shield her from the world. The sweatshirt she wore pulled tight across her broad shoulders, reminding everyone of the physical mismatch that had turned her life upside down. Quincy reached over at one point to pat Grace's arm, murmuring something reassuring, but none of them could shake the underlying dread.

Finally, Keesha mustered the courage to speak. "Rodriguez wants me to see him tomorrow," she said, her tone betraying how much she hated the idea. "At the juvenile ward."

Grace's fork slipped from her fingers, clattering onto the plate. The sound felt amplified in the tense hush. "Mom, no—he'll try something." Her voice, so low and resonant, still startled Keesha sometimes. She could see the flicker of tears in Grace's eyes, though, the pure fear that no deeper vocal cords could mask.

Keesha reached for Grace's oversized hand, clasping it in hers. "Detective Rodriguez will be there," she reassured, her voice husky. "Cameras, wires, guards. He won't be able to do anything without us knowing." If only I could promise you absolute safety, she thought, staring into her daughter's transformed face.

Grace's eyes glistened. "He's still dangerous. Even if he can't push his way into your thoughts like before, he knows how to manipulate people. He'll try to break you."

From across the table, Quincy spoke up, his voice a quiet rumble. "We can't let him run free. If there's even a chance to learn how to reverse this body-swap, we have to take it." He paused, setting his fork down. "But I don't like it either, Keesha. You know I don't."

Grace squeezed Keesha's hand, frustration and guilt warring on her borrowed features. "Promise me you'll be careful," she whispered. "I can't—I can't stand the thought of him hurting you again."

Keesha forced herself to meet Grace's gaze, summoning all the maternal ferocity she had. "I promise," she said, her words both vow and determination. "He's not the only one who's changed. I'm not letting him do to me what he did before."

They finished dinner in near silence. The weight of the bullet hole in the wall and the plywood on the door seemed to press in on them, physical reminders of a siege that was far from over. When Keesha collected the plates, she noticed a small speck of blood on the floor from a nail Quincy had hammered in earlier, no bigger than a drop. Still, it felt symbolic—no matter what they did, the violence in their lives kept leaving its mark.

Later, Keesha found herself alone in the living room, staring at the boarded-up front door. The lamp flickered, plunging the room into an erratic dance of light and shadow. She pressed a hand to her face, feeling the burn of tears she refused to let fall. Tomorrow, we face him again, she told herself. And we walk away with answers—one way or another.

Morning arrived too quickly, dragging with it a tense chill that seeped into Keesha's bones. She dressed plainly—jeans and a fitted sweater, her hair in a tight braid that made her feel marginally more in control. Over the years, she'd learned how a small routine—like braiding her hair or tying her shoelaces—could provide a sliver of steadiness. This morning, she needed every bit of steadiness she could muster.

She sat in the kitchen, her hands wrapped around a mug of lukewarm coffee she couldn't bring herself to drink. Each sip only reminded her of how her stomach churned with dread. She glanced at the clock. Thirty minutes until I leave.

Grace emerged from the hallway, silent and somber, wearing a sweatshirt that barely fit. They caught each other's eyes in the hallway mirror—Keesha, short and tense; Grace, tall and tired. The reflection looked like two strangers, yet she felt an unmistakable bond pulling them together. That was her daughter, regardless of the body, regardless of the madness.

Wordlessly, Keesha opened her arms, and Grace folded her into a hug. The warmth of that embrace resonated with memories of how Grace used to climb into her lap for storytime, how she used to babble excitedly about her day at school. As big as she was now, Grace still needed her mother's comfort. "We'll get through this," Keesha whispered, her words muffled against the soft fabric of Grace's sweatshirt. "No matter what."

Outside, Detective Rodriguez and Quincy waited by an unmarked sedan. The dull sky overhead threatened more rain, matching Keesha's mood. Quincy's eyes caught hers the moment she stepped onto the porch, a silent vow of protection in his gaze. He touched his collar, where a small listening device was clipped underneath his jacket. Keesha nodded—she wore a similar device beneath her sweater, its presence feeling heavier than its actual weight.

Grace hovered on the porch steps, uncertain, looking more childlike in that moment than she had in days. Keesha turned, meeting her daughter's eyes. I'll come back, she willed her gaze to say. No matter what happens. With a final, trembling smile, she slid into the passenger seat, while Rodriguez took the driver's side and Quincy climbed in back.

The drive passed in brooding silence, tension radiating from everyone. Keesha watched the cityscape roll by—the tired corner store, the graffiti-strewn walls, a school bus rolling past full of oblivious children. She felt an ache, wondering if Grace would ever return to that world—a normal life, normal school days. Could they reclaim any semblance of what was stolen?

When they arrived at the juvenile facility, two uniformed officers led them through sterile hallways that smelled of antiseptic and fresh paint. The overhead fluorescents buzzed like insects, adding to Keesha's mounting unease. They stopped outside a room flanked by one-way glass, and Keesha peered through the window. Her heart clenched. She saw Grace's body—slight build, bound to a table by metal cuffs. But the posture, the defiant tilt of the chin, was unmistakably Darius.

Rodriguez touched her earpiece. "Audio feed is live," she said quietly. Then she squeezed Keesha's arm. "We're right here," she added, a promise laced with urgency.

Keesha swallowed and pushed the door open. The moment she stepped inside, the scent of bleach and stale air assaulted her nose. Darius—wearing Grace's ten-year-old face—looked up, a slow, calculating smile curving what should have been innocent features. The sight made Keesha's stomach twist.

"Hello, Keesha," he said, his voice a quiet mockery. "I've been waiting." The bored drawl in that child's tone was monstrous—like an actor in the wrong costume.

She forced herself to stand tall, summoning every ounce of courage. "You asked for me. Start talking."

He leaned forward as much as his cuffs would allow, rattling them with growing impatience. "We both know why you're here: to save Grace. I might have a way to swap us back... but you'll have to give me what I want."

Keesha felt her anger spark. She could never forget how he'd toyed with her before—his illusions, the way he got into her head. He can't control me if I don't let him. "If you have a solution, then out with it," she demanded, her voice sharper than she expected.

A small smile tugged at Grace's young lips, but the expression was purely Darius—cruel and self-assured. He rattled off his demands: no armed guards, a secret location, a "psychic ritual" to realign their minds. Everything about it screamed trap. But Keesha also heard the faint ring of possibility. What if he's telling the truth? What if this is the only way to free Grace?

"Take it or leave it," Darius said, leaning back. The unnerving confidence in that little girl's face made Keesha's skin crawl. "I'm your only chance," he added softly, twisting the knife of guilt deeper.

Keesha gave two sharp knocks on the door, the code that signaled the officers to open it from the outside. As she stepped out, her breath came in a rush. It felt like she had been holding it the entire time.

Rodriguez was waiting in the corridor, her eyes reflecting a mix of concern and frustration. "He wants a private location for some so-called ritual?" she asked, voice bristling.

Keesha nodded, rubbing at her temples. "He claims it's the only way to swap him and Grace back." She took a shaky breath. "But for all we know, it could be a trick. Just another bid for freedom."

The detective's mouth tightened into a grim line. "We'll find another way," she said. "Don't let him manipulate you."

Keesha looked past Rodriguez to the glass window, where she could just barely see the outline of her daughter's small body, weighed down by chains meant for criminals. The cruelty of the image struck her all over again. "We'll see," she managed. "I won't let him call the shots. But if this is our only lead..."

Her words trailed off, but the implication hung in the corridor: How far would she go to save Grace? Quincy caught her eye, and she saw her own turmoil mirrored in his expression. Whatever it takes, he seemed to say silently, though the caution in his eyes reminded her not to walk into the lion's den blindly.

They turned to leave, the clacking of their shoes on the polished floor echoing like a gavel's final strike. Keesha could still feel Darius's gaze through the wall, a cold hand on her spine. She remembered the nights when she used to lie awake, convinced she felt his presence just outside the window. He'd made her doubt her own perceptions, turned her life into a labyrinth of fear. But no more. This time, she reminded herself fiercely, she had allies. She had a reason to stand her ground—and that reason was Grace.

One step at a time, she told herself. That mantra had carried her through countless nights when Darius's threats seemed insurmountable. Now, as her heart pounded in her ears, she vowed silently: I will free Grace, whatever it takes.

But even as she repeated that promise, dread lingered in the pit of her stomach, whispering that the cost might be more than any of them could bear. If Darius's words were true, what would he demand in return for reversing this mind-swap? And if he was lying, could she survive another brutal confrontation?

She pushed away the questions as they emerged from the facility into the pale morning light. Quincy touched her shoulder, grounding her, and Rodriguez pressed her lips into a thin line of resolve. The fight for Grace's mind—and her very soul—wasn't over. And as Keesha looked up at the expanse of sky overhead, she felt a grim determination take hold: no matter how dark this road becomes, I will walk it for my daughter.

Chapter 2: Lines in the Sand

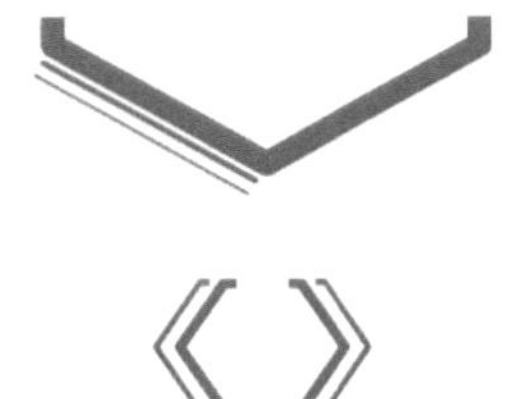

A COLD DRIZZLE SHEETED over the windshield, washing the city in tones of dull pewter. From her seat in Detective Elena Rodriguez's sedan, Keesha could almost believe the world was drowning in its own sorrow. Buildings rushed by in a watery blur, their silhouettes distorted by rivulets of rain that traced frantic paths across the glass. Each tremor of the wipers felt like a jolt against Keesha's nerves, which were already wound painfully tight. Inside the car, the atmosphere was no less charged—every breath Keesha drew felt constricted, as if she, too, were riding the edge of a storm.

They had left the juvenile detention center only moments ago, but Darius's proposition echoed relentlessly in Keesha's mind: a so-called ritual to swap himself back into his old body at an unknown location. Keesha's hands lay clasped in her lap, her knuckles white against the gray fabric of her coat. The day was still young, yet the weight of his words pressed on her shoulders like a week's worth of sleepless nights.

Detective Rodriguez, seated beside her, had scarcely spoken since they pulled out of the detention center's parking lot. She drove with uncharacteristic tension, her usually confident grip on the steering wheel betraying her unease—fingers rigid, jaw set. Despite the silence, Keesha could practically feel the detective replaying the interrogation with Darius, analyzing his every shift in tone or posture. Finally, Rodriguez cleared her throat, shattering the hush inside the car.

"I'll drop you at your place," she said, voice carefully measured, "then head to the station. I have a meeting with Dr. Flores lined up—we need to figure out how to approach this... 'offer.'" She shot Keesha a sidelong glance, her usually steady gaze laced with a frank worry Keesha hadn't seen before. The detective was often their rock, but even she looked rattled.

Keesha swallowed against the dryness in her throat. "All right. But, Elena..." She hesitated, choosing her words with care. "Time isn't exactly our friend here. Grace is—she's getting headaches. Bad ones. I'm worried."

Rodriguez's expression softened. She'd seen the toll this was taking on Grace—on all of them. "I know," she said gently. "We can't let Darius's demands back us into a corner, but ignoring him might cost Grace more than we realize. Dr. Flores has been monitoring Grace's condition, but from everything she's said, the tension in Grace's brain could worsen. We'll do our best to find a solution that doesn't let Darius run free."

Keesha turned to the rain-slicked window, meeting her own reflection in the wavering glass. Her features looked worn, her eyes underscored by bruised-looking shadows. *What if Darius isn't bluffing?* That question had been eating at her for days. She recalled the chilling sight of her daughter's face contorted with an adult's lethal intelligence—an expression that no ten-year-old should ever wear. Even with bulletproof glass and an armed guard between them, Keesha had felt that old fear coil in her stomach. "Just promise me," she said softly. "Promise me we won't dismiss the possibility he's telling the truth."

Rodriguez's lips pressed into a thin line, but she nodded. "I promise we'll consider it. If there's a genuine method to reverse what's happened, we need to know. Flores and I will consult the DA and see if we can craft a plan that doesn't hand Darius the upper hand."

Silence reclaimed the car as they navigated the final stretch of slick roads. The wipers thumped in steady rhythm, smearing the outside world into shapeless grays. A sting of memory tore through Keesha—she recalled how Darius, in the early stages of their relationship, used to drive her home on rainy nights, one arm draped over the seat as he told stories about how he'd grown up on the rough side of town. Back then, she'd had no inkling of the darkness lurking behind that charismatic smile. *How easily we can be deceived by the people we love...*

Yet as the hush fell between them again, Keesha's mind turned to a memory of the house before the bullet holes and plywood—a gentler time that felt a world away. She pictured a quiet Tuesday evening when Grace was only eight. The kitchen smelled of chicken broth and rosemary; a pot of soup simmered on the stove. Grace, clad in fuzzy socks, danced through the hallway humming some pop tune she'd picked up at school. Every so often, she'd skip into the living room to show Keesha a new step she'd invented.

Keesha had watched from the sofa, smiling over the rim of her tea mug. She remembered how the lamplight made the space feel cozy, the coffee table scattered with crayons and drawings of castles and dragons. Grace had insisted they tape her latest masterpiece—a lopsided sketch of a pony—onto the fridge door. The biggest concern that night was whether or not they'd have enough milk for breakfast the next morning. No illusions, no talk of psychic tethers or body-swaps—just a mother, her child, and the warmth of a safe home.

Her memory lingered on the gentle *tap-tap* of Grace's slippers on the hardwood floors, the easy conversations they'd shared. Quincy might have arrived mid-laughter, groceries in hand, teasing Grace that she should choreograph a routine for him next. Keesha had teased back, saying Quincy's rhythm needed work. They'd all ended up giggling, the house ringing with a lightness so distant now that it could be a dream.

Keesha blinked, returning to the present as the wipers smacked another sheet of rain aside. The warmth of that memory felt bittersweet—both a reminder of why she fought so hard and a painful testament to how far they'd fallen from normalcy.

When they finally pulled up to Keesha's house, the plywood over the doorway and the patched bullet holes presented a stark reminder of their new reality: safety here was paper-thin. Detective Rodriguez parked and turned to Keesha with a curt, regretful nod.

"I'll be in touch as soon as we have something concrete," she said. "Keep your phone on—and don't make any moves with Darius without calling me first. Understood?"

Keesha managed a shaky nod. "I promise," she breathed. Her nerves felt raw, but she was grateful for Rodriguez's steady presence.

Sliding out into the wet chill, Keesha hoisted her purse over her shoulder. The drizzle seeped through her jacket in seconds, chilling her to the bone. She watched the detective's car merge back into traffic, the taillights bleeding red through the rain until they vanished altogether. Alone, Keesha faced the battered remnants of her front porch, remembering how she and Grace would sometimes watch storms roll in while sharing jokes about the neighbors. That simpler time felt like a postcard from a lost world. Now, every gust of wind carried the echo of Darius's name, a haunting promise that the storm was far from over.

Inside, the house was quiet save for the faint hum of the heater. Soft shadows pooled in corners, and the partial patch over the bullet hole in the living room wall seemed like a bandage on a wound that refused to heal. Keesha lingered in the entryway, letting her damp jacket slide down her arms, the water dripping onto the floor. The staccato of raindrops against the plywood on the door followed her like a ghost she couldn't shake.

A muffled voice drifted from the kitchen. She recognized Quincy's deeper tones. He was on the phone, speaking in hushed urgency. She could hear the tautness in his voice even before seeing the worry etched on his face. Keesha found him leaning against the counter, phone pressed to his ear.

"Yeah, I'll let her know," he said, brow creased, "Thanks for the heads-up."

He hung up, noticing Keesha by the threshold. "Hey," he said quietly, slipping his phone into his pocket. "How'd it go? You alright?"

She took a shaky breath and crossed her arms over her chest, as if warding off an internal chill. "As all right as I can be, I guess. Rodriguez dropped me off—they're planning to meet with Dr. Flores to figure out how to handle Darius's *offer.*" She grimaced at the word. "Any news here?"

Quincy set his phone aside, absently rubbing the back of his neck. "Just a call from one of the lawyers. They needed more of Grace's medical records, said the courts are still baffled by how to classify all this. Legal definitions don't exactly cover mind-swapping."

Keesha's gaze flicked to the living room, where they'd all huddled in fear during Darius's last intrusion. "I'm worried," she admitted. "About Grace. About the headaches. We don't have a lot of time."

Quincy moved closer, resting a hand gently on her shoulder. "Me too." The warmth of his touch steadied her. "We'll figure out a way—some path through this. It's just... complicated."

"Complicated" felt like an understatement. They were wandering through a nightmare no one had prepared them for. *Psychic phenomena, body-swaps, rituals*—it all sounded like the plot of a cheap thriller, yet here they were living it. Keesha offered Quincy a half-smile, then willed her feet to carry her toward the dining room, where she heard the quiet clink of ceramic against wood.

They found Grace—still trapped in Darius's towering body—hunched at the small dining table, cradling a lukewarm mug of tea in her large hands. Her eyes lifted when Keesha and Quincy entered, and though the face belonged to Darius, the relief was undeniably Grace's.

"Hey, Mom," Grace murmured, her voice still unsettlingly low. "You're back." Despite the incongruous baritone, Keesha could detect the flicker of a child's concern in that single statement.

Keesha forced a reassuring nod. "Rodriguez dropped me off," she said, easing into a chair beside Grace. The table felt cramped with Grace's imposing frame, even though the real Grace was just ten years old. *He's stolen more than her body... he's stolen her place in her own home.*

Grace took a sip from her mug, then grimaced. "It's cold." She set it down, as if it had lost all appeal. "Not sure if that's because my head hurts or because it's *his* taste buds."

"Want me to heat more water?" Keesha offered, already half-standing.

Grace shook her head. "No, I'm fine." A pause, then: "The headache's better than earlier, but it's still there. Kinda... fuzzy." She pressed two big fingers to her temple. "Like static."

Quincy moved behind her, resting a careful hand on her shoulder. "We'll keep an eye on it. If it gets worse, we call Flores."

Grace let her gaze wander to the window, where the rain coursed down in silvery streaks. "I just—did you see him?" she asked, voice subdued. "At the detention center?"

Keesha exhaled, remembering too well the cold glint in her daughter's eyes when possessed by Darius's mind. "Yes. He's... making demands," she said gently, not wanting to overwhelm Grace. "He claims he has a *ritual* that can swap you two back. Detective Rodriguez wants to figure out how to proceed without giving him total freedom."

Grace's borrowed jawline tensed, a subtle clench that made her look older than she was. "He's lying," she said. "Or at least he's not telling the whole truth. He'll try to run if we bring him anywhere isolated."

"We're aware," Quincy said softly. "But if there's even a grain of truth in his claim, we have to explore it. Right?"

Grace dropped her gaze to her empty mug. "I know," she whispered. "I just hate feeling like... like a bargaining chip in his game."

Keesha's heart twisted. She reached out and squeezed Grace's forearm. Despite the disparity in their sizes, the gesture carried a world of maternal reassurance. "We won't let him take advantage again," she said firmly. "Not this time."

Their conversation was interrupted by Keesha's phone buzzing on the kitchen counter. She snatched it up, her pulse quickening at the sight of Dr. Flores's caller ID.

"Keesha here," she answered, voice taut.

"Keesha," came Dr. Flores's familiar, slightly raspy tone. "I just finished a preliminary talk with Detective Rodriguez. We've been poring over Grace's most recent brain scans."

Keesha gestured for Grace to join her so she could listen in. "What did you find?"

"Well, as we suspected," Flores said, "the neural synapses that correlate with stress and emotional processing are under significant strain. This could explain the persistent headaches Grace is experiencing. It also suggests there *is* an active psychic or neurological link between Grace and her original body—Darius's body—wherever he is."

Keesha pressed the phone to her ear, swallowing. "So the longer this goes on..."

"The more damage or discomfort Grace might endure," Flores confirmed. "Look, I'm not trying to frighten you, but I need you to understand the urgency. This link could intensify if Darius becomes more agitated or if he attempts any new psychic maneuvers."

Grace overheard enough to frown deeply. She mouthed, *What do we do?*

"Dr. Flores," Keesha said carefully, "is there a safe way to test or confirm Darius's claim without giving him free rein?"

"Rodriguez and I discussed a *controlled environment*," Flores said. "Somewhere secure, ideally with medical equipment and discreet law enforcement presence. We'd try to coax or replicate the conditions under which Darius performed the initial swap. But this time, *we* manage it. We don't let him hold all the cards."

A fragile surge of hope flared in Keesha's chest. "That's... that's good news. At least it's a plan."

"It's still very conceptual," Flores cautioned. "We'd need approval from the DA, and we might consult a parapsychology specialist—someone willing to take these phenomena seriously. In the meantime, keep Grace's stress levels as low as possible. If the headaches worsen or she experiences anything new—visual distortions, auditory hallucinations—call me immediately."

Keesha thanked her, then hung up. When she turned around, Grace was gazing at her, eyes filled with a mix of anticipation and dread.

"Well?" Grace asked, voice trembling.

Keesha relayed the conversation. "They're working on a plan—a controlled scenario. Something that might let us force Darius's hand safely."

Grace's reaction was swift. She stood, pacing the confines of the kitchen with large, uneven steps. "I'm in," she blurted. "I don't care how risky it is. I can't stand living like this—never knowing if he'll yank me out of my own mind."

Quincy took a step forward. "Just remember, we're not rushing into anything without thorough preparation," he said, voice calm but firm. "No one's jumping headfirst into a trap. We'll weigh every detail."

Grace paused, one hand still pressed to her temple. "Right. Sure." But the desperation in her tone undercut any casual agreement. Her eyes flicked to Keesha, pleading. "Just don't let them stall forever."

Keesha's chest tightened. She recognized in Grace a mounting panic, like a caged animal that senses time running out. It was a feeling

Keesha knew all too well—she'd felt it herself, those last terrible months with Darius, when every night she'd wonder if she could escape the illusions he planted in her head. "We won't," she promised, summoning a steadiness she didn't fully feel. "We'll stay on it, day by day."

Afternoon arrived in a hush. The rain slowed to a persistent mist that blurred the windows and dulled the sunlight into a milky glow. A sense of waiting pervaded the house, as though all three inhabitants were bracing for whatever news would come from Dr. Flores and Detective Rodriguez next.

At one point, Keesha found herself standing in the hallway leading to Grace's old bedroom, her eyes wandering to the pencil marks on the wall. Each line denoted Grace's growth over the years—*Grace: 4'2", Age 8; Grace: 4'5", Age 9;* and so on. Keesha traced these markings with trembling fingertips, recalling a day when Grace had bounced on her tiptoes, excited to see she'd grown another inch. There had been laughter in this hallway, bright and unfiltered. Now, that laughter was replaced by tension and dread.

As if summoned by her thoughts, memories of Darius surfaced. She recalled a day, shortly after Grace's eighth birthday, when he had stood in this very spot, glaring at the lines as though they were a personal affront. She'd never understood why it bothered him so much—maybe because it symbolized Grace's progress, her bright future, her independence. He despised any sign that someone else might thrive beyond his control. *He wanted me small and fearful, and he wanted Grace to look at him like some all-powerful figure.* Keesha clenched her fists, feeling a pulse of anger surging through her.

The old floorboard creaked. She turned to see Quincy approaching, his expression mirroring her quiet turmoil. "You okay?" he asked gently, resting a hand on the wall just above the top pencil mark.

Keesha inhaled shakily. "I'm remembering the day Darius yelled at me for letting Grace mark her height," she said. "He said it was pointless, that she shouldn't get too proud... That's who he was—someone who couldn't stand anyone else's growth or happiness."

Quincy nodded, lips thin. He knew a piece of their history, but never the whole of it. Over time, he'd pieced together enough to hate Darius for what he'd done to both mother and daughter. "He can't take that away now," Quincy said quietly. "Grace is still growing—just... on pause, in a nightmare. But we'll bring her back."

Keesha mustered a brittle smile. "Yes. We have to." She closed her eyes for a moment, letting the memory pass. *I won't let him define us anymore.*

When they returned to the living room, they found Grace kneeling by a shelf filled with old paperbacks and photo albums. She had pulled one of the slender volumes into her large hands—a dog-eared paperback on lucid dreaming and controlling nightmares, purchased back when Keesha was searching for anything that could help with her own night terrors.

"Mom," Grace said, turning the book's yellowed pages, "did you actually read this?"

Keesha sank onto the couch. "I did... a long time ago. I was having nightmares about—well, about your father, about the illusions he used to plant in my head. I thought maybe if I could learn to control my dreams, I could fight them."

"Did it help?" Grace asked, flipping through a chapter on "Dream Awareness."

"Not much," Keesha admitted. "But maybe it'll be different for you. You're... more naturally receptive to these... energies, I guess." She wasn't sure what word to use anymore. Psychic powers? Spiritual illusions? The boundaries between science and the impossible were bleeding together.

Grace set the book down, eyes flicking to the chipped coffee table, then to Quincy hovering nearby. "Even if it doesn't work, I have to try," she said simply. "If he attacks me again in my sleep, I want to be ready."

A sudden wave of protectiveness washed over Keesha. She hated that her daughter—once so full of carefree jokes and doodles—had to steel herself against psychic assaults. "We're not alone in this," she reminded Grace. "Flores, Rodriguez, they're all in our corner."

Grace ran a hand across her stubbled chin, looking pensive. "I know. But he's cunning. He always finds a way to slip through cracks. And I'm... I'm scared one day I'll wake up and he'll have replaced me again. Or that I'll be stuck in this body forever."

Quincy and Keesha exchanged a worried glance. Finally, Quincy said, "I've got a friend—ex-military, retired now—who does security consultations. Let me call him. He can help fortify the house, maybe set up cameras or an alarm system that *truly* works. The plywood on the door is just a temporary fix."

Grace managed a small nod. "That makes sense." A moment later, she added, "I'm sorry. I know it costs money and time to keep reinforcing the house."

"Don't apologize," Keesha said firmly. "Nothing is more important than your safety."

Grace didn't argue, but her eyes flickered with guilt all the same. She set the lucid dreaming book back on the shelf with a sigh, then stood. In the borrowed body, every movement looked too big for the cozy space—like a giant roaming a dollhouse.

The evening settled in slowly, a blanket of pale mist creeping over the streets. Streetlights glowed in watery halos, and sporadic cars passed by, their tires hissing through puddles. Keesha decided to make a simple dinner—vegetable soup and fresh bread from a local bakery. They ate at the dining table, the overhead light a small circle of warmth in an otherwise shadowy house.

Conversations around the table were sporadic, mostly updates about the day or quiet reassurances. Grace tried to sip some soup but ended up pushing the bowl away when another headache spike hit.

"You sure you don't want some painkillers?" Keesha asked softly, reaching for Grace's arm.

Grace shook her head. "Dr. Flores said it might mask any signs if something changes. I'd rather feel it than be caught off guard."

A flicker of pride intermingled with sorrow in Keesha's chest. *She's so brave, and she shouldn't have to be.* Quincy gently pressed a cool cloth to Grace's temple, and Keesha watched her daughter lean into his care, eyes heavy with fatigue.

By the time dinner was finished and the dishes were stacked in the sink, an uneasy stillness had descended on the house. Keesha found herself drifting to the living room window, looking out at the faint lights of neighboring houses. In one of them, she could see the flicker of a TV through sheer curtains—someone else's normal evening, so far removed from the chaos within her own walls.

Behind her, Grace and Quincy spoke softly about something—an old memory, perhaps, or a random observation about the day. Keesha caught snippets of their voices, the low rumble of Quincy's comforting baritone and Grace's deeper-than-normal replies. It struck her how quickly they'd all adapted to the dissonance in Grace's body. Yet each time she caught sight of that stubbled jaw or broad torso, it still jarred her. *I won't let it be permanent.*

They were nearly done tidying up when bright headlights swept across the makeshift boards covering the window, making Keesha jerk around instinctively. A moment later, a firm knock sounded at the door—three quick raps that resonated in the tense hush.

Quincy signaled for Keesha and Grace to remain back. He approached the door cautiously, pressing his ear to the plywood. "Who is it?"

"It's Rodriguez," came the muffled reply. "Open up."

At her voice, Quincy lifted the hastily installed deadbolt and carefully opened the door. Detective Elena Rodriguez stepped inside, water dripping off her hooded raincoat and pooling on the doormat. Her hair was plastered to her head, and her cheeks were flushed from the chill. She pushed the hood back and exhaled.

"Sorry for showing up so late," she said, sliding out of her coat. "But I have news, and it couldn't wait."

Keesha felt her nerves spark with a mix of hope and anxiety. "From Dr. Flores?" she asked, ushering Rodriguez away from the drizzle.

Rodriguez nodded. "Flores, plus a specialist at the university who at least *entertains* the notion of psychic phenomena. We're not talking tabloids; this is a legitimate psychologist who studies fringe mental processes—stuff that overlaps with neurology." She gave a wry shrug. "It's the closest we've got to an expert on mind-swapping, for lack of a better term."

Grace edged closer, arms folded protectively across her chest. "And? Does this mean we have a plan?"

Rodriguez's gaze flicked to the bullet hole in the wall and then to Grace's borrowed face. "We're still working on it," she admitted. "Right now, the best idea is a controlled environment, like Flores told you. Somewhere with hidden surveillance, quick medical access, and enough security to ensure Darius doesn't slip away. But in order for him to *perform* any 'ritual,' he has to believe it's *his* show."

Keesha bit her lip. "Meaning we pretend to go along with his demands?"

"Exactly," Rodriguez said. She peeled off her soggy gloves and stuffed them into a pocket. "We feed him just enough desperation—tell him Grace's condition is deteriorating fast and that we'll do anything to save her, including letting him lead us to some special location or method. Meanwhile, we guide him toward *our* chosen site, which we present as a neutral middle ground."

Quincy paced behind the couch, arms folded. "If he catches wind of the trap..."

Rodriguez set her jaw. "We'll keep it subtle. We'll have only a few people on-site, maybe disguised as hospital staff or building maintenance. Everything else can be monitored via remote cameras. If Darius truly has a way to swap minds, we need him to attempt it. That's when we intervene."

Grace swallowed, the bob of her Adam's apple visible in the adult throat. "He'll sense a setup if we're not careful," she said. "He knows I'm desperate, but he also knows we hate him."

Rodriguez offered a grim smile. "You can hate someone and still do business with them. He's counting on your desperation to overshadow your caution."

A heavy pause settled. Keesha felt a swirl of emotions—relief that a plan existed at all, fear that it involved toying with Darius's manipulations, and guilt for having to pretend she was *begging* him for help. Finally, she broke the silence.

"What do we do next?" she asked.

Rodriguez glanced at the phone on the kitchen counter. "Tomorrow, we'll schedule a call or video conference with him at the detention center, or possibly an in-person meeting if the lawyers sign off. We'll feed him the line that Grace is deteriorating, that we believe *only* he can fix this. We'll ask him to specify the time, place, or what's needed—but we'll push him toward certain logistical constraints."

Keesha nodded, pressing a hand to her sternum as though to steady her heart. "I can do that." *I've lied to Darius before to protect Grace, I can do it again.*

Grace's gaze flicked to the floor. "I just hate giving him what he wants," she said softly, "even if it's just an illusion of control."

Rodriguez reached out, briefly touching Grace's shoulder. "I know. But that illusion might be exactly what we need to beat him at his own game."

They settled around the dining table once more, cups of hot tea steaming between them. Detective Rodriguez opened a small notebook, each page already scrawled with bullet points and question marks. She clicked a pen and began scribbling:

1. Negotiation Tactics

- We propose a private meeting to finalize details.
- Keesha will emphasize Grace's worsening condition.
- We steer Darius toward a 'safe' location, presumably a warehouse or clinic site with hidden security.

2. Medical Oversight

- Dr. Flores onsite with specialized monitoring equipment.
- Possibly the parapsychology specialist, incognito.
- Real-time scanning of Grace's and Darius's neurological activity during attempt.

3. Security Protocol

- Undercover officers disguised as staff.
- Surveillance cameras, panic buttons, remote locks.
- Snipers or perimeter patrol if absolutely necessary (though not openly visible).

4. Legal Framework

- DA's office remains skeptical.

- We document everything as a medical procedure combined with law enforcement oversight.

As Rodriguez outlined each point, Keesha could almost see the shape of a final confrontation taking form. There was a methodical clarity to the detective's approach that steadied her nerves.

"Now, the big risk," Rodriguez continued, drumming her pen on the table, "is that Darius might try to sabotage our setup the moment he realizes it's not truly 'his' environment. If he feels threatened or cornered, he could lash out—maybe even harm Grace if that psychic tether still exists. That's why we have to stage everything carefully."

Grace leaned forward, pressing her forearms against the worn wood. "Then maybe we can let him think *I'm* in charge of the location," she offered, voice grave. "I know how he thinks. If I suggest a place that's off the grid, he might believe it's *my* idea, so long as we plant the right clues."

Keesha's stomach turned at the idea of Grace having to manipulate the man who'd shattered her life. But she recognized the strategic value. "Are you sure you're up for that, honey?"

Grace's eyes flickered. "I hate it," she admitted. "But I *know* him—this constant push-and-pull of control. It might be easier for him to accept if it looks like I'm making the concessions, especially if you and I act at odds." She gave Keesha a pained look. "He used to divide us—make us question each other. We can turn that into an advantage."

The suggestion sent a chill down Keesha's spine. She remembered all too clearly the nights when Darius had pitted them against each other, playing the "disciplinarian" father while making Keesha look like the fearful or overprotective mother. It had been a twisted power game. Now Grace was proposing they weaponize that dynamic. *Maybe it's the only way...*

"Let's not finalize that angle just yet," Rodriguez cautioned, though her tone suggested she found the idea compelling. "But keep it in mind.

Darius's biggest weakness is his ego—he'll jump at any chance to feel superior or 'in control.' If it looks like Grace is buckling to him, he might drop his guard."

Quincy, who had been scribbling in his own small notepad, spoke up. "What if Darius tries to forcibly swap back before we're ready?" His voice wavered, betraying his worry.

Keesha shuddered. It was a valid fear. "We'll have to rely on Dr. Flores's monitoring," she said. "Any sign of unusual brain activity, we pull the plug." Then she realized how precarious that was—relying on a piece of equipment to protect Grace from a psychic assault. *But what other choice do we have?*

They continued brainstorming well into the night, the pages of Rodriguez's notebook filling with potential pitfalls and contingency plans. By the time the detective clicked her pen one final time, the tea in everyone's cups had long gone cold.

"We're in uncharted territory," Rodriguez said, echoing the sentiment she'd voiced before. She closed her notebook with a soft snap. "But at least we have a direction. Flores and I will refine this tomorrow morning. One step at a time."

Keesha breathed out a sigh that tasted like both relief and dread. Grace stared at the tabletop, lost in thought. Quincy set a comforting hand on her shoulder, and she responded with a tight nod.

Rodriguez stood and gathered her papers, stifling a yawn. She glanced out the window at the thin haze of mist under the streetlight. "I should go get some rest. I'll call you tomorrow morning, let you know what the DA says."

Keesha walked her to the door, feeling the detective's weariness in every line of her posture. "Thanks for coming out so late," she said. "I know you have a million other cases."

Rodriguez shook her head, zipping up her coat. "Right now, this is top priority. None of my other cases involve a kid in a stolen body." She paused, turning her dark eyes on Keesha. "We'll bring her home. Truly."

Keesha swallowed hard, nodding. “Thank you.”

With that, Rodriguez slipped into the damp night, her figure receding into the glow of the streetlights until it was swallowed by darkness.

For a time, Keesha, Quincy, and Grace simply sat in the living room, exhaustion pressing down. They had a plan—tenuous, incomplete, but a plan nonetheless. And yet each of them could sense the tension building, the sense that tomorrow might crack open a new level of danger.

Eventually, Grace rose from the couch, her posture betraying her fatigue. “I’m going to try to sleep,” she announced, though Keesha suspected sleep would not come easily. “Staying up just makes me think too much.”

Keesha stood as well, wrapping her arms around Grace’s tall frame in an awkward embrace. She could feel the ripple of taut muscle beneath the sweatshirt—evidence of Darius’s adult strength. “Goodnight, baby,” she murmured, voice thick with emotion. “Call me if you need anything.”

Grace squeezed her back gently, careful not to crush her. “Night, Mom. Night, Quincy,” she added, her deep voice wavering. Then she withdrew toward the hallway, shoulders slumped in a posture that reminded Keesha of a child burdened with a too-heavy backpack.

Quincy watched her go, then turned to Keesha. The lines on his face seemed deeper than ever. “You should rest too,” he urged softly. “I’ll do one more check around the yard, make sure everything’s locked and quiet.”

Keesha nodded, grateful for the gesture of security. “All right,” she managed. “But don’t stay out there too long—it’s cold.”

He gave a small smile. “I’ll be fine.” Pausing, he touched her elbow gently. “We’re going to get through this, you know. I don’t know how, but I believe it.”

A wave of emotion crested in her chest. She thought of the first time Quincy had come into their lives—when Grace was seven, and he'd been a helpful neighbor who offered to fix a broken fence. He'd always been the type to step in when help was needed, never asking for anything in return. "I believe it too," she whispered, grateful for his steadiness.

Once Quincy slipped outside, flashlight in hand, Keesha found herself in the living room, alone with the hush of the late hour. She leaned back against the couch, staring at the bullet hole—now partially mended but still visible. The house carried a thousand echoes of what used to be. On the coffee table lay the remains of their notes from the evening's strategy session. She ran her hand across the scribbled pages, a swirl of arrows and question marks capturing their collective fear and hope.

She turned off the main lamp, leaving only a small side table lamp aglow, casting a warm puddle of light that didn't quite reach the corners. Outside, the wind rattled the plywood sheets nailed across the damaged front door. The sound grated on her nerves—a reminder of how vulnerable their once-cozy home had become.

Wandering to the window, she peered through the narrow gap. She could just make out Quincy's silhouette as he paced the perimeter, checking locks, making sure no one had tampered with anything. The watchfulness reminded her of ancient sentinels guarding a fortress under siege. *Our fortress is battered, but it's ours,* she thought. *We won't let Darius tear it down.*

She was about to turn away when a faint memory flickered through her mind—an image of Grace, seven years old, dancing barefoot in the living room to pop songs on the radio, Darius nowhere in sight. A day of laughter and childish silliness. Tears pricked Keesha's eyes. That was what she was fighting for: her daughter's carefree spirit, her chance at normalcy.

As midnight ticked closer, she finally left the window, too exhausted to keep vigil any longer. She flicked off the last lamp and made her way to her bedroom, pausing only to crack Grace's door open. The sight inside nearly broke her: the hulking form sprawled atop a twin bed that seemed comically small. Grace's breathing was ragged, her face turned toward the wall. Yet Keesha could hear the faint hitch of a nightmare in her breathing. She stepped into the room, crouched by the bed, and laid a gentle hand on Grace's forearm.

"Shh," she whispered, "you're safe here."

Grace's eyes opened, just for a moment, confused in the dark. Then she exhaled, seeming to settle. Keesha stayed a minute longer, waiting until Grace's breathing deepened into something resembling rest. She kissed the back of Grace's large hand—a gesture so familiar yet tinged with sadness in this borrowed flesh—and slipped from the room.

In the hallway, she leaned against the wall, heart pounding. The lines in the sand were drawn, indeed. Darius had forced their hand by offering a twisted bargain, and they were preparing to meet him head-on—on his own psychic battleground. *But we have more strength than we used to,* she reminded herself. *We have each other.*

Outside, the misty rain continued its quiet lament, and the wind carried the faintest moan through the loosened plywood. In that subtle symphony of water and wood, Keesha heard the promise of another storm looming. Yet a fragile ember of hope also glowed in her chest: *Grace is alive, we have allies, and we're not giving up.*

She thought of the bullet hole, the patched door, the unyielding love that had kept them going through every assault. Tomorrow would bring new challenges, new plans—and the looming confrontation with a man who refused to release his hold on their lives. But as she finally crept into her own room and sank onto the bed, she clung to the single thought that guided her through all this darkness: *For Grace, I will face any storm—even if I have to walk through hell to bring her back.*

And with that vow echoing in her mind, Keesha allowed her eyes to close, bracing herself for whatever nightmares the night might bring—and whatever battles tomorrow would demand.

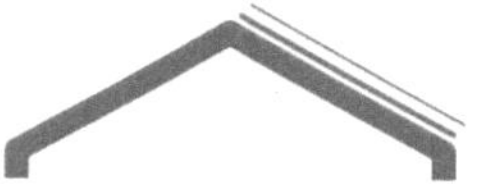

Chapter 3: Redwood Shadows

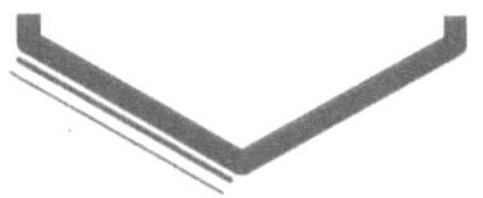

A pale dawn filtered through thinning clouds as Detective Elena Rodriguez pulled up to the curb outside Keesha Marshall's house. The unmarked sedan hummed with an undercurrent of tension, the engine sounding uncommonly loud in the morning stillness. Keesha stood by the newly repaired front door, arms folded across her chest in a show of measured resolve. A sideways glance at Quincy, hovering protectively beside her, reminded her that neither of them had truly relaxed in days.

When the car door opened, Rodriguez stepped out, a thick file tucked under one arm. Even from a distance, Keesha could see the dark crescents under the detective's eyes and the stray wisps of hair escaping her loose bun. Exhaustion radiated from her in palpable waves. The sight stirred a twinge of empathy in Keesha—*they were all running on fumes*—but it also strengthened her resolve. If Elena could keep pressing forward despite everything, so could she.

Behind Keesha, Grace shifted uneasily, standing in the threshold. Her borrowed adult body—tall, broad-shouldered, wearing clothes hastily purchased to fit—was a perpetual reminder of what Darius King had stolen. Keesha couldn't help the familiar pang that shot through her heart whenever she looked at Grace's gentle eyes set in that imposing face. The incongruity never ceased to twist her emotions into knots: fierce love, protective anger, and a mounting desperation to undo what had been done.

Rodriguez reached them, nodding a curt hello. "You called me," she said without preamble, her tone brisk. "Said there was intel on Redwood Ridge?"

Keesha gestured for her to come inside, trying not to let her anxiety show. "Yes. Someone phoned late last night—anonymously. He said he used to run errands for Darius, back when... well, back when Darius had more direct influence over people. He mentioned a cabin in Redwood Ridge that Darius referred to as an 'anchor point' for his powers."

Rodriguez's eyebrows rose. "Redwood Ridge? We scanned Darius's known properties, but that region never came up under his name. If it's real, it could be registered under a proxy. Or it might be entirely off the books."

Grace cleared her throat, producing a jarringly low sound. "Then we have to investigate," she said, voice trembling with a combination of determination and lingering fear. "If he's planning to use Redwood Ridge for that... ritual, we can't let him get there first."

Rodriguez studied Grace's face with a sympathetic furrow in her brow. "You're right," she allowed. "If there's a remote place that matters to Darius, we need to know why. Could be something he's been preparing for years."

Before anyone could reply, the sound of footsteps announced Dr. Miriam Flores's arrival on the porch. She carried a laptop case slung over her shoulder, her expression drawn but alert. "Morning," she greeted, then gave Grace a once-over. "I've been up half the night reviewing brain-scan data," she explained quietly. "Grace, the stress markers in your scans have intensified again since yesterday. That tether between you and Darius..."

Dr. Flores hesitated, casting a worried glance at Grace. "...It's growing stronger."

Grace's shoulders slumped. Keesha immediately reached out, curling an arm around her daughter's waist—an intimate, protective gesture complicated by the fact that Grace's waist was now muscled and broad. "You can feel it, can't you?" she asked softly.

The adult lines of Grace's face twisted in discomfort. "He was in my head again," she admitted. "Last night, I had dreams—no, more like nightmares. But in them, he spoke to me. Laughed."

A grim hush settled over the group. Rodriguez's gaze hardened. "We can't let him gain any more psychological ground," she said. "The DA's office is close to dropping charges against the person they're calling 'Darius King.' If we can't prove who he really is, he may walk. That means your body—your real body, Grace—could end up free to vanish if Darius plays his cards right."

From behind them, Quincy inhaled, his breath as steady as he could make it. "So Redwood Ridge is our best lead," he said. "If we can locate that cabin, maybe we can lure him there under our conditions. Or investigate first, see if it's even real."

Keesha shut her eyes for a moment. *Lure him, corner him, anything.* "What if we plan a sting at the cabin? Have a team on standby?" she suggested, pressing a hand to her temple where a dull ache was brewing.

Rodriguez inclined her head but kept her stance guarded. "Possible," she said. "But Redwood Ridge is remote. Getting backup there fast is a challenge, and Darius may have counters we haven't seen yet. We have to be strategic."

Dr. Flores joined her, arms crossed. "We also can't overlook Grace's condition. If the tether strengthens further, she might be vulnerable during a confrontation—even if Darius can't physically reach her, he may try to exploit the connection."

At that, Grace's large hands curled into fists, knuckles whitening. Keesha squeezed her side, as if to say *we won't let it happen.* The intensity in Grace's eyes bordered on desperation. "I can't keep living like this," she whispered, voice resonant. "Every night, I'm afraid he'll drag me out of my own mind."

No one spoke for several seconds. The wind carried the faint hum of a passing car, punctuating the collective tension. At last, Rodriguez nodded. "Let's take this inside," she said. "We'll make a plan."

They made their way into the living room, which still smelled faintly of new paint where bullet holes had been hastily patched. The memory of Darius's last assault lingered like a cold presence in the walls. Grace and Quincy veered into the kitchen, needing space and maybe a calming drink, while Keesha and Rodriguez set up near the couch. Dr. Flores hovered close by, her laptop case clutched to her side.

Rodriguez placed her thick file on the coffee table and flipped it open. "If Redwood Ridge is genuine," she began, "Darius could have stashed journals, ritual objects, or something else that amplifies these so-called powers. We've seen no sign of them in his other properties or personal effects."

Keesha glanced at the coffee table, recalling the many frantic hours spent there, combing through old family photos, trying to prove Grace's identity. "We can't let the possibility slip by," she said, her tone quiet but firm. "Grace's life hinges on this."

The detective's gaze rested on Keesha with an unspoken mix of sympathy and respect. "I'm sorry," she offered gently. "I know this is brutal to relive. But we do have one advantage: if Redwood Ridge is remote, it might mean fewer innocent bystanders. We can coordinate a more controlled operation—though it also means Darius has more freedom to set traps."

Keesha gave a curt nod. "Whatever it takes," she said. "I'll do anything to protect Grace."

Glancing at the hallway, Dr. Flores added, "If we confront him, Grace will need some form of protection—psychic or medical. I've been brainstorming ways to dull or interrupt the tether, possibly using mild sedatives or neurological blockers. It's experimental, but we have to try."

Rodriguez rubbed the back of her neck, exhaustion plain on her face. "And if this Redwood Ridge rumor leads nowhere?"

Keesha pressed her lips together, forcing herself not to dwell on that possibility. "We keep searching," she replied. "But I have a gut feeling it's real. Darius used to talk about going 'off-grid' if things went south. Said he had a place he could vanish into."

A short silence followed, thick with the weight of old trauma. Finally, Rodriguez reached for her laptop. "Let's see if we can confirm it."

An hour later, the house buzzed with activity. Detective Rodriguez had commandeered the dining table, her laptop connected to a portable hotspot as she searched property records, tax documents, and old legal briefs tied to Darius's known associates. Dr. Flores claimed a corner of the living room, flipping through obscure articles on telepathy, neurological phenomena, and unorthodox medical interventions. She made phone calls every few minutes, her voice low and urgent as she tried to gather more data.

Meanwhile, Keesha found herself in the role of impromptu assistant, dashing between Rodriguez and Flores to supply fresh coffee, gather blank paper, or scribble notes. The routine kept her grounded, even as her nerves hummed with anxious energy. She couldn't help occasionally glancing toward the kitchen window, where she caught sight of Grace's silhouette on the back patio.

Outside, Quincy was guiding Grace through basic physical conditioning. The morning sun had climbed higher, revealing a crisp blue sky—a stark contrast to the chaos inside Keesha's chest. She paused at the window, watching her daughter attempt push-ups with those large arms, her movements unsteady. Quincy, patient as ever, encouraged Grace to find her center of gravity. Keesha's heart contracted; Grace had been a slender child who once disliked gym class. Now she was grappling with the strength and mass of a grown man's body. *Will we ever return to normal?*

Through the glass, she noticed a faint shimmer around Grace—hardly visible, but reminiscent of the flickers they'd seen when Darius first demonstrated his mind-altering abilities. Grace was unaware of it, too focused on the motions Quincy coached her through. *Is that her own psychic power?* Keesha wondered, a chill skittering down her spine. She remembered Dr. Flores's theories that Grace might have absorbed some lingering abilities from Darius. If so, it could be a double-edged sword.

Back inside, she heard Rodriguez let out a small whoop of triumph. Keesha hurried over to the dining table, finding the detective pointing at a highlighted line of text on her screen.

"Got something," Rodriguez announced, glancing at both Keesha and Dr. Flores. "A hunting cabin on the outskirts of Redwood Ridge, registered under a shell corporation formed about twenty years ago. The corporation is connected to a lawyer who once handled Darius's finances."

"That's him," Keesha breathed, her adrenaline spiking. "Has to be."

Rodriguez nodded, lips pursed. "It's an hour north of the main highway, buried deep in the forest. We don't have exact details—just an approximate location. It's definitely suspicious."

Flores peered at the laptop. "Coordinates are here?" she asked, tapping the screen. "We could arrange for local law enforcement to keep an eye on the nearest roads."

"Exactly," Rodriguez agreed. "We'll do it quietly. If Darius catches wind that we're onto him, he might move on. Or worse, he might decide to lure *us* in on his own terms."

Keesha could practically hear her pulse in her ears. "At least we have a direction," she said. "We're not shooting blind anymore."

Not long after Rodriguez's discovery, Grace returned from her training session looking flushed and worn. At Dr. Flores's urging, she retreated to her old bedroom for a short rest. The small bed was woefully inadequate for her current body, but Grace tried to make the best of it, draping her long legs over the footboard. She stared up at the ceiling where glow-in-the-dark stars still faintly clung—a relic from her childhood. The sight filled her with a bittersweet ache.

She didn't realize she was drifting off until the edges of her vision began to blur. Slowly, sleep crept in... and with it came that familiar chill.

Grace...

The voice seeped into her thoughts like oil on water—dark, insidious. Even though it reverberated in her mind, Grace recognized it as Darius's, shaped to sound like her old child's voice. A mocking mimicry that made her skin crawl.

You're too weak for this body, the voice whispered, mingling with a sudden spike of pain. Grace's temples throbbed, and she dug her nails into the bedsheet. "Stop," she muttered under her breath, though her voice sounded distant.

This was always my fate. I'm only letting you borrow it, Darius hissed in her mind. *Don't get comfortable, little girl.*

Tears sprang to Grace's eyes as waves of dizziness overtook her. She wanted to scream but forced herself to remain quiet. Her mother and Quincy were working so hard—she couldn't keep scaring them. Instead, she squeezed her eyes shut and drew upon the breathing exercises Quincy had taught her. *Inhale for four... hold... exhale for four.*

Slowly, the voice receded, leaving a faint echo. The headache persisted, but the worst of it passed. For a moment, Grace lay there trembling, the aftershocks of the psychic intrusion washing through her. She hated how helpless it made her feel, how easily Darius could disturb her thoughts. The tether felt like chains wrapped around her soul.

A knock at the door brought her back to the present. "Grace?" Keesha's voice. "Can I come in?"

Grace cleared her throat, trying to steady her pulse. "Sure."

Keesha entered, eyes immediately darting over Grace's disheveled state. "Nightmare?" she asked, concern etched on her face.

Grace debated brushing it off, but the genuine warmth in her mother's eyes disarmed her. "He... got in my head again," she admitted. "It's like I can hear him whenever I'm alone or drifting off."

Keesha's jaw clenched, a flicker of anger burning in her gaze. She stepped forward and pressed a hand to Grace's forearm. "I'm sorry," she whispered. "We're close to a breakthrough—Rodriguez found something at Redwood Ridge. We'll follow that lead and put an end to this."

The fervor in Keesha's promise warmed Grace's heart. She managed a weak nod. "I believe you," she said, more to reassure her mother than herself.

By late afternoon, Rodriguez had made discreet contact with the local sheriff's office near Redwood Ridge. Their resources were limited—only a few deputies covering a large, forested county—but they agreed to monitor the main highway for any sign of a small child who might match Grace's real physical description, or any suspicious vehicles rumored to be tied to Darius.

"They'll keep it subtle," Rodriguez told the group as they gathered in the living room, where she'd hung a large map of Redwood Ridge on the wall. The region was dense with evergreen trees—towering redwoods and pines, dotted with a few winding roads. "If they spot Darius, they'll ping us immediately. Until then, we start planning how *we* might approach that cabin."

Quincy set down a cup of coffee, newly brewed, and leaned in. "I can scout it first if needed," he offered quietly. "Go in civilian style, no badges, no official presence. That way we don't risk tipping him off."

Keesha shot him a look of gratitude mixed with concern. "That could be dangerous," she said. "If Darius is already there—"

"I'll be careful," Quincy promised. "Better one person slip in than a whole convoy that might spook him."

Grace stood near the map, arms folded protectively over her chest. Her new posture reminded Keesha of how Darius used to stand—though Grace's eyes held none of his malice. "If we do find him," Grace said, voice steady yet threaded with unease, "will I have to... face him directly to trigger the swap? Or can Dr. Flores do something medically?"

All eyes turned to Flores, who had her notes spread across a coffee table. She grimaced. "I'm developing a sedation protocol—something that can keep you *aware* but shield your mind from sudden psychic intrusion. In theory, if we corner him and initiate the conditions he claims are needed for a 'ritual,' it could force a swap. But he has to at least *attempt* it. We can't do it unilaterally, not with our current technology."

Grace's shoulders slumped a bit. "So I have to rely on him?"

Flores nodded, sympathy etched into her features. "I'm afraid so. *And* on us protecting you if he tries to twist it for his own escape."

Rodriguez tapped a finger on the Redwood Ridge map. "We'll position plainclothes support around the perimeter—once we confirm he's there. The second we have eyes on him, we move in. If we can catch him off-guard, we might coerce him into performing this swap under monitored conditions. But that's a lot of 'ifs.'"

Keesha listened, her stomach twisting with each new detail. None of this was guaranteed. They were pinning their hopes on Darius's arrogance, on his belief that he could outsmart them. *But I know him,* she thought. *He'll want that control. He'll want to gloat.*

She reached for Grace's hand—a large, calloused hand that still felt foreign to her—and squeezed gently. "Stay strong," she murmured. "We're almost there."

Dusk settled in a slow crawl of purple and gray, hinting at a clear night sky. Keesha stepped onto the porch for a moment of quiet, arms wrapped around herself as a gentle breeze ruffled her hair. The boards creaked beneath her feet—a reminder of the night Darius's bullet had splintered them.

Grace joined her, carefully lowering herself onto the porch steps. The motion was still awkward in that body, and Keesha felt a pang of sorrow at the sight of her daughter's large frame dwarfed by the weight of confusion and dread.

"I keep thinking about Redwood Ridge," Grace said, gazing at the fading sunlight. "Imagining tall trees, a lonely cabin. It feels like something out of a nightmare."

Keesha settled beside her, close enough to feel the residual warmth of Grace's body. "It might be," she acknowledged softly. "But we won't face it unprepared."

The adult lines of Grace's face were softened by the gathering shadows, making her eyes stand out dark and reflective. "Mom," she said, voice wavering. "I just... I need you to be safe, too. What if he tries to hurt you again—like before?"

Memories flashed through Keesha's mind: Darius's illusions that left her reeling, the manipulations that nearly broke her spirit. She inhaled, steadying her voice. "He won't," she said firmly. "Not this time. I'm not the same woman I was back then. And I'm not alone now—I have you, Quincy, Rodriguez, Flores... We're a team."

Grace's gaze flicked downward. "I hate that you have to fight so hard to protect me."

Keesha wrapped an arm around Grace's shoulders. "That's what mothers do," she murmured, pressing a kiss to the short-cropped hair. "We protect our kids, no matter what it costs."

A trembling smile curved Grace's lips. "I love you," she said. "Thank you."

They sat in silence for a while, the evening air growing cooler around them. In the distance, a dog barked, and a car's headlights swept briefly across the street. For a moment, Keesha dared to imagine a future beyond Redwood Ridge—a future where Grace had her real body back, where they could enjoy an autumn evening without this ever-present cloud of danger.

Night fell fully, and one by one, the day's preparations wound down. Detective Rodriguez packed up her files, murmuring that she'd check into a nearby motel and resume calls first thing in the morning. Dr. Flores left with a stack of research papers under her arm, determined to refine the sedation formula that might protect Grace's mind.

Quincy spent the evening quietly walking the perimeter of the property, ensuring the new locks and reinforced doors were secure. Keesha watched him through the window, grateful for his thoroughness. She knew he was exhausted—the tension rarely left his face anymore. And yet, he continued, unwavering.

In the living room, Keesha paused by the wall where the bullet hole had once gaped. Now, it was half-patched and spackled, a faint scar on the drywall. She couldn't help placing her palm against it, as though checking for a heartbeat beneath. The house had become a symbol of their resilience—battered, but still standing.

Quincy slipped inside, footsteps soft on the floor. "All seems quiet," he said, voice low. He caught her gaze on the wall and brushed his fingers over hers gently. "We're mending, piece by piece," he added.

Keesha let out a shaky exhale. "I hope so," she said. "Sometimes I feel like we're just taping over the wounds, waiting for the next assault."

He pulled her into a brief hug, the warmth of his chest steadying her. "We'll face it head-on if it comes," he murmured. "We have no other choice."

Later, as they all prepared for bed, Keesha discovered Grace dozing in the old recliner in her bedroom—the same chair Keesha had once used to read bedtime stories. Grace's body looked awkward in it, with knees sticking out and arms dangling over the edges. Yet her expression, smoothed by sleep, seemed more like the little girl Keesha remembered: the child who used to sprawl across the living room rug, drawing pictures of butterflies and talking about her day at school.

Keesha retrieved a blanket, carefully draping it over Grace's shoulders. The motion caused Grace's eyes to flutter open, blinking in the dim light.

"Oh," Grace mumbled, voice thick with drowsiness. "Sorry. I—didn't mean to fall asleep here."

Keesha shushed her gently. "It's okay," she whispered. "You look comfortable enough."

Grace yawned, rubbing her eyes with the back of one large hand. "Did we hear anything else from Rodriguez? Or Dr. Flores?"

Keesha shook her head. "They're done for the night. Tomorrow, we'll pick up where we left off." She hesitated, then laid a hand on Grace's cheek, stubble scratching her palm. "Sleep well, baby. You need the rest."

Grace managed a faint nod before her eyes drooped closed once more, exhaustion claiming her. For a long moment, Keesha simply watched, torn between sorrow for the body Grace had been forced into and fierce maternal pride for how bravely she was enduring it.

Unable to sleep herself, Keesha headed back to the living room, where Quincy sat on the couch staring at the notes they'd compiled. The lamp's warm glow accentuated the lines of fatigue on his face.

"Couldn't sleep?" he asked quietly.

Keesha sank down beside him. "Too wired," she admitted, letting her head drop against the back of the couch. She scanned the papers—maps of Redwood Ridge, printouts from property registries, and Dr. Flores's typed analyses about the tether. "It feels like we're on the cusp of something big," she murmured.

Quincy nodded, flipping a page. "When we do track him down," he said, "it'll be dangerous. I'll go first, Keesha. I can't let you walk into a trap unprepared."

She reached for his hand, fingers interlacing. "Thank you," she said softly. "But you know I won't stand by if Grace's life is on the line."

A small, rueful smile tugged at Quincy's lips. "I know," he conceded. "That's why I love you. Stubborn and fearless when it comes to Grace."

They sat in companionable silence for a few minutes, the hush of the house broken only by the faint hiss of the air vents. Eventually, Quincy set the notes aside and pulled Keesha closer, letting her rest her head on his shoulder. Outside, the wind picked up, rattling the boards on the repaired door. Both of them stiffened at the noise—a reminder of how quickly the night could turn.

At last, Keesha gently disentangled herself from Quincy's embrace, pressing a light kiss to his cheek. "We should try to rest," she murmured. "We'll need clear heads tomorrow."

Quincy nodded and stood, heading down the hallway to the spare bedroom he'd adopted as his own. Keesha lingered, switching off lamps one by one until the living room was swallowed by dimness, lit only by slivers of moonlight filtering through the blinds.

She paused at the window, gazing out at the quiet street. This place—their home—had become a fortress of tension and determination. *But Redwood Ridge waits,* she thought, picturing towering trees and a hidden cabin. *What secrets has Darius left out there?*

A swirl of images flashed in her mind: Grace's frightened expression, the bullet hole in the wall, Darius's cold sneer. Beneath it all, an ember of hope burned. They finally had a lead that could turn the tide—an opportunity to force Darius's hand and reclaim Grace's rightful body.

In her bedroom, she found Grace still curled in the recliner, the blanket rising and falling with each slow breath. Keesha knelt by her side, smoothing the blanket over Grace's broad shoulders once more. *Soon,* she told herself, *we'll end this.*

Outside, the moon emerged from behind the thinning clouds, casting a soft glow on the patched bullet holes and the makeshift repairs around the front door. The wind whispered through the nearby trees, as if calling them onward. A part of Keesha quivered with anticipation—even fear—but another part firmed with determination, echoing the silent vow in her heart:

Darius King, you won't hold my daughter hostage any longer. We're coming for you—and for Redwood Ridge. And this time, we'll make sure you have nowhere left to run.

The night stretched on, filled with the unspoken promise of the coming confrontation. Mother and daughter—even in mismatched bodies—were bound by unbreakable love. Tomorrow would be one step closer to Redwood Ridge, one step closer to unraveling the final strands of Darius's twisted hold. The shadows might be gathering, but Keesha refused to cower. She would face them head-on, fueled by the single truth that mattered: *Grace deserves her life back, no matter what.*

Chapter 4: Deepening Shadows

The next morning arrived beneath skies the color of tarnished steel, a cold wind scraping against the windows and raising goosebumps on Keesha's arms. She'd managed only a few hours of fitful sleep, haunted by dreams of Redwood trees reaching for her like gnarled hands. The moment her eyes opened, a hard knot formed in her stomach, a relentless reminder of everything they'd be facing soon.

She rose before dawn, the house still cloaked in a dim hush. Outside, the early light revealed leaden clouds that threatened more rain. *It fits the mood,* she thought grimly. Even the weather seemed to acknowledge the tension coiled in her heart.

By the time she padded into the kitchen—feet chilled on the worn linoleum—she knew coffee would only jangle her nerves further, so she set the kettle to boil for tea instead. Each bubble in the heating water sounded loud in the silence, a mirror to the rising anxiety in her chest.

A soft rustle in the hallway signaled that Quincy was already awake. He emerged wearing a faded gray T-shirt and jeans, his hair still rumpled from sleep. In the dim overhead light, she could see the worry etched into his features. No words were needed; the mutual look they exchanged held a thousand unspoken concerns.

He offered a faint smile. "Morning," he murmured, stepping into the kitchen. He looked at the waiting kettle, then back at her. "You trying a gentler start to the day?"

Keesha shrugged, her grip tightening on the edges of the countertop. "Coffee feels too harsh right now," she admitted quietly, gaze flicking to the patch of the plywood-covered door. "I already feel like I'm on pins and needles."

Quincy nodded, sympathy in his eyes. "I get that," he said. Then his expression shifted, more serious. "I'll be heading out soon. I told Elena I'd help scout Redwood Ridge in person, see if we can confirm the cabin's exact location. She and I will coordinate with the local cops—quietly—so Darius doesn't suspect a thing."

Keesha's stomach knotted. She tried to steady her voice. "You're sure you have to go yourself?" Even as she asked, she knew the answer. She'd grown accustomed to Quincy's steady presence, his willingness to take on the more dangerous tasks so she and Grace could stay a step removed.

"It's best I go," Quincy said, resting a hand gently on her shoulder. "Elena needs backup, and I have experience doing recon." He hesitated, reading the fear behind her eyes. "I'll keep it simple: in, gather intel, and out. No heroics."

Keesha released a shaky breath, pushing a mug toward him. The kettle had just reached a soft whistle, steam curling into the air. "Be careful," she said, her voice almost a whisper. "If something goes sideways, promise me you won't push it. Just come back."

Quincy's eyes softened. "I promise." He wrapped his free hand around the mug she'd prepared, letting the warmth seep into his palms. "We won't let Darius catch us off guard this time."

Yet *safe* was a word that felt hollow to Keesha. Darius had an uncanny ability to slip through cracks and exploit any opening. She forced the thought aside, not wanting to dampen Quincy's reassurance, and swallowed her worry with a sip of tea.

A flicker of movement from the hallway made them both turn. Grace—trapped in her borrowed adult body—stood there quietly, half-hidden in shadows. She wore a heavy hooded sweatshirt that made her broad frame look even more imposing. In the half-light, Keesha noted the strain in her daughter's eyes.

"Morning, Grace," Quincy greeted gently. "I won't be long out there, I promise."

Grace nodded, folding her arms protectively. "I know," she said, her voice low with fatigue. "Just... watch your back."

A small, sad smile ghosted across Quincy's face. "Always."

Within half an hour, the living room was populated by hushed voices and subdued tension. Detective Elena Rodriguez arrived with a leather messenger bag slung over her shoulder, her hair in a tight ponytail that highlighted the worry etched into her features. Close behind her was Dr. Miriam Flores, dragging a rolling suitcase filled with medical gear—electrodes, wires, sedation vials. The sight of so much equipment made Keesha's stomach clench. *How had their lives come to this?*

Grace lingered near the wall, where a faint scar remained from the bullet hole Darius had left behind. Her hood cast a shadow over her face, and Keesha's heart twisted with sympathy. She hated seeing her once-carefree daughter so on edge, glancing at the door as if Darius might storm in at any moment.

Rodriguez stepped forward, her boots creaking on the living room floor. "We're heading out," she announced, her tone brisk. "Quincy and I will drive to Redwood Ridge, link up with a local deputy who's willing to help off the record. Once we've got a lay of the land and confirmed the cabin's location, we'll call."

Keesha, arms folded, tried to mask the tremor in her voice. "And us?"

"Stay put for now," Rodriguez insisted. Her gaze swept from Keesha to Grace, then back again. "We can't tip our hand if Darius is monitoring anything, or if he still has an ally. We don't know how far his influence goes. Last we heard, he was still in juvenile lockdown, but we can't be sure he's as powerless as they claim."

Dr. Flores shifted her weight, worry flitting across her face. "If he senses we're making a move, he could escalate—psychically or otherwise. We need to remain cautious."

Grace swallowed audibly. "He might feel it," she said, her voice carrying a hint of the child she truly was. "Like... if I panic or something, maybe he'd sense that."

Flores inclined her head. "We just don't know the exact mechanics of this tether. I hate dealing in hypotheticals, but better safe than sorry."

A tense hush settled over them. It broke only when Quincy and Rodriguez exchanged a final nod and slipped out the door, their footsteps fading on the porch. Keesha watched through the window as they climbed into Rodriguez's unmarked sedan and drove off into the gray morning. Once they were gone, an ache settled in her chest—part fear for Quincy's safety, part dread that they were heading toward a confrontation long overdue.

With Quincy and Rodriguez en route to Redwood Ridge, the house seemed both quieter and more claustrophobic. Keesha found herself pacing from room to room, channeling her nerves into mundane tasks. She reorganized the papers on the dining table, which documented Grace's identity struggles: medical scans, legal forms, outlandish headlines that had begun to circulate. When that no longer occupied her, she wiped down the already-clean kitchen counters.

Grace tried to help, but she kept knocking her hip against furniture, misjudging how much space her borrowed body took up. Each collision was a reminder of the dissonance she lived with. At one point, Keesha heard Grace grunt in pain or frustration; she rushed over to find Grace rubbing her temple.

"You all right?" Keesha asked, concern spiking.

Grace's broad shoulders lifted in a shaky sigh. "It's like I can feel him—Darius—at the edges of my mind," she murmured, tapping a fingertip against her temple. "Not words, exactly, but... like a background hum that gets louder if I let my guard down."

Seated at the dining table with her laptop open, Dr. Flores glanced up. "Any illusions? Visual distortions?"

"Not yet," Grace replied, her voice subdued. "But I keep expecting it."

A wave of anger swept through Keesha. She wished more than anything that she could reach inside Grace's head and yank out whatever tether Darius had installed. "We'll manage it," she said softly, crossing the room to offer Grace a gentle squeeze on the shoulder. "Just keep telling us if it gets worse."

Grace nodded, tension carving lines into her otherwise unfamiliar face.

Around midday, a thin band of sunlight broke through the heavy cloud cover, illuminating the backyard with a muted glow. The reprieve felt like a gift, and Keesha seized on it. She led Grace outside for a breath of fresh air, hoping a change of scenery might ease the suffocating anxiety.

The backyard was small, mostly grass with a battered old swing set in one corner—remnants of Grace's childhood. Now, those swings looked too small for her towering frame. Quincy had spent time teaching her some basic martial stances as a way to master her new strength. Grace practiced them now in slow, deliberate movements, arms sweeping in arcs that required careful control.

Keesha stood to one side, watching with cautious pride. "You're getting good," she said. "I remember how you used to hate P.E. class. Now look at you."

Grace lowered her arms, cheeks flushing. "It still feels wrong," she admitted. "Like I'm wearing a costume I can't take off. Sometimes I... I want to lash out with this strength, just to see if it's real. But I'm terrified that's *him*, not me."

A pang shot through Keesha's chest. "You're still you," she murmured. "No matter how strong this body is, your heart and mind belong to Grace." She stepped closer, resting a hand on Grace's arm. "We just have to keep reminding ourselves of that."

Grace's mouth curved into a small, sad smile. "Thanks, Mom."

They continued the practice for several more minutes, Grace breathing deeply to chase away the creeping dread of Darius's presence. In those moments, the tension in the air seemed to dissipate—just a bit. The sun warmed them, and the act of moving gave Grace something tangible to focus on.

They were still outside, halfway through another sequence of stances, when the sliding door burst open. Dr. Flores rushed onto the patio, her voice urgent. "Keesha! Grace! Come in—quickly."

A jolt of fear shot through Keesha. *What now?* She and Grace hurried inside, leaving footprints of dew across the kitchen floor. Dr. Flores placed her phone on the counter and hit speaker mode. Detective Rodriguez's tense voice crackled over the line.

"Is Grace with you?" Rodriguez asked, her tone clipped by static.

Keesha's heart pounded. "Yes, she's right here. What's going on?"

Rodriguez let out a sharp exhale. "Darius is gone. He escaped the juvenile ward less than an hour ago."

The color drained from Keesha's face. "*Escaped?* How is that possible?"

"Apparently, he faked some kind of seizure—or used a remnant of his power to spook the staff. While they were distracted, he slipped through a security door. A guard was found unconscious, so it looks like someone on the inside might have helped. We don't know how far he's gotten."

Dr. Flores pressed a hand to her temple. "If Redwood Ridge really is his anchor point—"

"We suspect that's where he'll head," Rodriguez confirmed grimly. "Quincy and I are still en route. We've alerted the local sheriff's department. If Darius has a car or an accomplice, he might beat us there. We'll do our best to intercept him on the roads, but he could also be traveling at night or taking back routes."

A wave of terror slammed into Keesha. *Darius—free again—in Grace's real body.* "What do you need us to do?" she asked, trying to keep her voice from shaking.

"For now, stay put," Rodriguez repeated firmly. "He might try to come after Grace, but we're not certain. He could also go straight to Redwood Ridge. Just don't engage him alone, okay?"

Grace's eyes were dark with anger and fear. "He knows everything about us," she managed through gritted teeth. "Our routine, where we live—everything."

The detective's voice softened. "I know. We'll do everything possible to catch him before he reaches that cabin. Keep your phone on. If he contacts you or if you see anything suspicious, call me immediately."

The call ended, leaving a charged silence in its wake. Keesha stared at the phone, her fingers trembling. *Darius was free. He has Grace's rightful body.* Any illusions that he might be under lock and key were shattered.

"We can't just stay here," Grace burst out, pacing in the small kitchen, her large hands flexing with restless energy. "If Darius shows up, we're—"

"I know what Rodriguez said," Keesha began, arms folded protectively across her chest. "But maybe she's right that it's safer to wait for them."

Grace shook her head, jaw clenched in frustration. "Every time we sit and wait, something goes wrong. He's always one step ahead. If we want to protect ourselves—or get my body back—we have to be proactive."

From across the room, Dr. Flores cleared her throat, her expression conflicted. "I understand the impulse, but Redwood Ridge is remote and dangerous. If you arrive without backup, you could be walking into a trap."

"I hate doing nothing." Grace's voice trembled, betraying her young age beneath the deep timbre of her borrowed vocal cords. "What if he sets up that ritual before we can stop him?"

Keesha's maternal instincts warred with her memories of Darius's cunning. She looked between Grace and Dr. Flores, feeling the weight of the decision. "What if we position ourselves closer but not at the cabin?" she suggested, voice subdued. "That way, we're not sitting ducks here, and we can still link up with Rodriguez faster if something goes down."

Flores paused, considering it. "A motel near Redwood Ridge—maybe half an hour away. That might be a compromise."

Grace exhaled, some tension draining from her posture. "That's all I want," she admitted. "I can't stay here waiting for him to break in again."

Though fear still twisted inside her, Keesha nodded. "Let's do it. We'll pack essentials, keep a low profile. If we need to move quickly, we can."

Flores hesitated but ultimately agreed. The idea of staying put when Darius was on the loose felt unbearable. *At least if we're closer,* Keesha reasoned, *we have a chance to react in time.*

They packed hastily—some clothes, first aid supplies, Dr. Flores's medical equipment, and enough snacks to last a day or two. Keesha took the driver's seat in her aging sedan, Dr. Flores beside her with a phone clutched in one hand, and Grace in the back, hood pulled low over her face.

As Keesha started the engine, she caught a glimpse of the house in the rearview mirror. *Bullet holes, plywood patches, and the weight of too many nightmares.* She had half a mind to lock the door and never look back. But this was still their home—if they survived Darius, she dreamed of truly restoring it.

Dr. Flores seemed to read the melancholy in her expression. "You'll rebuild," she said softly, tucking a stray lock of hair behind her ear. "Once he's caught, once Grace is free again—this place can be a real home again."

Keesha managed a trembling smile. "One step at a time," she whispered, eyes returning to the road.

Grace leaned forward between the seats. "We will fix this," she said quietly, her gaze shifting between Keesha and Flores. "I know it's scary, but we're not powerless."

Keesha gripped the steering wheel, drawing strength from Grace's conviction. It occurred to her that Grace was still a child, but her trials had forged a determination well beyond her years. *She deserves a normal life,* Keesha thought fiercely. *We'll get it for her.*

As they drove north, the landscape changed, rolling hills rising on either side of the road, thick clusters of trees looming in the distance. Dr. Flores periodically checked her messages: *No sign of Darius yet. No updated sightings.* The tension mounted with every passing mile. Keesha felt her shoulders stiffen each time the phone buzzed, half-expecting news that he'd attacked someone.

They eventually reached a small roadside motel on the outskirts of a sprawling evergreen forest. A garish VACANCY sign blinked in red letters, and the paint on the exterior walls had peeled to reveal weathered wood beneath. It was far from welcoming, but it offered locked doors and proximity to Redwood Ridge—enough to satisfy their uneasy plan.

Their room was cramped: two narrow beds draped in threadbare blankets and a single wobbly table by the window. The musty scent of old carpet hung in the air, and the overhead light buzzed faintly. Dr. Flores set up her equipment on the table, checking vials of sedatives, laying out electrodes and reading materials in neat rows.

Grace went straight to the window, pulling aside the dusty curtain to peer at the parking lot. Beyond the row of parked cars, tall pines swayed in the afternoon breeze. "It's so quiet," she murmured, shoulders tensing as though expecting Darius to leap out from behind a tree.

Keesha joined her, resting a hand on Grace's shoulder. "Rodriguez said to hold tight," she reminded gently. "We're only about thirty minutes away from Redwood Ridge now, which means if they find him..."

"...We can be there," Grace finished. Yet frustration lingered in her eyes. "I'm sick of feeling trapped. It's like we're always hiding."

Keesha had no comforting answer. She felt it, too—this sense of constantly being on the defensive, never fully in control of their own fate. "I know," she said, her tone laced with empathy. "But we'll face him soon. And when we do, we'll be ready."

Behind them, Dr. Flores chimed in softly, "Let's review our emergency steps if he tries contacting Grace directly—via phone or telepathy. We document every detail, keep calm, and if the pressure in Grace's mind spikes, we use a measured sedative."

Grace sighed, a mixture of relief and resignation crossing her features. "All right," she conceded, stepping away from the window. "I just hate relying on sedatives to keep him out."

"Better than risking a complete mental attack," Flores said.

And so they settled in, each grappling with their own swirl of emotions, as the hours began to slide by in that stuffy motel room.

The sky outside shifted into swaths of bruised purple and orange, signaling the onset of evening. Keesha dozed fitfully on one of the beds, her mind drifting in and out of half-formed nightmares. A muted ring jolted her awake. She sat up, heart pounding, as Dr. Flores snatched her phone and answered.

She put it on speaker, and Rodriguez's voice came through, marred by faint static. "Flores? Keesha? You there?"

Keesha rubbed her bleary eyes. "We're here. Any news?"

"We're at the cabin," came Rodriguez's clipped reply. "It's definitely linked to Darius. Old receipts and personal effects confirm it. But there's no sign of forced entry or recent activity—no footprints, no tire marks. Could be he's not here yet."

Keesha felt both relief and renewed tension. "So we still don't know where he is," she said softly.

"Not exactly." The detective's tone carried frustration. "We've got a sheriff's deputy at the main highway, but Darius could be traveling the back roads or even hitching a ride. Quincy's scouting around the perimeter—there's a large clearing behind the cabin, big enough for vehicles. We're trying to set up a covert watch."

Grace leaned over the phone, brow furrowing. "So he could show up at any time?"

"Right," Rodriguez confirmed. "I'm sorry we don't have better intel. Where are you three right now?"

Keesha glanced at Dr. Flores, then at Grace. Guilt twisted in her gut as she admitted, "We came north. We're about half an hour from Redwood Ridge in a motel. We figured we should be closer."

A pause, then a sigh crackled through the speaker. "Well, it's not what I advised," Rodriguez said, "but maybe it's better you're close if something goes down. Just don't do anything rash, okay? If he appears, call me immediately. We'll coordinate a takedown."

Keesha swallowed. "Understood."

"Good. Keep your phone on. If all stays quiet, we'll regroup at dawn." There was a faint shuffle, as though Rodriguez were shifting position. "Stay safe."

The call ended with a faint click, leaving the motel room steeped in silence. Keesha let out a breath, the tension in her shoulders refusing to dissipate. At least Darius wasn't at the cabin—yet. But that also meant he could be anywhere, including en route to them.

Grace set her jaw. "He's out there somewhere, free," she muttered. "And I'm stuck here in... *this*." She gestured at her adult body in frustration.

Keesha reached for Grace's hand, her own much smaller fingers sliding over Grace's broad knuckles. "We'll get him," she promised softly. "One day at a time."

As darkness fell, the motel took on an eerie stillness. The parking lot lamps buzzed, drawing insects that flitted in circles. Inside, the hum of an old air conditioner provided a constant background drone. Dr. Flores prepped her sedatives, lining up syringes with carefully labeled doses. Keesha positioned herself by the window, keeping an uneasy vigil. Grace sat on the edge of the second bed, arms propped on her knees.

The hours passed slowly. Now and then, a car rumbled by on the nearby highway, and each time, Keesha tensed, half expecting the driver's silhouette to be Darius—her daughter's body inhabited by that dangerous mind.

Close to midnight, Grace gave a sudden gasp, clutching at her forehead. Keesha was at her side in seconds. "What is it? Is he—?"

Grace nodded, her face contorting in pain. "He's pushing," she choked out, pressing a palm to her temple. "Like he's *digging* at the tether."

It felt like a punch to Keesha's gut. *Even from a distance, he could do this?* "Stay with me," she urged, voice trembling.

Dr. Flores rushed over, already drawing a small dose into a syringe. "I'll give you just enough to dull the link," she explained, her tone steady but urgent. "It won't knock you out completely. Just... insulate you."

Grace's breath came in ragged gulps, sweat shining on her brow. She jerked back her hoodie sleeve, baring a muscled forearm that still seemed so wrong to Keesha's eyes. Flores administered the injection swiftly, then laid a calming hand on Grace's shoulder.

"It'll help," Flores murmured.

Moments later, the tension in Grace's posture began to ease. Her breathing slowed, though her eyes were still wide with lingering terror.

Keesha sank onto the bed beside her, smoothing back a tuft of short hair that once had been long and curly. *Another reminder of how everything had changed.*

"Thank you," Grace managed once the worst had passed. Her gaze flicked toward the window. "He's out there, and he's not stopping."

Keesha's heart broke at the fear in her daughter's voice. "We'll stop him," she whispered fiercely. "I promise."

They huddled in a tense quiet for the next few hours, only the whir of the air conditioner and the faint drip of a leaky faucet breaking the silence. Dr. Flores eventually drifted into an uneasy doze, needing rest in case her medical skills were required again. Grace reclined on her bed, fighting off the sedation but too wired to truly sleep.

Keesha perched on the edge of the remaining bed, phone in hand, glancing at the clock every few minutes. *1:30 A.M... 2:15 A.M... 3:00 A.M...* Sleep felt impossible. Each time she closed her eyes, she pictured Redwood Ridge: towering evergreens, a rickety cabin, and Darius's smug grin as he prepared some monstrous ritual. *No,* she told herself. *We'll be there to stop him.*

At some point, Grace let out a soft, fitful snore—exhaustion finally pulling her under. Keesha crept closer, tucking a blanket over her daughter's oversized frame. The incongruity struck her again: large hands, muscled arms, the faint stubble along the jaw. Yet the furrow of Grace's brow was heartbreakingly familiar. She remembered smoothing that brow when Grace was a toddler, chasing away nightmares with a lullaby.

Unable to help herself, Keesha began humming that same lullaby under her breath, the soft notes filling the cramped motel room. *Maybe it can keep some of the nightmares away,* she thought. If nothing else, it soothed her own nerves, reminding her of simpler nights when Grace had been small and unafraid.

Eventually, Keesha's own exhaustion took hold. She settled against the pillows, phone on the bedside table, set to maximum volume. *No matter what,* she told herself, *we'll be ready for the call.* Outside, the forest exhaled a breeze that brushed against the window, whispering like a distant warning.

As she drifted into a light, restless sleep, her mind returned to the Redwood trees. She saw them looming tall, their branches interwoven to create a skeletal roof. Somewhere in that dream-forest, Darius lurked, wearing a ten-year-old's face with a twisted adult's cunning. *We're coming for you,* she vowed silently, *and this time, we're not letting you slip away.*

The motel walls felt like a paper-thin barrier against the storm gathering in her dreams. Yet for the moment, three weary souls found a fragile reprieve from the terror outside. Morning would come soon enough, and with it, the next step in their ever-tightening confrontation with Darius King—and the psychic tether that bound him so cruelly to Grace's mind.

Chapter 5: The Gathering Storm

A leaden sky pressed down on the motel the next morning, pale light seeping through the thin curtains like a reluctant warning. Keesha startled awake from a shallow doze, her body tense and the sheets beneath her damp with anxiety. For a disorienting moment, she forgot where she was—until the cramped dimensions of the motel room set in. Dr. Miriam Flores perched at the small table, her eyes rimmed with fatigue as she typed on her phone. The hush in the room felt dense, as if the walls themselves were listening.

Grace stirred on the other bed. Watching her tall, broad-shouldered form shift under the thin covers made Keesha's stomach lurch with the same jolt of incongruity she felt every morning. *She should be a ten-year-old girl, fussing about school or cartoons,* Keesha thought miserably. Instead, Grace was still sedated from the dose she'd needed to blunt Darius's psychic tether.

Outside, a car door slammed, and Keesha's heart tripped. She forced herself to exhale when it turned out to be just another motel guest. Dr. Flores offered a wan smile, the kind that said *I understand your fear, but there's nothing I can say.*

"You got a bit of sleep," Dr. Flores observed softly, closing her phone. "Better than nothing."

"Some," Keesha answered, running a hand over her damp brow. "No calls from Rodriguez or Quincy?"

Flores shook her head, worry flickering in her expression. "Not overnight. I've checked my phone every hour. Nothing."

That *nothing* weighed on them. It could mean Darius was nowhere near Redwood Ridge—or that he'd already outmaneuvered them. The possibilities echoed in Keesha's mind like phantom footsteps. She forced the thought away and turned to Grace, who was sitting up with a bleary, heavy-lidded gaze.

"Mom?" Grace muttered, pressing a hand to her temple. "Dr. Flores?" A flash of awareness crossed her features, and then resignation settled in. "No updates yet?"

Keesha managed a sad smile. "No. But we'll get some soon."

Grace gave a small, grim nod, the lines of stress around her eyes a stark reminder that no one in this room was truly rested.

An hour later, the motel room buzzed with a fraught kind of routine. Keesha sipped lukewarm coffee, trying not to dwell on the bitter tang that matched her mood. Grace poked half-heartedly at a microwaved breakfast burrito, eventually giving up on it altogether. Dr. Flores went through her medical kit, triple-checking sedation vials and heartbreakingly aware that she might need them at any moment.

Then Keesha's phone rang—a harsh jangle that made them all jump. She fumbled for it. "Rodriguez?"

"Yes, it's me," Detective Elena Rodriguez's voice crackled against a weak signal. "We've got movement. Locals found a stolen sedan abandoned near the cabin. Footprints leading into the woods—likely Darius."

A jolt of alarm lit through Keesha's chest. *He's already there.* She pressed her free hand to her sternum. "He's at Redwood Ridge."

"Almost certainly," Rodriguez confirmed. "Quincy and I are at a trailhead with the local deputy. We're early, but we need more manpower—and that means you three if the ritual possibility still stands."

Keesha felt Grace's gaze lock onto hers, the silent question flaring between them: *Are we really doing this?* She nodded at Grace, who swallowed hard and gave a terse nod back.

"We'll come," Keesha told Rodriguez, voice wobbling despite her best efforts to be steady. "What's the plan?"

"Meet us at the ranger station off Route 14. We'll brief you there, then head in. Think you can be here fast?"

Keesha closed her eyes, bracing herself. "We'll manage."

"Good. Be safe—but hurry."

The call ended, leaving the motel room hushed again. Dr. Flores exhaled through parted lips, snapping her suitcase shut with a decisive click. Grace stood slowly, hoodie rumpled, tension thrumming in every line of her borrowed body. She looked simultaneously too big for her old life and too fragile for this one.

Keesha forced a tremulous smile, crossing to press a quick hug to Grace's broad shoulders. "We'll handle this," she said, uncertain whether she was trying to reassure her daughter or herself.

The drive was far from pleasant. A chill drizzle swept over the windshield, the wipers thumping a frantic rhythm against the rising tension in the car. Keesha clutched the steering wheel so hard her knuckles whitened, darting anxious glances at the forest looming beyond the misty two-lane road.

In the passenger seat, Dr. Flores' fingers hovered near her phone, ready for any last-second call from Rodriguez. Grace sat in the back, hood pulled low, absently rubbing her temple when a flicker of pain jostled her. Each time she did, Keesha's pulse spiked with protective fear.

They finally turned into the gravel parking lot beside a small ranger station. Detective Rodriguez's sedan was there, along with a sheriff's SUV. Quincy emerged from the SUV, relief momentarily softening his usually stoic features. Keesha parked next to him, and the three travelers spilled out, stiff from tension.

"Keesha," Quincy said, voice low, scanning each face in quick assessment. He nodded to Grace, brow furrowed with concern, then turned to Dr. Flores. "I'm glad you made it okay."

Rodriguez joined them, a cap shielding her dark hair from the drizzle. She looked more exhausted than Keesha had ever seen her, yet her eyes gleamed with determination. "We'll start soon. Come inside."

The ranger station's main office was a cramped, utilitarian space lined with detailed maps of the Redwood Ridge area. A single overhead light cast a weary glow. Deputy Rhodes, heavyset and calm, acknowledged them with a polite tilt of her head. Her collected demeanor gave Keesha a sliver of reassurance.

On a worn wooden table lay a spread of satellite images and hand-drawn sketches marking the cabin's location, probable entry points, and vantage spots. Rodriguez pointed to a particular area circled in red. "We think Darius is here, in the thicker forest around the cabin. Tracks lead that way."

Grace inhaled shakily, stepping closer to study the layout. Quincy gave her shoulder a faint squeeze, a silent *we've got your back*. "So... how do we approach?" she asked, voice rough with uncertainty.

Deputy Rhodes cleared her throat. "We'll keep it quiet—no lights or sirens. Locals will hold the perimeter. Detective Rodriguez and Quincy will confirm if Darius is actually in the cabin or off in the woods. If he's inside, we act fast."

The tension in the room thickened. Keesha slid her gaze to Rodriguez. "If he's there... I assume we try to capture him?"

Rodriguez nodded grimly. "Yes. But there's the matter of the 'ritual' he wants," she added, looking at Grace. "We're still not sure how real or dangerous it is. If it's the only chance for you to get your body back, do we risk it?"

Grace clenched her borrowed fists. "If we don't, I might be stuck like this forever. But if it's a trap—"

"Then we stop him," Quincy said, tone unyielding. "We won't let Darius hurt anyone else."

Dr. Flores fiddled with her sedation kit, expression taut. "I'll administer a partial blocker to Grace's mind if we need it. It might dull any psychic assault Darius tries. But if we want a real swap... sedation might also hamper that connection."

A heavy quiet settled over them, each mind churning with possibility. Finally, Keesha exhaled, resolve firming. "We do this carefully. If we see a chance to swap them back safely, we try. But if it's clearly a ruse—"

"We end it," Grace finished in a whisper. The flicker of despair in her eyes cut Keesha to the core.

They drove in a small convoy: Deputy Rhodes led, Rodriguez and Quincy in another vehicle, and Keesha with Grace and Dr. Flores close behind. The forest thickened around them, branches arching overhead like a canopy of silent watchers. A soft rain tapped at the windshield, intensifying the sense of walking into something ancient and treacherous.

Eventually, Rhodes signaled them to stop at a narrow, muddy path. They parked on the shoulder, engines ticking in the cold damp. The plan: Rhodes's team would fan out on the perimeter. Rodriguez, Quincy, Keesha, Grace, and Dr. Flores would advance along the trail leading to the cabin.

The chill seeped through Keesha's jacket as she stepped onto the soggy ground, the wind carrying the sharp scent of wet pine. She caught Grace's eye; her daughter's face was drawn, each breath tense. Without a word, Dr. Flores produced a syringe from her kit, administering a small dose to Grace's upper arm.

Grace flinched at the prick, swallowing. "I'll be fine," she insisted, though her voice wavered. "Better than letting him waltz into my head."

Quincy checked his handgun, tucking it securely in its holster, while Rodriguez did the same. Keesha's pulse hammered at the memory of past violence Darius had wrought. *We can't afford another bullet hole near Grace.* She shook the thought away.

"Stay alert, everyone," Rodriguez murmured. "He may sense us coming."

They slipped single file down the winding trail, the hush broken only by the slap of rain on leaves and the squelch of their boots in mud. Keesha walked close behind Grace, ready to catch her if sedation made her unsteady. Every step felt like a countdown to an inevitable confrontation.

After twenty minutes, the dense pines began to thin, revealing a small clearing ahead. Through the curtain of drizzle, Keesha spied a cabin—weathered, with a sagging roof, perched at the clearing's far edge. A thin spiral of smoke rose from a metal chimney pipe, barely visible against the gray sky.

They pressed behind a cluster of soggy underbrush. Rodriguez raised her hand, signaling them to halt. Quincy peered out, scanning for signs of life. His eyes narrowed at the faint wisp of smoke. He gestured: *someone used the stove recently*.

Keesha's heartbeat throbbed in her ears. *He's here.* She felt Grace tense beside her, shoulders rigid with apprehension. Dr. Flores hovered behind, sedation kit still in her grip, the corner of her mouth twitching with unspoken dread.

Rodriguez motioned that they should split. She and Quincy would approach from the left; Keesha, Grace, and Dr. Flores would edge around the right. Step by step, they crept forward, the wet grass tugging at their ankles.

Grace inhaled in short, shallow bursts, each breath layered with anxiety. The sedation hadn't fully numbed her ability to sense Darius's psychic presence, which flickered like a dark heartbeat in the background of her mind.

At last, they converged in front of the porch, a worn structure missing several boards. An ax leaned against a stump nearby—fresh wood chips scattered at the base. *Someone's been here recently,* Keesha thought, heart kicking into overdrive.

Quincy swept around the porch's corner and signaled a clear, though his tense posture suggested he didn't trust appearances. Rodriguez nodded, then gently tested the cabin door. It creaked open, unlocked.

Darkness stretched inside. The scent of damp wood wafted out, carrying faint traces of ash. Rodriguez drew her firearm, flicked on a flashlight, and slipped past the threshold. Quincy followed. They vanished for a moment that felt eternal.

Then Quincy's voice came, low and urgent: "Clear." He emerged, waving for the others. One by one, they entered, forming a tight knot in the cramped main room.

The space was bare—a table, two rickety chairs, and a battered wood stove. A battered candle, half-burned. A faint warmth still radiated from the stove's embers. Keesha noted the scorch marks near the hearth. Something had burned recently.

Rodriguez surveyed the corners. "No sign of him. Either he left, or he's hiding." Her flashlight roved over the walls, revealing carved symbols, half-familiar from the warnings Dr. Flores had given about "ritualistic" setups.

Quincy exhaled. "Maybe he stepped out... or maybe he's deeper in the woods." Anxiety hummed in his voice, a rare note for someone usually so collected.

Keesha swallowed. "If he's not here, then where—?"

Grace wandered to the table, spotting a yellowed parchment scrawled with runes and cryptic notes. She lifted it carefully, eyes darting across bizarre symbols. A flicker of recognition darkened her brow. "This is... instructions for some ceremony. My head aches just looking at it."

Dr. Flores leaned closer, her breath catching. "Could be his plan for swapping you two back. Or something worse."

A chilly gust rattled the door. Quincy turned, shining his flashlight on the walls. More carved runes glowed in the gloom, matching those on the parchment.

Grace let out a sharp hiss, dropping the parchment. "He's close. I can feel him—like a wire tightening in my skull."

As if summoned, a faint thud sounded from a back hallway. Keesha's pulse spiked. Quincy and Rodriguez exchanged a grim nod, drawing their weapons and gesturing for the others to follow.

In the narrow corridor leading to what might be a bedroom, they found Darius—short, lithe, wearing Grace's pre-teen form—poised like a cornered animal. Grace's heart hammered at the sight of her own younger face twisted with cunning. For a heartbeat, no one moved. Then Darius lunged, slamming into Rodriguez, sending her careening into Quincy. He dashed back down the hallway before they could recover.

"Stop!" Rodriguez barked, spinning to chase him. Grace broke into a sprint, ignoring Keesha's shout to wait. She couldn't watch him slip away again.

Keesha and Dr. Flores raced behind, fear pounding in their chests. They reached the cramped back room, dusty and piled with firewood. **Darius** stood near a door leading outside, chest heaving from adrenaline. His eyes burned with the same defiance Keesha remembered from their final days living under his control.

"That's far enough," Rodriguez commanded, weapon raised. Quincy mirrored her stance, hand near his holster.

A wry grin twisted across Darius's tween features. "Rodriguez. Took you long enough."

Time seemed to slow, every detail amplified: the faint drip from the leaky ceiling, the musty smell of wet wood. Grace hovered behind Rodriguez, her adult frame stiff with rage and heartbreak. Quincy edged sideways, poised to block any escape. Dr. Flores lingered near the hallway, sedation syringe tucked against her side. Keesha could almost feel the cabin's oppressive runes throbbing with tension.

Darius spread Grace's slender arms with mock bravado, blocking the exit. "You're here to finish this, I take it?"

Rodriguez's grip tightened on her gun. "You're not walking out again, Darius."

He let out a low laugh. "We'll see." Then his gaze landed on Grace, a barbed challenge in his eyes. "How's my old body treating you? Feel that aggression? Or do you just savor the strength?"

Grace's cheeks darkened, jaw clenching. "Shut up."

Keesha's heart twisted. She remembered how Darius would *needle* them until they snapped. She forced her voice to steady. "Darius, you can't run forever. You need to face what you've done."

He arched a brow. "Oh, Keesha. Still the optimist, are we? I'll show you who holds the power." His gaze flicked to the carved walls. "These symbols... they're not for decoration."

Grace strode forward, ignoring Rodriguez's warning hand. "You said there's a way to swap back," she hissed. "All your talk about a 'ritual.' Was it a lie?"

Darius's ten year old face tilted in a half-shrug. "There is a method—risky for both of us. That sedation you're on might ruin it. But maybe you'd rather I keep this body permanently?" He aimed a toxic smile at Keesha. "She'll never be your little girl again."

Rodriguez's patience cracked. "On the ground," she ordered, stepping forward with her gun. "Now."

A malicious light gleamed in Darius's eyes. "Shoot this body, Detective? Are you sure you want to chance that bullet in Grace's heart?" He turned to Grace, voice dropping low. "If you want your life back, you'll have to face me—no sedation, no cops. This is your last chance."

Grace sucked in a breath, torn between fury and longing. "You used to control me," she whispered. "Not anymore." But Darius had already pivoted, leaping for the door.

Rodriguez lunged to intercept, Quincy moving in sync. Darius swerved abruptly, darting back toward the main room. Grace charged after, adrenaline roaring through her. Keesha and Dr. Flores hurried behind, fear screaming in their veins.

Darius slid to a stop near the battered table, snatching up a half-burned parchment. Grace halted, confronting the twisted reflection of her younger self. The flicker of candlelight made the carved runes on the walls dance ominously.

"Don't!" Grace pleaded, voice cracking. The tension swelled, each breath hammered by dread.

Quincy and Rodriguez arrived, forming a semicircle. Guns at the ready, eyes locked on Darius. Dr. Flores lingered, sedation kit in hand, uncertain when or how to act. Outside, thunder rumbled, a storm intensifying.

Darius's grip on the parchment tightened. "You want the swap? Let's see how brave you are." His tone dripped scorn. Then he soared forward, ramming into Grace with unexpected force. They crashed into the table, toppling the candle. Flames licked at the scattered notes.

"Grace!" Keesha yelled, surging forward. Quincy tried to yank Darius off, but the petite pre-teen frame wriggled free, snatching a shard of broken glass from the floor. He pressed the sharp edge against Grace's adult forearm, drawing a crimson line.

"Stay back!" he snarled, voice high and frenzied. Grace froze, pain etched across her face, while Keesha's entire world narrowed to that single blade point.

Lightning exploded outside, making the cabin windows vibrate. For a heartbeat, no one breathed. The small flames near the candle sputtered, threatening to spread among the strewn papers.

Dr. Flores hovered, stricken, sedation syringe trembling in her hand. Quincy and Rodriguez exchanged a frantic look—one misfire could be lethal to Grace's body. Grace herself stood pinned by the shard, bleeding lightly.

Keesha forced her legs to move, stepping forward. "Darius," she said, voice wavering yet resolute. "We'll do the ritual—together. But let Grace go. We can't do it if she's half-dead."

He scoffed, pressing the glass a hair deeper. "Why should I trust you?"

Keesha raised both hands in surrender. "No sedation," she lied, ignoring Dr. Flores's sharp intake of breath behind her. "No cops, no illusions. Let us try your method. Please."

Grace exhaled shakily. "Yes," she whispered, eyes flicking to her mother. "Mom... do it."

Darius hesitated, eyes darting among the circle of faces. Rain battered the roof in a relentless drumbeat. "Fine," he said at last, stepping back—though he kept the shard aloft. "But if this is a trick, I'll cut deeper."

"Understood," Keesha managed, heart pounding. Dr. Flores nodded minutely, tucking the syringe close, biding her time.

Darius marched Grace into the middle of the room, forcing Keesha and Dr. Flores to follow. Rodriguez and Quincy hovered near the walls, guns half-lowered but ready. Darius stomped out the small fire with Grace's heavy boot, smoke curling in the stale air.

"Stand there," he ordered, guiding Grace to a spot near the runes carved in the floorboards. "Focus on the tether."

Grace winced, pressing a hand to her temple. "Alright," she muttered, voice fraught with dread. Keesha watched with her heart in her throat. *If he tries to kill her, we're done.* Dr. Flores took up position behind them, sedation kit clutched like a lifeline.

Darius began breathing in deep, exaggerated inhalations. Grace mirrored him, though the sedation hampered some of her connection.

Still, something palpable stirred in the air—a crackling energy. The carved symbols on the wall seemed to flicker as thunder rattled the cabin.

Keesha's stomach churned. *This feels real.* She glanced at Dr. Flores, who stood rigid, eyes darting between the runes and the pair in the center. Quincy and Rodriguez shifted tensely at the perimeter, uncertain how to intervene.

Grace's face twisted in concentration. Darius's features contorted in turn, locked in a psychic struggle. For a few seconds, the tension felt like a living entity, swirling between them. Then Grace let out a pained cry, buckling slightly as if an invisible cord yanked her. Darius's brow knit, sweat beading at his temple. The air pulsed with something akin to static.

Keesha couldn't stand still. She moved closer, ignoring the risk. "Grace? Are you okay?"

Darius snarled, shifting his focus. "Stay back!" He brandished the glass shard, momentarily weakening the mental link. Grace swayed on her feet, disoriented. Seizing the moment, Dr. Flores lunged forward, stabbing the sedation needle into Darius's shoulder. He roared, slashing the shard across her arm. Flores stumbled back, clutching the wound.

Rodriguez and Quincy surged in, but Darius fought to keep consciousness. The cabin erupted in frantic motion—Quincy managed to clamp an arm around the thrashing ten year old, while Rodriguez stomped out a patch of newly sparked embers near the stove.

Grace doubled over, reeling from the abrupt severing of the tether. Keesha rushed to her side, catching her child's large frame in shaky arms. "Grace! Stay with me."

Through the smoke and the flicker of lightning, Darius's eyes went glassy from sedation. He spat a final curse and collapsed against the table. The shard clattered uselessly to the floor.

In the frenzied aftermath, Rodriguez barked into her radio, calling for medical backup. Quincy wrestled Darius's limp elementary school girl body into handcuffs, forcibly pinning him to the wall while the sedation overtook him. Dr. Flores pressed a bandage to the bleeding slash on her own arm, grimacing from pain and frustration.

Grace trembled, leaning on Keesha. Her head swam with leftover psychic noise, her mind still anchored in the wrong body. The ephemeral connection had ripped away too soon for any successful swap. She could feel it in the hollowness behind her eyes.

"We have him in cuffs," Quincy said, voice wavering with adrenaline, "but we didn't finish the swap."

A ragged sigh escaped Rodriguez as she stomped out the last flame. "At least he's not running again. We got him... but this isn't over."

Tears pricked Keesha's eyes as she cradled Grace's face. The same foreign stubble beneath her palms, the same helpless ache in her chest. *All that risk... and we're still here.* She brushed tears from Grace's cheeks with shaking fingers. "Baby, I'm so sorry."

Grace swallowed, exhaustion radiating from her every pore. "He... wasn't going to let it happen, was he? Not really."

Dr. Flores knelt beside them, wincing at her own wound. "We'll set up a controlled environment," she promised softly. "We won't let him decide the terms again."

Grace's borrowed shoulders shuddered in a silent sob. Keesha held her tight, feeling the patter of rain intensify outside, as if the storm itself mourned with them. Her gaze flicked to Darius, half-conscious against the wall, the tween's features etched in sedation and simmering hatred.

Lightning flashed, throwing the carved runes into harsh relief. The storm raged, but no bullet holes or new tragedies had claimed them tonight—only a fractured attempt at a ritual, scarring them all further. Yet Keesha clung to Grace and refused to let despair close in. *They'd survived.* It was enough for now.

Rodriguez slid her gun back into its holster, kneeling to help Dr. Flores with her bleeding arm. She shot a look at Keesha—exhausted, but oddly resolute. "We'll get him back into custody, and from there... we'll keep fighting," she murmured, voice threaded with empathy. "This isn't the end."

Keesha nodded, her words coming in a hushed vow against Grace's trembling shoulder. "No. We won't stop until Grace is free."

And so, as the wind whipped the cabin and water dripped through the ruined rafters, the battered group found their uncertain resolution. Darius, in chains but not broken. Grace, still trapped but alive. Keesha, shoulders braced against the storm, determined to see her child truly returned—no matter what horrors they had to face next.

Outside, thunder shook the sky, and the Redwood Ridge trees stood like silent sentinels, bearing witness to a battle only half-won. But inside, Keesha whispered a single promise:

This is not over. We will find a way.

Chapter 6: Fault Lines Exposed

The rain-soaked wind rattled the cabin walls, as though the storm itself recoiled from the dark ritual nearly performed inside. Detective Elena Rodriguez stood by the makeshift hearth, radio in hand, her voice low but urgent as she requested urgent medical backup. Nearby, Quincy crouched beside Dr. Miriam Flores, his brows knitted in concern as he helped wrap her injured arm with gauze from a small first-aid kit.

Keesha hovered over Grace—still trapped in Darius's body—offering a cool cloth to her daughter's brow. With each shaky inhale, Grace seemed to find a fraction of composure, clinging to her mother's presence to hold back the echoes of that aborted mind-swap.

A few feet away, Darius King slumped against a scorched table, cuffed wrists hidden behind his stolen pre-teen form. Even sedated, he exuded the same menace that had dogged the Marshalls for years; the flickering lamplight played cruelly across the youthful angles of Grace's real face. Keesha tried not to stare at it too long—seeing her daughter's features twisted by Darius's hatred tore at her soul.

Keesha's voice was subdued as she pressed the cloth to Grace's forehead. "Just breathe, baby," she murmured. "Easy, now."

Grace's borrowed chest heaved. "I almost... let him in," she managed, voice wavering in that incongruously deep timbre. "He was pulling at me, trying to drag me into—into his darkness."

Keesha winced; she could still picture the two of them locked in that psychic struggle. "But you didn't," she said firmly, brushing damp hair (or was it sweat?) from Grace's brow. "You fought him off."

A flicker of guilt crossed Grace's face. "I only held out because Dr. Flores sedated him," she murmured. "I'm still stuck. And now we're all back to square one."

Meanwhile, Quincy tied off a strip of gauze on Dr. Flores's arm, apologizing under his breath when the motion caused her to hiss in pain. "How bad?" he asked, his jaw tight.

Flores forced a pinched smile, clearly trying to minimize her own wound. "A few stitches, maybe," she replied, voice taut from adrenaline and discomfort. "But Grace..." Her gaze drifted to the tall figure hunched against Keesha. "She endured worse."

Rodriguez finished speaking into her radio and stepped over, rain dripping from her hairline. "Paramedics are on the way," she announced. "The deputy's sending a four-wheel-drive rescue unit, but the roads are a mess in this storm." She surveyed the scene—Flores's bloodied sleeve, Darius's limp form, and Grace trembling under Keesha's care. Her shoulders sagged with frustration, as if the night's failure pressed on her conscience. "At least we have him sedated again. Once we get everyone out of here, we can transfer him somewhere more secure."

Grace coughed, her lungs still raw. "He was so close," she whispered. "Like he was prying at my mind with claws—trying to yank my consciousness out."

Keesha laid a hand on Grace's temple, an oddly maternal gesture that felt surreal given the adult shape of her daughter's borrowed body. "But you held on. You survived."

Grace lowered her gaze, voice heavy with a sense of defeat. "Because he got sedated before he could finish. I'm still in the wrong body. This was supposed to end here, Mom." She swallowed, blinking back tears.

From across the room, Quincy rose, tension in the set of his jaw. "It didn't end," he conceded, "but we've got Darius locked down—for now. No more halfway ceremonies on his terms."

Rodriguez nodded, crossing her arms. "Exactly. Next time, we do this in a secure facility, with a plan. No candlelit rituals, no improvised sedation. We'll call in every expert we need."

A thunderclap rippled through the cabin, shaking its old beams. For a beat, no one spoke, sharing a single thought: *We almost ended this nightmare—but it persists.*

Eventually, sirens cut through the roar of rainfall. Deputy Rhodes arrived with a small team, the red glare of emergency lights slicing the sodden darkness. Two paramedics, weighed down by ponchos and gear, hurried across the flooded clearing. The cabin's interior smelled of singed parchment and wet timber, amplifying the claustrophobic atmosphere.

One paramedic knelt beside Dr. Flores, gently examining her arm. Flores gritted her teeth, forcing a wry half-smile that didn't reach her eyes. The other paramedic approached Darius's slumped form but froze when Rodriguez held up a cautionary hand.

"Careful," the detective warned. "He's extremely dangerous."

Though sedated, Darius stirred, lids fluttering. The venom in his eyes belied his sluggish movements. "You haven't won," he rasped, Grace's young voice startling in its malice. "This is just a delay."

Quincy loomed, arms folded in silent warning. Nearby, Grace watched with haunted eyes, absently pressing a cloth to the shallow cut Darius had inflicted on her forearm—her daughter's *real* body had done that, and the irony twisted Keesha's gut.

Despite the swirling mud and rain, the paramedics carefully loaded Dr. Flores and Darius into one ambulance, with an armed officer accompanying them. Then, Keesha, Grace, Quincy, and Rodriguez climbed into a second rescue vehicle, the battered lamplight of the cabin fading behind as they pulled away. The ride was agonizingly slow—dirt roads transformed into slippery quagmires by the relentless downpour.

In the back of the ambulance, Grace gripped the bench seat, knuckles white. Keesha sat close, their roles reversed from every hospital trip of the past: Grace large and haggard, Keesha hovering anxiously like the mother she'd always been. Rodriguez and Quincy whispered up front, hashing out logistics:

- Darius would be secured in a high-security hospital ward, not a juvenile facility.
- Dr. Flores would receive proper treatment for her injury.
- Grace—stuck in Darius's adult body—would wait for yet another plan to free her.

Keesha rested a hand on Grace's shoulder, recalling the endless times she'd promised her child safety. *How many times have we thought we had Darius contained?* she wondered bitterly.

They reached a regional hospital just after midnight, the storm still raging outside. Flashes of lightning revealed the grim expressions on every face as they dashed through the downpour into the ER. The overhead fluorescence was jarringly bright, antiseptic smells and the buzz of triage staff creating a surreal sense of normalcy.

Hospital personnel hustled Dr. Flores to a curtained area, ignoring her protests that she was "fine" except for a slash that needed stitches. Their attention shifted to Darius, whose sedation and restraints were quickly upgraded under Rodriguez's direction. Even amid the confusion, a sharp-eyed nurse paused at the sight of Grace, arms scratched and clothes streaked with mud.

"Sir, are you hurt?" the nurse asked, and Grace visibly flinched at the address. It stung each time someone used the wrong pronoun—and yet how could anyone know the truth?

"I'm okay," she managed in that low voice, each word forcing her to acknowledge the dissonance of being seen as a grown man.

Keesha stepped in protectively, her tone tight. "We've got it under control. Just—just let us handle it."

The nurse hesitated, evidently sensing tension she couldn't place, then nodded and moved on. Within half an hour, Darius was wheeled to a secure wing typically reserved for violent psychiatric patients. Even the beep of monitors couldn't mask the anxiety that pervaded the corridors. Quincy and Rodriguez exchanged clipped words with hospital security, ensuring top-tier precautions against Darius's formidable cunning.

Meanwhile, Keesha guided Grace to a small, sterile exam room far from prying eyes. The glaring overhead light made Grace flinch; the chemical sting of antiseptic revived flashbacks of her old surgeries. *Except it's all backward now,* Keesha thought, a surge of sorrow fueling her determination to help her daughter reclaim her rightful body.

Shortly after, Dr. Flores arrived, her arm bandaged and face pale but resolute. She leaned against the doorframe, exhaustion and resolve battling in her features. "I've arranged a sealed wing for us. Minimal staff, fewer chances for Darius to manipulate anyone. Once he's stabilized, we can do a thorough neuro assessment." She paused, meeting Grace's eyes. "Then we'll try another swap attempt—but on our terms."

Grace perched on a steel stool, arms folded protectively over her borrowed chest. "What if it fails again?"

Flores's gaze softened with empathy. "We can't guarantee success, but we'll have an actual medical team, not a half-burned cabin. We'll use sedation, EEG scans, maybe controlled hypnosis—anything to keep Darius from fighting us in the final stretch. We won't let him ambush you again."

Keesha exhaled, some tension easing from her shoulders. "What do you need from us?"

Flores mustered a faint, determined smile. "Time. We'll have to monitor Grace, refine the sedation. If we can coax Darius's mind into a state where he can't fully resist, Grace might slip back into her real body before he regains control."

Rodriguez stepped in, her face drawn but relieved to see everyone safe for the moment. "We'll maintain guards on Darius around the clock—no repeat escapes. Quincy's working out a rotation schedule with local officers."

Quincy nodded, arms crossed. "We've learned the hard way how clever he is." His gaze flickered to Grace, regret warring with protectiveness. "But we won't be caught off-guard again."

A beat passed, the group collectively grappling with the enormity of the next steps. Then Grace broke the silence, her voice trembling with both longing and fear. "Just... promise me you'll stop if it gets too risky. I'm tired of putting everyone in danger just so I can get back to normal."

Keesha laid a hand on Grace's forearm, eyes glimmering. "We're not giving up on you. No matter what."

An hour later, the storm tapered to a steady drizzle, and a nurse escorted Keesha and Grace to a modest private room in the sealed wing. Quincy and Rodriguez stayed behind to finalize Darius's transfer into a high-security chamber. Dr. Flores departed for her own wound care, vowing to return soon for more scans.

The private room was stark—a single bed, a chair, and a medical monitor. When the door clicked shut, Keesha felt exhaustion crash over her like a wave. She sank into the lone chair, pressing her palms to her eyes, trying to keep tears at bay.

Grace eased onto the bed, face etched with worry. "Mom?" she asked quietly, seeing her mother trembling.

Keesha dropped her hands, sorrow shining in her eyes. "I'm sorry," she whispered, voice raw. "You've been so brave, and I—I wish I could do more. I hate that he still holds any power over you."

Grace hesitated, then approached, her tall frame offering a protective gesture that felt oddly reversed. "It's not your fault," she insisted, heartbreak lacing her deep timbre. "He chose this path. Not you."

Keesha's tears slipped free. "But I brought him into our lives. You should've never had to face this."

Grace's eyes filled with compassion. "We both survived him before, and we will again." She knelt beside her mother, dwarfed by her own towering presence, and gently rested a calloused hand on Keesha's knee. "Don't blame yourself."

They stayed like that for long moments, mother and child locked in a poignant role-reversal—Grace offering comfort in the body of a man Keesha once feared. Finally, Keesha's tears ebbed, and she rose, pressing a kiss to Grace's forehead. "We'll set things right," she promised, her voice quieter but firm.

Night deepened, quiet settling over the sealed ward. Outside, the rain tapped a subdued rhythm on the hospital's roof. Keesha dozed fitfully in the chair, jerking awake whenever Grace shifted on the bed. Memories of bullet holes, mind-control illusions, and half-failed rituals haunted her fragmented dreams.

Sometime past three in the morning, Grace jerked upright with a strangled gasp. Keesha jolted, heart hammering. "Grace?" she asked urgently, voice husky from lack of sleep.

Grace pressed a hand to her temple, eyes unfocused with panic. "He's... still in my head. Even sedated, I feel his anger—like a muffled scream."

A chill slid down Keesha's spine. She forced calm into her tone. "We'll talk to Dr. Flores, get you a blocker dose." She reached out, taking Grace's larger hand in hers, the incongruity still jarring. "We're safe here. He can't hurt you."

Grace's chest rose and fell in quick breaths. "I know," she breathed, "but it's like a nightmare I can't wake from."

Keesha gripped her hand tighter. "We'll keep fighting," she repeated, though each repetition tasted of desperation. She glanced at the door. *If only Rodriguez or Quincy were awake to help.* But they needed rest too. Everyone did.

Grace nodded, swallowing hard. After a moment, she leaned back, letting her mother's presence settle her frayed nerves. "Thank you," she whispered.

Morning came with a dull glow through the ward's small window. The rain persisted, but gentler now, as if the storm had spent its worst fury. Dr. Flores reappeared, arm in a proper sling. She carried a portable EEG machine, an IV drip, and a set of small electrodes.

"Good morning," she said gently, voice subdued. "I'm sorry for the early start, but it's best we gather data before anything changes with Darius's sedation."

Grace nodded, forcing herself upright. "Where do we start?"

Flores set up her equipment, explaining each step. "We'll do an EEG first, see how your neural patterns react if we apply mild external stimuli—like focusing on images of your old body or hearing recordings of your voice. It might provoke the tether."

Keesha's heart skipped. "You mean... we risk him sensing us?"

Flores let out a weary breath. "A small risk, but we'll be ready. If we detect any psychic 'feedback,' we'll give Grace a blocker. We're in a controlled environment this time." She tried to smile reassuringly at Grace. "No candlelit arcane symbols or last-ditch sedatives—just medicine and science."

Grace swallowed, her eyes flicking to Keesha. "I'll do it," she said softly. "I have to."

Rodriguez and Quincy arrived then, each holding a to-go coffee. The detective's hair was damp, her eyes ringed with fatigue, but she mustered a firm nod as she took in the equipment. "We'll be outside. Just holler if you sense any shift in Darius."

Keesha watched them go, anxiety twisting her gut. Then she turned back to Grace, who now lay on the bed with electrodes mapping her brain activity. Dr. Flores tapped a small screen, lines of shifting data reflecting every breath Grace took.

In that sterile, cinder-block room, the hush felt charged with both trepidation and hope. The overhead lights buzzed, the beep of hospital machinery marking time in steady increments. *We are trying again,* Keesha told herself, *and this time we're prepared.*

Outside, the rainclouds gradually thinned, allowing a sparse wash of dawn's light into the windows. Gray and gold mingled over the horizon, a faint but promising sign that the storm might soon pass. Keesha glanced once at that subtle brightness, willing it to be an omen of success.

Yet as she looked down at Grace—her beloved daughter in a stranger's frame—she knew their battles were far from over. Even if Dr. Flores's plan offered a glimpse of salvation, Darius remained a looming threat behind heavy doors. A single psychic slip, a single moment of carelessness, and he could tear Grace's mind free or incite another wave of violence.

Still, as Keesha laid a hand over Grace's, she felt a stubborn kernel of determination ignite in her chest. They had survived the worst once, twice, and many times more. They would face whatever came next.

"Ready?" Dr. Flores asked, her finger hovering over a switch that would start the EEG test. Grace took a deep breath, then nodded.

Keesha smoothed down the corner of Grace's bedsheet. "We're with you," she said softly. "Always."

And with that, the next phase of their long fight began—fault lines laid bare, but hearts steeled to forge a path back to the life Darius had stolen. Outside, the clouds broke just enough to let in a slender, golden ray, a small but defiant promise of morning.

Chapter 7: Deeper Waters

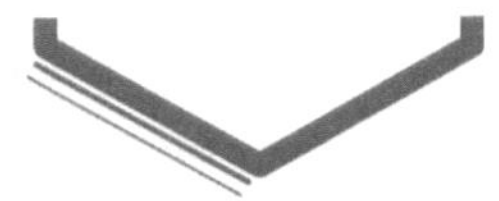

Morning light spilled weakly through the sealed ward's narrow windows, illuminating a hive of controlled chaos. The muffled hum of medical equipment mingled with the scuff of hurried footsteps and the low murmur of anxious conversation. Two armed officers stood watch at either end of the corridor, their grim expressions testament to how seriously they took this peculiar threat.

In a small, private exam room, Keesha hovered at Grace's bedside. The child she remembered—ten-year-old Grace, with a shy smile and love of art—was barely recognizable in the imposing adult form sprawled on the hospital bed. Wires snaked from Grace's scalp to a portable EEG, while monitors tracked her vitals in a steady chorus of beeps. Dr. Miriam Flores sat beside a rolling cart, adjusting the IV line and wincing at the tug on her own injured arm. Next to her stood Dr. Kunal Patel, a neurologist with a calm demeanor that seemed at odds with the extraordinary situation.

Grace lay with her gaze fixed on the overhead fluorescent lights, hospital gown bunched around muscular shoulders that weren't truly hers. A fresh bruise discolored one forearm—the final reminder of Darius's glass shard from the cabin. An IV line trailed from the other arm, delivering the careful balance of sedation blockers and medication Dr. Flores had concocted.

Keesha perched on a plastic chair, trying not to let her worry show in every breath. "How's your head?" she asked gently, smoothing the thin blanket across Grace's knees.

Grace drew in a shallow breath, the large chest rising beneath the gown. The incongruity still tore at Keesha's heart. "Quiet," Grace admitted in that deep, dissonant voice. "Dr. Flores's meds must be working—he's not pulling at me as strongly."

Flores, a sling still stabilizing her bandaged arm, nodded from her seat. "That's the blocker," she said. "But to attempt a real separation, we need to find the sweet spot—if we block Darius's influence too much, we also lose the chance to align your consciousness with your original body. It's going to be a delicate dance."

Grace's eyes flicked to Dr. Patel, who folded his hands thoughtfully. "Exactly," he said in a soft, precise tone. "We'll monitor your brain waves while tapering the blocker. If we see any spike indicating Darius is forcing a connection, we'll increase it again. Our goal is to see whether your consciousness can stand on its own 'frequency,' separate from his."

Grace's throat bobbed with tension. "Like two radio stations," she murmured. "He's the static, and I'm trying to tune him out."

A bittersweet pang lanced through Keesha. The analogy reminded her of the times Grace, at just five or six, would fiddle with the radio, half-lost in laughter when static crackled. She reached for Grace's hand, ignoring the size difference that never felt right. "We'll get there," she whispered, voice tight with emotion.

Flores offered a small, tired smile. "Darius remains heavily sedated. Detective Rodriguez and Quincy are ensuring that if he so much as stirs, we'll know."

Keesha stroked Grace's knuckles. A sliver of hope nestled under her worry. *We have a plan now, a real one,* she told herself. But as she saw the dark circles under Grace's eyes, she knew how fragile that plan truly was.

At the far end of the corridor, Detective Elena Rodriguez and Quincy stood with two uniformed officers just outside Darius's secured room. They peered through the narrow window in the door, glimpsing the sedated figure on the bed. Even in the stolen prepubescent body, Darius exuded a malicious aura that put them all on edge.

One officer consulted his notes. "He's stable for now—heart rate normal, sedation level holding. He tried mumbling a few hours ago about illusions, but we raised his dosage."

Rodriguez's brow creased. "We can't let him sweet-talk or influence the staff again. Keep his sedation as high as possible without risking medical complications." She glanced at Quincy. "If he even hints at coming around, we'll have to up the dose again."

Quincy's gaze lingered on Darius's form beyond the glass, a mixture of loathing and protectiveness warring in his expression. "What if sedation isn't enough?" he asked quietly. "If he tries some psychic trick at the worst moment—?"

Rodriguez set her jaw. "Then we do whatever it takes to protect Grace. I won't let him slip away again." A faint tremor edged her voice, revealing the strain of the many times Darius had outmaneuvered them.

They exchanged a silent understanding: *If a line had to be crossed to save Grace, so be it.* The unspoken truth settled over them like a warning, crackling with the tension of an unfinished war.

Back in the exam room, Dr. Patel fixed the final EEG electrode to Grace's temple. Dr. Flores readied a syringe filled with a small amount of medication designed to reverse the psychic blocker. Keesha stood beside Grace, every muscle taut.

"All right," Flores said softly. "We'll reduce the blocker incrementally. Grace, you might feel dizziness or a lurch, like a door in your mind swinging open."

Grace swallowed, nodding. "I'm ready," she whispered, though her voice wavered.

Flores pressed the syringe into the IV port. Patel tapped a few keys on a portable monitor, and the EEG waveforms jumped in lively lines of color. Keesha forced herself to remain outwardly calm, one hand braced on Grace's shoulder.

At first, nothing happened. Then Grace inhaled sharply, the IV lines quivering with her movement. "I— I sense something. A corridor, or... a glimmer. Not him, exactly, but like an echo of his presence."

Flores glanced between Grace and the monitors. "Elevated alpha and theta waves. That's the dream or trance state," she confirmed. "Keep going, Grace. Keep describing what you feel."

Grace's eyes shuttered halfway. "He's sedated, but not... gone. It's like he's in another room of my head. I can almost hear him pacing." A tremor ran through her. "I'm trying to focus on *me*. My memories. My name: Grace Marshall."

Keesha leaned closer, voice trembling with emotion. "Yes, baby. Remember all the times you drew pictures, how we pinned them to the fridge."

Grace's lashes fluttered, tears pooling. "Yeah... my old hands were so small. I used to hold crayons and swirl color everywhere. I... I remember." A fleeting smile crossed her features, heartbreakingly out of place on the hard lines of Darius's adult jaw.

Flores adjusted the drip again, eyebrows pinching. "Her readings are stable. Good sign." Dr. Patel monitored a wave spike, biting his lip. "He might be stirring, but we're keeping him at bay."

Keesha squeezed Grace's arm, tears stinging her eyes. "That's right. You're Grace Marshall, an artist, a dreamer. This body isn't yours."

Grace let out a shuddering breath. "He hates that I'm saying that. Even sedated, I can sense his fury."

Across the corridor, in Darius's room, the sedation monitors flickered. Darius's eyelids jerked, his body twitching against the restraints. The guard stationed inside stepped closer, anxiety fraying his composure.

Rodriguez and Quincy rushed to the door, leaning in to see. Darius's petite face contorted in a grimace, a gasp escaping his lips. For a split second, that withering glare locked onto the window, saturating the air with dread. Then his head lolled back, sedation reclaiming him.

Quincy exhaled, tension riding his voice. "He's still too stubborn to stay fully under."

Rodriguez whispered into her radio: "Flores, watch out. He's twitching again."

Dr. Flores heard the warning crackle through her earpiece. She glanced at Dr. Patel. "We can't risk giving him another sedation boost without damaging Grace's real body."

Patel's attention snapped back to the EEG. "We have to keep going but watch for a surge." He looked at Grace. "Focus, Grace. Keep that mental thread of your own identity. Picture your real hands, your real face."

Grace's chest hitched, her eyes tight with strain. "He's pushing back," she choked out. "Like a wave smashing the door I'm trying to hold shut."

Flores reached for an IV dial. "I'll give you just a hair more blocker to dull his push. Hang on."

Keesha's nails dug into her palms. "You've got this, sweetie," she murmured, forcing her own fear aside.

Grace's muscles tensed, her borrowed frame seizing with a shiver. "I—my name is Grace," she repeated, voice breaking. "I'm not you, Darius. I'm not you!"

Patel's monitor beeped frantically. "Alpha wave overload," he warned. "Her mind's pushing against Darius's sedation-driven broadcast. We need to either pull her out or she'll—"

Grace let out a ragged moan, sweat dripping down her temples. "I feel a crack," she gasped. "Like I can break free if I just—"

Flores's and Patel's eyes locked, each torn between continuing and risking Grace's safety. Keesha's heart thundered in her ears, her hands shaking on Grace's shoulder.

Then Grace convulsed, body arching off the bed, a wrenching cry spilling from her lips. The EEG screamed with red spikes. Keesha fought panic, tears flying from her eyes as she leaned over her child. "Grace, stay with me!"

For a moment, it felt as though the entire room held its breath. Grace's cry faded into a choking gasp. Her limbs went rigid, then released, leaving her slumped on the bed.

Keesha bent down, voice trembling. "Grace? Talk to me!"

A heartbeat later, Grace's eyes flickered open—unfamiliar eyes in an unfamiliar face, yet a flicker of relief glimmered there. She raised a shaking hand, cupping Keesha's cheek with surprising gentleness.

"Mom," Grace murmured, voice husky. "I... cut him off. I don't hear him the same way, or feel him. It's like I slammed a door." She sagged back, gasping for air.

Keesha sobbed in relief. "Oh, thank God. It's okay, baby. I'm here."

Flores quickly studied the EEG, her good hand swiping tears from her own cheeks. "Her readings are calmer—less interference. I think she might've severed a major part of the tether."

Dr. Patel's shoulders relaxed. "She's stable now. This is... progress."

For a minute or two, the room was wrapped in a stunned hush. Machines beeped a slow staccato, and Grace's ragged breathing began to even out. Keesha stroked her daughter's brow, tears of mingled hope and exhaustion sliding unchecked.

Eventually, Flores cleared her throat, drawing closer. "Grace, do you still sense him at all?"

Grace closed her eyes, testing the mental space. "It's like... a distant echo. He's there, but quieter—like he's behind a wall." She flexed her borrowed hands. "Still not me, though."

Keesha swallowed a lump in her throat. "So he's not controlling you anymore, but you're still... stuck?"

Grace's gaze fell. "Yeah," she answered, voice hoarse. "We haven't reversed the swap. But at least I'm not fighting him every second."

Flores nodded carefully. "We'll take it. One step forward. Rest now—you've been through a lot."

Grace managed a slight nod, eyes half-closing as fatigue claimed her. Keesha brushed a lock of hair from Grace's brow, inwardly marveling that it didn't feel like the hair she'd once braided when Grace was younger. *One day,* she vowed silently, *we'll get you back fully.*

Outside the exam room, Keesha briefed Rodriguez and Quincy on the outcome. Quincy exhaled in relief, shoulders loosening from an unspoken tension. Rodriguez's eyes gleamed with a cautious hope.

"Any sign of Darius waking?" Keesha asked, arms wrapped around herself.

Rodriguez shook her head. "He stirred, but sedation dragged him under. Good thing, too. If he'd regained full consciousness during that procedure, who knows what he would've done."

Keesha nodded, lingering anxiety flickering across her face. "So... Grace is stable, but no full swap yet."

Quincy patted Keesha's shoulder. "We'll keep him contained until we figure it out. No more near-escapes. The staff is on high alert."

A part of Keesha's heart unclenched. "Thank you," she breathed, meaning the words far beyond mere politeness. Rodriguez gave a firm nod in acknowledgment, and they parted ways, each bracing for the next chapter of this battle.

Late afternoon brought a gentle drizzle rather than the torrential storm of the previous night. Inside Grace's hospital room, the hum of monitors and antiseptic smell felt oddly lulling. Dr. Flores quietly checked the IV lines while Keesha read texts from friends who had no idea how drastically her world had changed.

Occasionally, Grace would stir, briefly opening her eyes. Each time, Keesha offered water or a comforting smile. Though still in the wrong body, Grace at least bore a lighter expression—no longer cringing with every flicker of Darius's will.

Flores finished her last vitals check and set down the chart. "Her stats are better," she said quietly. "Tomorrow, if she's strong enough, we can attempt a more structured approach."

Keesha forced a weary laugh that held little humor. "I'm almost afraid to hope. But we have to try."

Flores's gaze softened. "We do. She's proven it's possible to push him out. Now it's about guiding her back into her rightful place."

That night, while Grace slept under a gentle sedative, Keesha found herself standing outside Darius's locked room. The ten year old body within was so painfully familiar: the shape of Grace's cheeks, the arch of her eyebrows. But the occupant was all Darius, tethered to machines that dripped sedation into his veins.

Rodriguez hovered in the hallway, arms crossed. "You okay?" she asked softly.

Keesha stared through the glass at the still form. "I'm not sure I'll ever be okay, seeing my daughter's body like this," she confessed. "It's wrong on every level."

Rodriguez's voice was gentle. "One day soon, we'll fix that. We're not giving up."

They stood in shared silence, tension thrumming like an undercurrent. Darius remained motionless except for the mechanical rise and fall of his chest. At times, a small twitch of his fingers would remind them all of the danger lurking under sedation.

Finally, Keesha swallowed and turned away from the window. "I should get back to Grace."

Rodriguez offered a tight nod. "Rest if you can. Tomorrow's another big day."

Keesha allowed a final glance at Darius's unconscious form before heading down the corridor. Quincy gave her a reassuring nod as she passed, continuing his vigil near the security desk. She marveled at how many people had united to protect her child—despite the unimaginable strangeness of the situation.

And as she returned to the room where Grace lay, she found that fragile sense of determination still glowing in her chest. Even though the path was fraught with danger, they had proven that Darius's grip could be severed, at least partially. The next step might be riskier still, but each day brought them closer to the end of this nightmare.

Slipping inside, she saw Grace's imposing form curled under a thin blanket, lines of fatigue still etched on that borrowed face. Yet Keesha spotted a subtle peace in her daughter's features, as though Grace no longer wrestled a constant psychic battle in her sleep.

Moving to the bedside, Keesha brushed a gentle hand over Grace's short hair, tears threatening again at the mismatch of such a gesture. "We'll finish this," she whispered, voice scarcely audible over the beep of monitors. "No matter what it takes."

Grace murmured something unintelligible, lost in a sedative haze, but Keesha swore she glimpsed a faint flicker of a smile. Taking her daughter's hand, she settled into the chair, letting her eyes drift shut. Tomorrow they would wade into deeper waters, forging a path toward reclaiming the life Darius had stolen.

And in that hush, lulled by the quiet beep of machines, mother and child—mismatched in body and soul—prepared for the next step. No illusions of an easy victory remained, but hope glimmered like a distant light beneath the darkest waves.

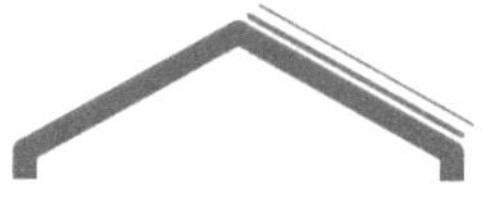

Chapter 8: Psychic Chess

Morning light seeped thinly through the sealed ward's narrow windows, pooling across the hospital floor in a pale hush. The faint hum of machines and whispered footsteps underscored the tenuous calm, as though even the walls sensed the precarious balance within. Keesha Marshall sat beside her daughter's bed, exhaustion etched into the lines of her face. She'd spent the night perched on a too-small chair, arms folded on the mattress, watching Grace's uneven sleep.

Grace—trapped in Darius's adult body—looked too large for the crisp hospital sheets. The faint beep of her heart monitor and the soft hiss of the IV pump provided a fragile lullaby. Each time a nurse entered to check vitals, Keesha tensed, half-expecting to see fear spark in the nurse's eyes at the sight of Grace's imposing form. If Darius woke enough to exploit someone's mind, the consequences could be catastrophic.

Dr. Miriam Flores slipped into the room, her own arm still bound in a sling from the injury in Redwood Ridge. She walked with a slight stiffness, but her eyes were alert. "How's she doing?" she asked softly, tipping her chin toward Grace.

Keesha rubbed her gritty eyes. "No seizures, but she kept muttering in her sleep. We had to increase the sedation-blocker dose once around four a.m. The nurse said her brain waves were spiking again."

Flores grimaced, glancing at the screens that captured Grace's EEG. "At least no full-blown psychic assault. I'll take restless over catatonic."

She exhaled, setting down a tray of fresh electrodes. "I'm thinking we try to tweak the sedation-blocker balance this morning. Dr. Patel agrees that if we block Grace's psychic sense too hard, she can't attempt reconnecting with her original body. But if we ease off too much..."

Keesha nodded, jaw tight. "Darius finds a way in."

Flores's gaze flicked to the monitors. "We have an advantage—he's still heavily sedated in another room, and we've got watchers stationed. But it's not a fail-safe. He's... incredibly stubborn, even under sedation."

Keesha clenched her fists, remembering Grace's tortured expression when she tried to sever the tether last time. "Is there no safer approach? Something that doesn't tear her mind apart?"

Flores set her sling-bound arm gently on the bed railing. "We're edging toward it. The data from yesterday shows Grace can resist if Darius is groggy and she has partial support from the blocker. She's stronger than we realized."

Keesha's gaze dropped to Grace's peaceful face, an echo of tears burning in her throat. "She's so brave," she whispered. "I hate that she has to fight again."

Outside in the corridor, Detective Elena Rodriguez and Quincy stood in low-voiced conversation with Deputy Rhodes and another officer. Their circle of grim expressions spoke volumes.

Through the small window in the exam room door, Keesha could see them exchanging files and discussing something with tense body language. *Probably new intel on Darius's associates,* she guessed, a surge of unease rising. The idea that Darius might have willing accomplices—people who'd attempt to carry on his twisted ritual or help him escape—made her blood run cold.

When Rodriguez finally slipped into Grace's room, she closed the door quietly behind her. "Morning," she said, wiping the fatigue from her eyes. "We've got some leads from Redwood Ridge locals: a couple of strangers poking around where Darius holed up. No hard proof yet, but we're worried it might be allies of his."

Flores's expression hardened. "Allies who could attempt a rescue?"

Rodriguez tilted her head. "Or finish what he started. We're not sure. Either way, we've doubled the guard. So far, no sign of an organized break-in, but we can't rule it out."

Keesha's chest tightened. "As if we didn't have enough to worry about. He can't do much under heavy sedation, right?"

Rodriguez's jaw worked. "We hope not. But I've seen how cunning he can be, even half-awake. If he manages to influence a staff member, it could undermine everything."

A soft moan cut through the tension. Grace shifted, the borrowed muscles in her arms flexing under the thin hospital blanket. Keesha hurried to the bedside, heart pounding with relief and worry. Grace blinked groggily, eyes struggling to focus on the sterile surroundings.

"You're safe," Keesha murmured, brushing the blanket aside to check her daughter's IV. "How do you feel?"

Grace swallowed, that deep baritone still jarring to hear. "Tired, but... better than the last time I was conscious. Less pain in my head."

Flores approached the monitor. "Vitals are decent. No headache spiking?"

Grace shook her head. "No. And I can't feel him—Darius—right now. It's... quiet."

A breath of relief escaped Keesha's lungs, though she knew it was temporary. "We were just talking about next steps," she explained, carefully meeting Grace's eyes. "Dr. Flores thinks we can try another approach to help you reconnect with your body."

Grace's expression flickered with a mix of hope and trepidation. "Okay," she managed, voice rough. "But not alone. I can't—" She winced at the memory of the last violent encounter.

"Never alone," Keesha assured her, gently covering Grace's forearm with her hand. The difference in size still made her heart clench with every touch.

Rodriguez crossed her arms, stepping closer. "We'll keep Darius sedated. Quincy and I will stand by. If he stirs, we'll handle it."

Grace tried for a shaky smile, gratitude lighting her borrowed features. "Thank you."

Flores drew a small rolling table over, where brain scans and sedation charts lay spread out. She tapped one graph, pointing out peaks of activity. "Grace, we think we can induce a mild trance—something closer to hypnosis—where you safely access your original psychic signature without letting Darius intrude."

Keesha felt her nerves fray at the mere thought. "You said that was risky if he wakes."

Flores nodded. "Hence the sedation and a partial psychic blocker. We'll watch your vitals, Grace, and if anything spikes, Dr. Patel will pull you out immediately. The idea is to nudge your consciousness toward your rightful body and see if we can anchor it there, inch by inch."

Grace closed her eyes briefly. "Every time I remember how close I came last time, my stomach flips. But... I want to try again. I want my life back."

Keesha's throat grew tight. "Baby, you don't have to rush. If you need more time—"

"No," Grace said, voice firm despite the weariness. "I can't stay in Darius's body forever."

Rodriguez cut in, gaze steady. "We'll keep him physically contained. He's locked down. Even if he stirs, we'll control him. Just focus on your end."

A flicker of determination sparked in Grace's eyes. "Then let's do it."

By midmorning, Dr. Patel arrived pushing a small cart of specialized equipment: a portable screen for guided imagery, a set of LED lights designed for therapeutic hypnosis, and additional sensors to refine the EEG's readouts. It felt almost surreal—like a science fair project colliding with supernatural warfare.

Grace eyed the gear warily. "Feels like we're staging a sci-fi experiment."

Patel offered a reassuring smile. "I admit it's unconventional. But we'll proceed gently. If at any point you feel uneasy, say the word 'Stop,' and we'll halt. Your safety is our priority."

Keesha hovered, arms folded tightly. "I'll be right here, Grace. Whatever happens."

From the doorway, Quincy leaned in. "Rodriguez and I have the corridor covered. If Darius so much as flinches, we'll know."

Flores helped Grace adjust her position, mindful of the IV lines. Then she tested the sedation drip. "Ready," she said, nodding to Patel.

The lights dimmed, leaving only a soft LED glow flickering across Grace's face. Patel's voice dropped to a gentle, rhythmic cadence, guiding Grace through a process of deep relaxation. Keesha watched her daughter's chest rise and fall in a slow pattern, tension melting from the borrowed muscles.

Flores monitored the EEG. "Alpha waves descending nicely," she murmured. She glanced at Keesha, her expression kind. "So far, so good."

Keesha squeezed Grace's hand, lips trembling with unspoken prayers. In the corner, a nurse discreetly took notes, while another hovered near the door, ready to fetch sedation backup if Darius stirred. The hush felt charged, as though the air crackled with invisible currents.

"Imagine a peaceful place," Patel murmured. "Somewhere you feel safe, Grace—like your old bedroom or a sunlit garden." He guided her deeper, watchful for the slightest spike on the EEG.

Grace's face relaxed, a ghost of a nostalgic smile curving her lips. "My room," she breathed. "Blue walls... sketches taped everywhere... I can smell the pencil shavings."

Keesha shut her eyes, remembering the sweet chaos of Grace's creative mess. *She's in there,* she thought, tears threatening. *She's still my Grace.*

After several minutes of calm, Patel introduced the idea of a "corridor" in Grace's mind leading to the tether. Keesha felt her heart tighten at the risk. Each time Grace approached that psychic link, it felt like stepping onto a minefield.

"You see a hallway," Patel said softly. "A door at the end. Behind it lies the tether to Darius. You don't have to open it wide—just sense its presence."

Flores tapped the EEG screen, noting a spike. Grace's breathing quickened. "It's dark," she murmured, brow crinkling. "He's there, but distant... sedated. I can feel him thrashing, though, like a storm under the surface."

Keesha's nails bit into her palms. "Stay calm, honey. We're all right here."

Grace let out a trembling exhale. "There's another path branching away from him. I see it, faintly—like a faint glow."

Flores leaned forward, voice low. "That's you, Grace. Your own true identity. Focus on it."

In Darius's room, an alarm beeped. His heart rate soared, sedation monitors flashing. A nurse called out, "He's spiking again!"

Rodriguez rushed in, with Quincy right behind her. Through half-lidded eyes, Darius's face contorted, lips moving soundlessly. Grace's diminutive form twitched under the restraints.

"That sedation level's near max," the nurse warned. "Another push might be dangerous."

Rodriguez exchanged a grim look with Quincy. "If we don't, he'll break free. Grace's attempt will be ruined." She turned to the nurse. "Increase it by point two, if that's safe. We can't let him wake fully."

The nurse swallowed. "I'll do it carefully."

Darius's eyelids fluttered, a low moan escaping him. Quincy set a hand on the pre-teen's shoulder, ready to restrain him physically if needed. "Stay down," he growled under his breath.

Grace's body tensed in bed. Her eyelids fluttered, sweat beading at her temples. "He's fighting me," she said in a tight whisper. "But he's not fully awake. I can... slip past him."

Patel offered encouragement. "Yes, you can. Picture your real self, Grace—your own face, your own hands. Let that image draw you closer."

Keesha bit back tears, remembering Grace's gentle features, her bright eyes. *Please let her make it this time,* she thought fervently.

Grace's lips curved in a fleeting smile. "I see my reflection. I'm—my old self. It's so close..." Her voice cracked with wonder. "I can almost step into it."

Flores's eyes shone with cautious optimism. "She's stable, EEG suggests a deeper identity alignment." She raised a brow at Keesha, a silent *This could be it.*

Keesha's heart thumped wildly. "Grace..." she whispered, voice trembling.

With a nod from Flores, Patel adjusted the LED pulses, guiding Grace to the brink. "Take that final step, Grace," he said gently. "Feel your consciousness slip back where it belongs. Darius can't stop you if he's this sedated."

Grace inhaled sharply, cheeks flushing with emotion. "I'm... going," she whispered. "It's like stepping through water—cold, but it's me on the other side."

Keesha gripped Grace's hand, tears streaking her cheeks. *Please, dear God, let this work.*

A sudden beep spiked on the monitor. Grace stiffened, mouth falling open in a silent gasp. The overhead lights flickered ominously, or perhaps it was Keesha's imagination. A harsh moan tore from Grace's throat. "He's... pushing again!"

Alarms shrieked, and Grace convulsed, the bed rattling under her. Flores cursed under her breath, scrambling for a syringe. Patel tried to revert the LED pattern, but Grace's vitals soared, heart rate spiking. Over the intercom, a nurse's frantic voice crackled, "Darius is thrashing, sedation near critical!"

Keesha cried out, "Grace, hold on!"

Grace's face contorted with agony, eyes rolling back. For a terrifying instant, her features twisted into a mimic of Darius's cold sneer. "No—" she rasped, voice distorted. "He's dragging me... down—"

Flores stabbed a second syringe into the IV line, reintroducing the stronger blocker. Patel forcibly ended the trance sequence. Grace's body jerked one last time, then slumped, monitors squealing in protest. For a heartbeat, Keesha feared her heart might stop from sheer terror.

Then Grace's chest heaved, and she let out a choked sob. The EEG lines plummeted from their chaotic spikes, though they remained tense. *We lost it again,* Keesha realized, devastation crashing over her.

Flores pressed a hand to Grace's brow. "She's alive, stable. Attempt aborted." Her voice shook, though she tried to hide it.

Keesha's tears blurred her vision. "Grace? Baby?"

Grace's eyes cracked open, exhaustion and heartbreak pouring through. "I was so close," she whimpered. "I felt... my body. Then he yanked me away again."

Keesha followed Dr. Flores out into the hallway once Grace's vitals steadied. Rodriguez and Quincy came from the opposite end, their own faces etched with tension.

"He nearly woke," Quincy said, voice rough. "We had to push sedation to the edge. Another minute, and we'd have needed restraints or worse."

Flores exhaled, pressing the sling more snugly against her body. "We had to abort on our side. Grace was in full convulsion. If we'd pushed one second longer..."

Keesha's hand trembled on the doorframe, anguish tightening her features. "It's too much. She can't take these collisions forever."

Rodriguez gave a slow nod. "We'll rethink our strategy. There must be a way to keep him fully distracted or subdued while she transitions."

Quincy's gaze burned with frustrated protectiveness. "He's like a cornered animal, refusing to let go. And we can't keep doping him like this forever—it's dangerous."

Flores glanced down the corridor, expression distant. "We'll figure something out. But these direct attempts are becoming all-or-nothing showdowns. The cost is too high."

That afternoon, they gathered in a cramped side office off the ward—Flores, Patel, Rodriguez, Quincy, and Keesha. An overhead lamp buzzed, casting long shadows on the table where scattered documents and EEG printouts lay.

Flores let out a weary sigh. "We keep hitting the same wall: Darius fights back the instant Grace nears a full re-merge. He's strong enough to resist sedation. We can't push sedation much further without risking organ failure."

Patel rubbed his jaw. "We might need a psychic distraction method—something to occupy Darius's mind while Grace transitions. Could be advanced illusions or a specialized neural loop that forces his cognition to chase false stimuli."

Keesha bristled. "Isn't that dangerous for whoever's feeding him illusions?"

Flores grimaced. "Potentially. But if we can automate it—like hooking him to a virtual reality brain feed that occupies his mental bandwidth—Grace might slip by undetected."

Rodriguez pursed her lips, arms folded. "Alternatively, we secure a bigger team of specialists. But that means more people at risk of mind manipulation. This entire operation has to stay under the radar."

Quincy placed both hands on the table, tension rippling through his posture. "We do what we must. Grace can't survive indefinite half-sedation in someone else's body."

A thick silence followed, each person confronting the weight of the problem. Finally, Keesha cleared her throat. "If it'll help Grace, I'm in. Whatever it takes."

Flores laid her uninjured hand over Keesha's. "We're all in this together."

That evening, after more sedation checks and a final consult with Dr. Patel, they let Grace rest in a private room again. Keesha settled into the chair by the bed, lulled by the steady beep of the heart monitor. The sky outside had darkened to a stormy gray, thunder rumbling low in the distance—a near-constant reminder of how precarious things remained.

Grace lay with her eyes closed, IV lines taped to her forearms, drifting between restless dozing and faint stirring. Keesha stroked her daughter's hair—short, coarse, not at all like the soft locks she remembered braiding when Grace was little. But it was Grace nonetheless. Each gentle touch carried a vow: *I won't abandon you, no matter how many times we fail.*

In the corridor, Rodriguez and Quincy paced, ever-watchful. Flores and Patel poured over research, brainstorming the next move in this high-stakes "psychic chess," where each misstep endangered Grace's life. Meanwhile, the distant pulse of Darius's sedation kept him in a forced slumber... for now.

Keesha let her eyes drift shut, exhaustion mingling with a fierce resolve. *We will find a way,* she promised silently. Even if it took illusions, advanced technology, or an army of determined allies. Darius's stranglehold might be powerful, but Grace was stronger than he could ever fathom.

She felt Grace shift, a faint murmur escaping her lips. Keesha leaned forward, heart pounding gently with love and determination.

Thunder rumbled again outside, echoing her convictions: Even in the deepest waters, there was always a path to surface.

"We're in this," Keesha whispered, brushing a kiss across Grace's temple. "And we'll keep fighting until you're free."

Grace's lips parted, a soft exhale of relief crossing her tired face. And in that small, fragile moment, mother and child found the tiniest measure of hope—enough to face the next day's tumult, enough to plan another gambit in the psychic chess match that had become their reality.

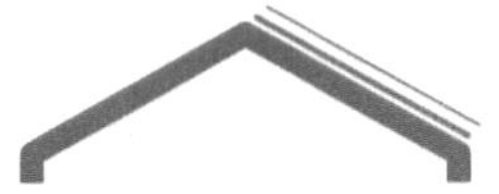

Chapter 9: The Widening Gyre

The sealed hospital ward weathered the storm in a hush that felt almost reverent. Beyond its tall windows, rain drummed steadily, matching the low hum of tension that threaded through every corridor. Dr. Miriam Flores had insisted on minimal foot traffic, warning nurses and guards that even the quietest disturbance might rouse the sleeping beast among them. If any place in the building could be said to house a tempest, it was the ward where Darius lay drugged, a mind both powerful and unstable, floating on the edge of consciousness like a shark in dark water.

Yet it was not only Darius that weighed on every mind. Grace, still trapped in the older man's body—long-limbed and coarse-featured—struggled against a deepening despair. Whenever she opened her eyes, she would check that Keesha was there, her mother's face an anchor in a world turned upside down. But she rarely spoke; exhaustion radiated from her in waves, and each breath felt like an echo of the psychic battles she had fought.

From her vinyl chair beside Grace's bed, Keesha watched her daughter's fitful dozing. She had hardly slept in days, plagued by half-remembered nightmares of Grace's screams. When she did drift off, it was only to jolt awake, convinced she heard Darius's mocking voice echo in the quiet. At times, she paced the small room, wishing she could force a resolution by sheer will. But the answer remained maddeningly out of reach.

Dr. Flores, Dr. Patel, Detective Rodriguez, and Quincy filled the roles of Keesha's battered army, each tirelessly gathering every resource they could find. Behind the ward's hushed doors, their discussions raged with medical jargon, parapsychological theories, and police protocols. This improbable alliance—part hospital staff, part law enforcement, part desperate family—was forging a new plan to outmaneuver Darius's terrifying will. No one had illusions about how little margin of error remained.

It was nearing midnight when Deputy Rhodes knocked softly on Grace's door. The gloom in his eyes spoke of bad news even before he opened his mouth. "Dr. Flores wants everyone in the conference room," he said, voice subdued. "She asked for you specifically, Ms. Marshall."

Keesha glanced at Grace, who lay curled on her side, monitors chiming a steady if fragile rhythm. Grace's sedation had settled her into a deep, uneasy sleep. Could Keesha risk leaving her, even for a short while? Yet if Flores was calling them together, it was surely important.

With a sigh, she rose, wrapping a thin sweater around her shoulders. "I'll be back soon, baby," she whispered to Grace, pressing a gentle hand to her borrowed brow. Then she followed Rhodes into the winding corridors, each step echoing as though the building itself were holding its breath.

At intervals, they passed an officer or nurse on duty, each exchanging solemn nods. Though no direct threat was visible, the tension in the ward felt like a taut wire—one sharp pluck and it would sing with chaos. Keesha's stomach clenched at the thought: if Darius awoke or somehow extended his mind beyond sedation, a single nurse could become his unwitting pawn.

Deputy Rhodes led her into a cramped conference room, where Flores, Dr. Patel, Detective Rodriguez, Quincy, and a visibly nervous nurse named Kaylin were gathered around a small rectangular table. The overhead fluorescent flickered ominously, the storm's occasional flashes illuminating their drawn faces.

Flores gave Keesha a tight nod. "Thank you for coming. We've discovered something... potentially game-changing," she began, wincing at the harsh buzz of the overhead light. Her injured arm rested in its sling, but her demeanor was all business.

Nurse Kaylin, a slight woman with curly hair pinned back, cleared her throat. "I've been analyzing the sedation logs for Darius and cross-referencing them with Grace's medical events," she said, spreading out messy printouts of EEG charts. The lines looped and spiked in patterns that made Keesha's eyes swim. "Notice these spikes here—and again, here. They match moments Darius either attempted a surge of power or Grace tried to push him out."

Keesha felt her stomach twist. Those spikes had coincided with Grace's seizures—the times Keesha had watched her daughter's face contort in agony. "So he's causing them?"

Dr. Flores nodded grimly. "Or reacting to them. We already knew Darius had a psychic link to Grace. But these logs confirm it's extremely sensitive. He feels every shift—like they're dancing on the edge of the same razor."

Kaylin pointed to another series of data lines that dipped sharply after the spikes. "Here's what's interesting," she said, gaining confidence. "After Darius exerts himself—or resists Grace's attempt—there's a brief lull in his brain waves. It's as if he depletes his energy and needs a minute to recharge."

Dr. Patel's eyes lit with possibility. "A refractory period," he murmured, turning to Floress. "If we time Grace's next move to that exact moment, Darius might be too drained to fight back effectively."

Detective Rodriguez frowned, arms crossed. "That means waiting until he's just spent his push, then pouncing on the window of weakness. But we still need a plan to keep him from lashing out the moment he senses Grace again."

Kaylin's voice softened. "Dr. Flores thinks we might... distract him." She glanced at Patel, who explained: "A neural feedback loop aimed at Darius. We've tested illusions on Grace's end, but never tried to occupy Darius's mind directly. We have older specialized equipment in the neuro lab that might flood his brain with illusions or conflicting signals—like a dream he can't wake from."

Quincy leaned forward, tension lining his brow. "So while he's chasing illusions, Grace can reclaim her body in that short window?"

Flores exhaled. "It's our best chance yet. But we have to be careful. If we over-sedate him or push illusions too far, we risk damaging his body—or accidentally letting him slip away entirely."

Keesha's throat felt tight. "You mean... he could die?"

Rodriguez's face darkened. "We're not looking to kill him. But if it's between that and letting him keep Grace's life hostage..." She trailed off, lips pressed thin.

Flores cleared her throat. "We want him alive. But we also want Grace free. Let's see if we can thread that needle. Kaylin, can you and Dr. Patel handle the illusions?"

Kaylin nodded, though she looked pale. "I'll do my best."

Dr. Patel turned to Keesha. "We'll need Grace in a controlled trance, too, ready to act when we give the signal. There's always risk, but if we coordinate sedation, illusions, and the timing of that dip in his brain activity, we might succeed."

Keesha's chest burned with mingled hope and fear. "Then let's do it," she whispered. "Let's get my daughter back."

Outside, the storm raged on, a low thunder rolling over the hospital's silhouette. Detective Rodriguez and Quincy stood near a wide window in one of the waiting areas, staring at the turbulent sky.

"Feels endless," Quincy muttered, arms crossed. "One front after another. Hard to believe it's noon."

Rodriguez rubbed the back of her neck. "Under normal circumstances, I'd say it's just an unlucky weather pattern. But after all we've seen... I wouldn't be surprised if Darius's presence stirred something up. Guess that's the paranoid cop in me talking."

Quincy's lips twisted in a humorless smile. "Paranoia might be the only sane reaction nowadays."

Deputy Rhodes approached with a nod. "They're nearly done calibrating the neural loop. You two are needed in Darius's room to handle sedation and security."

Rodriguez straightened, tension coiling back into her frame. "Let's go."

In a vacant ICU room repurposed for the attempt, nurses wheeled in an imposing machine bristling with leads and monitors. Dr. Patel's face was tight with concentration as he worked alongside Kaylin to calibrate the feedback signals. Everything had to be perfect: the illusions had to be neither so mild that Darius shrugged them off nor so chaotic that his system flatlined under the mental assault.

Quincy stood by the sedation pump, triple-checking the dosage. "We're near the safe threshold. One push beyond that could cause organ failure or put him in a coma."

Rodriguez stood at the foot of the bed, arms folded across her bulletproof vest. Darius lay strapped down, eyes half-lidded, monitors beeping a staccato that betrayed his erratic vitals. Thunder rattled the windows.

Kaylin hovered over a console. "We'll watch for that spike. Once it drops, we have a minute or two before he can surge again."

Rodriguez nodded, knuckles whitening on the bed's metal rail. "Let's make that minute count."

One room over, Grace was prepped with a simpler set of electrodes. Keesha stood close, stroking Grace's arm in a gesture that mingled maternal gentleness with steely resolve. Dr. Flores held the sedation-blocker drip, controlling how alert Grace remained.

Grace's heart drummed. "I'm ready," she said, her borrowed voice quivering with reined-in terror. She glanced at Keesha. "You'll be here, right?"

Keesha squeezed Grace's hand. "Every second, baby. I promise."

Flores pulled up a small LED rig. "Keep your eyes on the lights. Dr. Patel will speak to you via headset once the illusions begin on Darius's side." She met Grace's gaze, her own eyes reflecting sympathy. "You can do this."

Grace nodded, letting her eyelids grow heavy, sinking into the guided trance that had become a grimly familiar territory. Despite her exhaustion, a spark of hope drove her onward: If she succeeded this time, she could finally be herself again.

In Darius's room, the moment arrived. "He's peaking," Kaylin announced, eyeing a chaotic blip on the EEG. They waited with bated breath as the wave surged—and then dipped. "Now!" she called.

Quincy threw the sedation pump into partial override, letting a trickle more sedation flow. Patel tapped a sequence on the illusions console. A low hum arose, the machine feeding data into the battered girls form. Lights flickered and beeped, and Darius's eyes rolled beneath the lids. Muscles twitched, as if chasing nightmares. The illusions soared in complexity.

Rodriguez watched anxiously. "Is he taking the bait?"

Kaylin checked the EEG lines. "Yes," she whispered, the lines showing a swirl of frantic mental activity. "He's focusing on something. Let's keep it that way."

Grace felt Dr. Patel's voice resonate in her headset. "Grace, he's momentarily occupied. Find your reflection. Take it slowly."

She pictured the corridor again: the heavy door beyond which Darius lurked. This time, the darkness felt thinner, as if the swirling shadows lacked their usual teeth. She eased the door open, bracing for an attack, but met only a muffled sense of struggle—Darius locked in some hidden illusionary battleground.

Keesha stood at Grace's side in real life, whispering affirmations. "You're Grace Marshall. You're the bravest person I know."

Inside her mind, Grace found the luminous path that had once led her to a mirrored version of herself. The swirl of blackness was subdued, and she advanced, heart thundering. *This is it. I have to do this.*

In Darius's room, the illusions poured on, pushing his sedation-fogged mind deeper into chaotic visions: dissonant sounds, labyrinthine images that shifted too rapidly for him to anchor himself. His vitals spiked, but he couldn't direct his psychic lash at Grace.

Rodriguez watched the monitor with a clenched jaw. "Come on. Just another minute..."

Darius jerked, hands straining against the cuffs, a low, guttural sound escaping him. The illusions hovered at the brink of what his body could endure. If they pushed further, they risked stopping his heart. If they let up, he might lash out.

Quincy's face glistened with sweat. "He's fighting," he murmured. "We need to hold him in this net."

Grace advanced to the mirrored gateway, each step a test of her will. She pressed her hands against the shining surface. On the other side, her true self waited—shorter, younger, alive with the memories she had cherished. She pressed forward, feeling the mirror's surface yield like water.

A faint snarl reverberated through the corridor—Darius's presence, half-lost in illusions. Grace winced but kept going, summoning every ounce of courage. "I am me," she whispered, tears stinging her closed eyes. "I won't let him take me again."

She pushed, and the mirror parted. A surge of warmth flooded her senses—the sensation of returning to her rightful home. Her mind blurred with color, light, and an electric tremor that jolted her consciousness.

In a separate ICU bed, monitors began shrieking. Grace's original body spasmed once, the prepubescent limbs jerking against loose restraints meant for sedation safety. Nurses scrambled forward, Dr.

Patel at the forefront. "She's bridging!" he shouted. "Vitals are spiking—heart rate climbing!"

Keesha, standing on the sidelines, pressed a fist to her mouth, tears streaming. Was this a seizure or the final step? Then the lines stabilized. Grace's hands twitched, and her eyes fluttered open, disoriented but undeniably alive in the rightful form she had been denied.

"Grace?" Dr. Flores asked, voice trembling with cautious hope. The pre-teen turned her gaze, confusion flickering before relief took hold.

"Dr. Flores," she croaked, voice scratchy but her own. "I—" She lost words as tears blurred her vision.

Keesha stumbled forward, ignoring a nurse's attempt to hold her back. She cupped her daughter's cheeks, fingertips brushing the exact features she had kissed a thousand times before. "Grace," she whispered, breath catching. "My Grace."

They clung to each other, sobbing in relief.

But Darius's ten year old form—where it lay strapped in the other bed—began crashing. A new cacophony of alarms ripped through the ward. Kaylin's voice rang out from the console: "He's coding!"

Flores tore herself from the joyous reunion. "Stabilize him," she barked. Dr. Patel rushed after her to the adjacent room, Rodriguez and Quincy hot on their heels.

There, paramedics fought to keep the young girl's body alive: the illusions had forced him beyond sedation's safe boundary, and the psychic turbulence threatened respiratory collapse. Rodriguez hovered, shocked, remembering that this battered boy's body still belonged to Grace once. But now, if Darius died, there'd be no telling if some lingering tether might haunt Grace or if he'd simply vanish. None of them truly knew how these psychic bonds worked upon death.

A paramedic jolted Darius's chest with defibrillator paddles. "No pulse. Again—clear!" Another shock. The lines on the monitor wavered. Then a faint heartbeat flickered, slow and erratic. He was alive—for now.

Quincy watched, grim determination in every line of his face. "We wanted to stop him," he said quietly to Rodriguez. "But not like this."

She nodded, eyes heavy with weariness. "Either way, we can't let him free again. We keep him here, sedated, guarded. If he regains consciousness..." She let the sentence trail off, uncertain whether to hope for his survival or dread it.

In Grace's room, Keesha and Grace remained oblivious to the chaos for precious moments, lost in their embrace. Grace clung to her mother, trembling with exhaustion. Each breath soared with relief, tempered by the lingering trauma of Darius's infiltration.

Slowly, the room's reality seeped in. Nurses scurried in, checking the tween's vitals, adjusting IV lines. Dr. Patel returned, face streaked with sweat but carrying a tender smile. "He's stable," he said, answering Keesha's unspoken question about Darius. "Barely, but stable. Let's focus on Grace now."

Grace's eyelids drooped, her body weakened by the ordeal of reentry. "Am I... safe?" she whispered.

Keesha pressed their foreheads together gently. "Yes, baby. You're safe."

Flores joined them, wincing as she repositioned her injured arm. "We'll do more scans, but everything suggests you're truly back in your own body. It'll take time for you to heal—physically, psychologically. But you're home, Grace."

Tears rolled down Grace's cheeks. "Thank you," she breathed. "I almost gave up."

Flores's eyes misted in return. "I never doubted you."

Outside, the ward felt as though it had collectively exhaled. The immediate crisis—Darius's violent thrashing, the illusions, the precarious sedation—had subsided into a subdued hush. Deputy Rhodes watched from the perimeter, ensuring no unauthorized staff ventured near Darius's room. A handful of new guards stood by, rifles strapped, prepared for any last-ditch attempt by would-be accomplices.

Rodriguez leaned against a wall, pinching the bridge of her nose. She'd stared down criminals, conspiracies, and abusers, but never imagined she'd face something so far beyond the ordinary. Now she felt an odd mixture of triumph and sorrow: Grace was free, but Darius lay near death. And if he survived, a new wave of legal and moral complexities loomed.

She spotted Quincy approaching, shoulders stiff. "How are they?" she asked.

He gave a measured nod. "Flores says Grace is stable. Keesha's with her. They're... unbelievably relieved." He hesitated, gaze flicking to the door that led to Darius. "And him?"

Rodriguez pursed her lips. "Still critical. We might not know for days if he'll pull through. The doctors are worried about brain damage."

A pause settled, their shared tension easing only slightly. Quincy sighed, running a hand over his hair. "At least Grace is free. That's what matters."

Rodriguez nodded. "Yeah." *It is*, she told herself, but a pang of leftover guilt gnawed at her. She wondered if they'd robbed a child's body of life or if Darius's darkness had consumed it already. The lines had blurred so completely.

Through the night, doctors scanned Grace's newly reclaimed body. The results showed only minor muscle weakness, a bit of malnutrition from her time on sedation. The biggest wounds, they agreed, were intangible—the memories of Darius's invasive presence. But physically, she would recover.

In the early morning hours, the storm clouds finally parted, sunlight streaking the corridor with tentative gold. One by one, those who had fought all night stole a moment to marvel at the quiet day dawning. It felt like the hospital itself was breathing easier.

When Keesha woke in a chair beside Grace, the girl was already stirring, blinking against the soft glow. For a moment, panic flashed in Grace's eyes, as though she expected to see an unfamiliar man's limbs.

But a glance downward reassured her she was truly herself. The tension in her face released in a shaky exhale.

Keesha gently clasped Grace's hand. "How do you feel, honey?"

A flicker of a smile touched Grace's lips, though tears pricked her eyes. "I feel... real again. Everything's too bright and heavy, but... it's me."

Keesha's own tears welled. "You're home."

That day, Dr. Flores authorized a small, celebratory step: Grace could move to a regular room soon, as her vital signs stabilized. The halls still held guards, but the energy was different—less harrowing, more hopeful. Quincy came by with a small wave, eyes shining with relief, while Rodriguez informed them that a thorough investigation would continue for weeks, if not months. Keesha accepted it all with grateful solemnity.

Toward late afternoon, Grace managed to sit upright without dizziness. She glanced at Keesha, a hesitant grin forming. "So... we can go home soon?"

Keesha's eyes glistened. "Maybe. Dr. Flores wants a couple more days of observation, but yes—soon. We can pick up your drawings, your favorite snacks, whatever you want." She laughed softly, "I'll even get that brand of ice cream you love, the one with the chocolate chunks."

Grace chuckled, a sound that warmed the room. "That sounds... amazing."

Grace's laughter was like music to Keesha's ears, a precious sign that the girl she'd nurtured for ten years was truly back. Reaching out, she tucked a lock of hair behind Grace's ear—her ear—and the wave of emotion nearly overwhelmed her. They had faced a monstrous threat, a twisted psychic game that nearly destroyed them both. But they had survived.

Outside, the weather turned placid, pale sunlight washing the hospital grounds in a tentative promise of peace. And in that hush, mother and daughter—both scarred, both resilient—settled into the new reality. The gyre of dread and desperation that had consumed them was at last unwinding, leaving them space to heal and breathe.

Darius's fate remained uncertain, and no one could predict if he might rise again. But for now, in the stillness of this brightening ward, the bond between Keesha and Grace shone unbreakable, having emerged from the darkest vortex stronger than before. And that, they decided, was victory enough for today.

Chapter 10: The Gathering Shadows

A hush had settled over the sealed corridor—a quiet that should have brought relief after so many sleepless nights. Yet an undercurrent of tension still thrummed beneath the walls and floors, as if the hospital itself had learned to be wary. Darius might have been comatose, but his presence seemed to hang over everything like a dark curtain. His supporters remained unaccounted for, Redwood Ridge still held its secrets, and no one could shake the lingering sense that something—or someone—still lurked in the margins.

Grace awoke the next day to the sound of rolling carts and murmured voices. She blinked in the half-light, disoriented by the ever-present hospital smell—antiseptic and lingering coffee. For a heartbeat, fear jolted through her: *Am I still in his body?* But a quick glance at her own hands, small and pale, eased her panic. She was Grace Marshall again.

She heard Dr. Flores's soft footsteps before she saw her. The doctor peered into the room with the careful caution of someone who'd spent too many days bracing for the worst. When she saw Grace's open eyes, a warm smile creased her face.

"Good morning," Flores said, easing closer. Her right arm was still in a sling, and faint bruises mottled her visible skin—reminders of the night Darius had nearly broken free. "How are you feeling?"

Grace pushed herself upright, heart fluttering. She felt weak but alive. "Tired," she admitted. "But... better. Definitely better."

Keesha stirred in the vinyl chair, rousing from a light doze. Despite dark circles under her eyes, she shot Grace a tender smile. "You slept through the night. No nightmares?"

Grace shook her head. "No nightmares." And she realized it was true—no searing visions, no sense of Darius's presence dragging her into darkness. She closed her eyes for a moment, allowing the relief to wash over her.

Flores set a stethoscope gently against Grace's chest. "Deep breaths." She listened with a practiced calm. "Your vitals look strong. Once we have the results of the new bloodwork and the MRI, we'll have a better picture, but from everything I can see... you're well on your way to recovery, Grace."

A knock on the frame of the open door revealed Dr. Patel and Nurse Kaylin, both holding clipboards. Patel offered a small, encouraging nod. "We're going to monitor your heart rate and brain activity a bit more today—just to confirm there's no reemerging psychic tether. But so far..." He glanced at the readouts. "It all looks promising."

Keesha clasped Grace's hand, hope shining in her eyes. For a moment, they simply savored the calm—a lull in the storm that had consumed their lives.

Down the corridor, the ICU room that held Darius's massive, adult frame buzzed with a quieter, more somber energy. Armed officers posted by the door exchanged looks whenever a nurse went in or out. Machines beeped softly, charting the fragile line between life and death that Darius now walked.

Detective Rodriguez stood in the hallway conferring with Deputy Rhodes, her expression grim. "No changes overnight," she said, voice low. "His vitals are stable, but still critical. The doctors say it could be days, weeks, even months before he regains consciousness—if he does at all."

Rhodes shifted his weight, gaze straying toward the ICU's small window. "And Redwood Ridge? Any new intel from your contacts there?"

Rodriguez exhaled, frustration pinching her features. "Not much. The local PD scoured the cabin site, found traces of ritual paraphernalia—but no immediate leads on accomplices. It's like these people vanished into thin air. No new sightings, no chatter on phone lines. They may be lying low until they know if Darius..." She gestured toward the ICU bed. "...pulls through."

Rhodes glanced at the silent, hulking figure inside. Seeing the broad shoulders and scarred, muscular arms of the man who had terrorized them was jarring. "I just hope he stays comatose," the deputy murmured. "A man that size, with that kind of will... let's pray we don't have to find out what happens if he wakes up angry."

Rodriguez gave him a sidelong look. "He's got a full guard detail for a reason. Let's pray we don't have to find out."

By late morning, Grace was up and about with the help of physical therapy aides. She clung to a walker, concentrating intently on each move of her legs. Though her muscles remembered what to do, days of sedation and malnourishment had drained her strength. Keesha hovered protectively, arms outstretched to catch Grace if she stumbled.

"One step... two steps... keep your core engaged," the therapist intoned.

Grace's forehead beaded with sweat, but her eyes were determined. Inch by inch, she made her way across the room, never letting her gaze wander from the goal—a plain metal chair at the far wall. When she finally reached it, her breath came in ragged bursts, and the walker rattled as she set it aside.

"Good," the therapist praised, checking her posture. "You're making progress. Let's sit for a moment."

Grace collapsed onto the chair, limbs trembling. Still, she flashed a triumphant grin up at her mom. "I walked five whole steps," she joked, though tears of relief glistened in her eyes.

Keesha knelt beside her, her own smile wobbly. "And those five steps feel like five miles in the right direction."

From the doorway, Dr. Flores and Dr. Patel watched with subdued pride. It was a small victory compared to the psychic war they'd just waged, but it was a victory all the same.

Early in the afternoon, the bustle of the hospital returned to normal—code calls, routine check-ups, the occasional overhead page for staff. Grace, exhausted from therapy, napped in her bed while Keesha stretched her legs in the corridor. She was about to return with a cup of lukewarm tea when she noticed a figure stepping off the elevator at the far end of the restricted ward.

The man was tall and lean, dressed in a dark suit that seemed out of place in the hospital setting. He moved with a sort of self-assured precision, pausing to scan the signage. Something about him made Keesha's stomach tighten with unease.

She approached cautiously. "Excuse me," she said, tone polite but firm. "This is a restricted area. Are you looking for someone?"

The man turned, revealing piercing gray eyes and a narrow face. A practiced smile touched his lips as he reached into his pocket for a badge. "Agent Paul Weston," he said smoothly, flashing credentials that read *Federal Bureau of Investigation*. "I'm here to see Detective Rodriguez concerning an ongoing investigation."

Keesha studied the ID—a valid federal badge, from what she could tell—then summoned her resolve. "Right. Detective Rodriguez should be down that hall." She nodded toward the corridor leading to Darius's ICU. "Let me walk you."

Agent Weston dipped his head. "Thank you, Ms...?" He glanced at the name badge around Keesha's neck, courtesy of hospital security.

"Marshall," Keesha supplied. "I'm Grace's mother."

His expression flickered with curiosity. "Ah. Grace Marshall. I've heard quite a bit about her situation." He said it casually, but his eyes flicked to the sealed ward doors with a certain intensity. "Very unusual case."

Keesha's guard rose. "That's one way to put it," she replied coolly.

She led him to where Rodriguez was poring over a stack of paperwork with Quincy. At the sight of a stranger in a crisp suit, Rodriguez stiffened. "And you are?"

He introduced himself again, carefully handing over the badge. "I'm with the Bureau's special assignments unit. I was sent to consult on the Redwood Ridge incident. I understand we have a suspect in custody here—though I hear he's in no condition to talk."

Quincy raised an eyebrow. "Word travels fast."

Weston's mouth curved in a faint, humorless grin. "The Redwood Ridge site caught our attention months ago when we received reports of potential cult activity. Federal interest was minimal until local law enforcement flagged... certain irregularities." He looked meaningfully at the sealed ward. "I'm here to determine whether this suspect—Darius—has connections to broader criminal networks."

Rodriguez studied him, arms crossed. She was no stranger to bureaucratic interference, and there was something in Weston's stance that put her on guard. Still, the badge was real, and Redwood Ridge was definitely big enough for federal notice. "We can talk in the conference room," she said shortly. "Deputy Rhodes, keep an eye on that elevator. This is still a high-security zone."

The deputy nodded, moving to post himself by the doors.

Before Rodriguez escorted the FBI agent away, he gave Keesha a single, polite nod. "Thank you for your help. Ms. Marshall... I wish your daughter a speedy recovery."

But the way he said it—quiet, cool, calculating—made Keesha's skin prickle. She watched him disappear into the conference room with Rodriguez and Quincy, unsettled by the notion of yet another powerful organization peering into Grace's ordeal.

While the meeting with Agent Weston took place behind closed doors, Keesha returned to Grace's room. She tried to downplay her worry, not wanting to alarm her daughter, but she couldn't suppress the knot twisting in her gut.

Grace was awake now, picking at a bowl of soup. She looked up when her mother walked in, frowning at Keesha's tense posture. "Mom, everything okay?"

Keesha forced a smile. "Just some federal agent here to talk about Redwood Ridge."

Grace's brow furrowed. "Federal agent?"

"That's right. FBI," Keesha said softly. "He's consulting on the case. Probably routine."

Grace set her spoon down with trembling fingers. "It doesn't feel routine. Whenever Redwood Ridge is mentioned, I..." She trailed off, swallowing. The horrors of that cabin, the twisted circle of chanting figures, the creeping sense of something *wrong* in the air—it all lingered too close for comfort.

Keesha sank onto the edge of the bed. "I know. But you're safe here," she murmured, brushing a strand of Grace's hair from her forehead. "Rodriguez and the hospital staff aren't letting anyone near you without clearance. We'll cooperate if it helps keep you—and everyone else—safe."

Grace exhaled, shoulders slumping. "I just don't want any more trouble," she whispered. "I want it to be over."

Keesha squeezed her hand. "Me too, baby. Me too."

Meanwhile, in the conference room, Detective Rodriguez sat across from Agent Weston, her posture rigid. Quincy leaned against the wall, arms folded, eyes watchful. Weston flipped open a slim notebook and jotted down details as Rodriguez explained the timeline—Grace's disappearance, the infiltration of Darius into her body, the near-fatal confrontation in the hospital. He listened with a face carefully schooled into neutrality, though the occasional flicker of disbelief crossed his features.

"Let me be clear," Rodriguez said, voice unwavering. "There's documented evidence that some sort of... *psychic transference* took place. We have the medical records, EEG scans, and multiple eyewitness accounts. If you want to call it something else in your report, that's your business—but these are the facts."

Weston tapped his pen on the table. "I'm aware of the official version, yes. The Bureau has had rare encounters with cult-like groups claiming supernatural abilities. Most turn out to be smoke and mirrors, mental manipulation... but this Redwood Ridge matter is more elaborate than usual." He paused, glancing from Rodriguez to Quincy. "I assume you're still investigating any accomplices."

Quincy nodded. "Yes. We have reason to believe Darius had a network. Or at least, sympathizers. But they all went to ground after Grace's rescue."

Weston's gaze sharpened. "So you're telling me that right now, the only person who can confirm or deny Redwood Ridge's scope is lying in a coma? That's... inconvenient."

Rodriguez's lips pressed tight. "We have him under constant guard. If he ever regains consciousness, I'll make sure you're notified."

A silence settled, charged with tension. Finally, Weston closed his notebook. "I appreciate your cooperation. I'll review your files and consult with my superiors. If Redwood Ridge is part of a larger domestic threat, we'll escalate our response. In the meantime, I'll be staying nearby—in case circumstances change."

Rodriguez inclined her head. "We'll keep you updated. Just remember, Grace is a minor and a victim in this. She's not a resource for you to interrogate."

"Understood," Weston said, though a shadow crossed his features. "I won't disturb her without your permission."

The promise sounded polished but not entirely sincere. Quincy exchanged a subtle, uneasy glance with Rodriguez. It seemed they weren't done tiptoeing through bureaucratic minefields—no matter how battered the hospital or how scarred the people within it.

That evening, the hospital lights dimmed to night mode, a soft amber glow along the corridors. Despite the calmer day, anxiety lingered among the staff. People spoke in hushed voices about the FBI agent's arrival, about Redwood Ridge, about Darius's precarious state. A few even whispered the rumor that the storms might start up again; the weather forecast hinted at more unpredictable fronts rolling in.

In her room, Grace tried to settle into a doze. Keesha stayed by her bedside, a paperback novel abandoned in her lap. She couldn't concentrate on reading; every passing shadow outside the door made her tense.

Eventually, Grace's breathing evened out, her eyes fluttering shut. Keesha turned off the overhead light, letting the faint glow from the monitors serve as a nightlight. She was about to stand and stretch when a rustle at the threshold made her whip around.

Quincy stood there, face drawn with concern. "Didn't mean to startle you," he said softly.

Keesha pressed a hand to her racing heart, nodding for him to come in. He closed the door most of the way, glancing at Grace to ensure she was soundly asleep. Then he turned to Keesha, voice low. "We've run into a snag with the Redwood Ridge investigation. The local PD is spooked—says they don't have enough manpower to monitor every rumored safehouse. And the feds are only interested in what they can classify under federal statutes. They might not take this 'supernatural threat' angle seriously enough."

Keesha's brows drew together. "So Redwood Ridge's people could regroup?"

"It's a possibility." Quincy rubbed the back of his neck. "Rodriguez is pushing for additional patrols, but her department's stretched thin.

And with Agent Weston... I'm not sure we can count on him to see beyond the 'cult activity' label."

Keesha sighed, anxiety pressing her chest. "What about the hospital? Could they try to break Darius out?"

Quincy shrugged, expression grim. "We have security posted, but you know as well as I do—no plan is foolproof. We'll do our best."

He paused, glancing at Grace's sleeping form. "On the bright side, her scans look good. Dr. Flores is optimistic. It's just... I wish we could give you both the peace of mind that none of this will come back."

Keesha lowered her gaze to her daughter's pale face. "So do I. But I appreciate everything you and Rodriguez have done. Just... don't let them take Grace away for some 'investigation.' She's been through enough."

Quincy nodded firmly. "We won't. I promise."

His words carried the weight of conviction, but Keesha heard the unspoken reality: so many threads remained untied. If Redwood Ridge had a deeper network, or if Darius somehow awakened... the fight might not be as over as they'd hoped.

In the hours before dawn, Grace woke from a surprisingly restful sleep. The nightmares that used to jolt her awake had loosened their grip. She blinked, adjusting to the hospital's dim overhead panel. Keesha was asleep in the chair again, arms folded over a thin blanket.

Grace felt an odd mixture of hope and apprehension. *I'm free of him,* she reminded herself. *Darius can't hurt me anymore.* But beneath that reassurance lurked a nagging whisper: *Unless he wakes up. Unless Redwood Ridge tries again.*

She pushed the thought aside and focused on the present. The nurses had unhooked one of her IVs, freeing her from at least a bit of tether. She extended an arm, rotating her wrist, marveling at how it felt to simply *move* without another consciousness leering at the edges of her mind.

A soft knock sounded, and Dr. Patel entered, carrying a portable EEG machine. He gave Grace a warm smile. "Morning. Time for another test."

She nodded, letting him place the small electrodes around her temples. While he attached the leads, she shot a glance at Keesha, who slept on. "It's okay," Patel assured her quietly. "Let her rest. This won't take long."

Grace closed her eyes as he flipped the machine on, the gentle hum vibrating through the silence. She'd grown used to the swirl of lines on the little screen that charted her brain's rhythms. Patel studied the readout with practiced focus.

Her thoughts began to wander, drifting through half-formed images: Redwood Ridge's pine trees swaying ominously, the claustrophobic hush of the sealed ward. She felt her chest tighten with nerves, but she forced herself to breathe slowly. *You're safe. You're safe.*

At last, Patel nodded in satisfaction. "Everything seems normal. No sign of abnormal spikes or tether fluctuations. Just your own brain waves doing what they're supposed to."

Relief loosened Grace's clenched shoulders. "Good."

He detached the electrodes, carefully folding them away. "Dr. Flores will be pleased to hear this. We'll do one more EEG in the afternoon, then consider stepping you down from high-level observation."

Grace's heart fluttered. "Does that mean I might... get to go home soon?"

Patel's expression softened. "If you continue to stabilize, it's likely. We'll want you to have daily check-ups at first, but yes... home is on the horizon."

A small smile curved Grace's lips. *Home.* The word felt like a door opening to a future she'd nearly lost.

Down the hall, Agent Weston emerged from the ICU, wearing an unreadable expression. He'd spent nearly an hour studying Darius's condition, though no one seemed to know exactly what the FBI wanted with a comatose patient. Nurse Kaylin tried to keep a polite distance, but her unease was clear.

In the corridor, he crossed paths with Detective Rodriguez, who eyed him warily. "Find what you were looking for?" she asked, voice tight.

Weston shrugged. "I'm merely documenting the environment and verifying that your security measures are adequate. The Bureau doesn't want any... surprises."

Rodriguez stiffened. "We've handled plenty of surprises, Agent Weston. Our team knows the risks."

He offered a mild, almost smug nod. "I'm sure you do. Just remember, if Redwood Ridge's cult is as dangerous as you say, it's only a matter of time before they make a move. Let's hope you're prepared."

Before she could fire back a retort, he turned and headed for the elevators, leaving her with a storm of unspoken warnings swirling in her mind.

By the time the sun dipped low in the sky, Grace had managed another short session of walking—this one even longer than before. She still relied on the walker and felt fatigue dragging at every muscle, but her improvement was undeniable. Each successful step was a victory she savored.

Keesha watched her daughter with a proud, aching heart. She could almost forget the horrors that had brought them here. Almost.

Dr. Flores joined them after dinner, her sling now removed in favor of a stiff brace on her shoulder. She moved gingerly, but relief flickered in her eyes. "I have good news," she announced, scanning Grace's vitals. "Tomorrow morning, we'll run the final EEG for clearance. If it looks good, and you can walk a little more on your own, we'll arrange for discharge in the next day or two."

Grace's face lit up. "Really? That soon?"

Flores smiled, carefully setting aside her chart. "Your body's responding well. You'll still need outpatient therapy, but there's no medical reason to keep you in a hospital bed if you're stable."

Keesha swallowed a lump of gratitude. "Thank you," she whispered. "Thank you for everything, Dr. Flores."

Flores touched Keesha's arm gently. "We all fought for her. And she fought hardest of all."

Grace stared at her own feet—no longer alien, no longer overshadowed by Darius's presence. "I can't wait to just... be home," she said softly, her voice trembling with a mix of anticipation and fear. "I know it'll never be the same, but... it's mine."

Keesha gathered Grace into a gentle hug, tears prickling her eyes. "We'll make it ours again. Step by step."

Darkness fell gently that evening, the hospital windows reflecting the glow of street lamps. A quiet alert was sent out by Rodriguez's precinct—some rumor of suspicious activity near Redwood Ridge—but so far, it amounted to little more than a reported break-in at a vacant cabin. No direct link to Darius's cohorts. Still, it set everyone on edge.

In the ward, the soft beep of monitors served as a lullaby of sorts. Grace curled onto her side, letting her eyelids drift shut. Keesha, exhausted herself, stretched out in the chair with a pillow stuffed behind her head. In the background, the distant hum of the hospital ventilation sounded almost soothing now.

But outside Grace's window, beyond the hospital walls, the world was not so peaceful.

- In the police station a few blocks away, Detective Rodriguez pored over new files, brow furrowed, senses tingling with the suspicion that Redwood Ridge wasn't done.

- In a small motel on the outskirts of town, Agent Weston typed furiously on a laptop, sending urgent emails to nameless superiors and scanning reams of data about cultic practices and "anomalous" incidents.

- Somewhere much farther away, on a lonely stretch of road near the Redwood Ridge wilderness, an old station wagon pulled onto a dirt track. A figure emerged, hooded and quiet, heading toward a hidden structure among the pines.

Unseen by the hospital staff, the slender silhouette carried an air of grim purpose. A single candle flickered inside the cabin, illuminating the twisted shapes of arcane symbols scrawled on the walls. A hushed chant began, reverberating in the night air, stirring an ancient echo that refused to die.

If Redwood Ridge's faithful had gone to ground, they hadn't stayed idle. Whatever power they revered, whatever force they had attempted to harness through Darius, it still simmered beneath the surface—waiting for a chance to rise again.

Inside Grace's dimly lit hospital room, the machines continued their steady watch, charting every breath, every heartbeat. Grace slept fitfully, lulled by the knowledge that she was in her own skin at last. The battle she had fought was over, but the war—unknown to her—might only be shifting shape.

Keesha, too, drifted in and out of uneasy dreams. A part of her sensed the danger wasn't entirely past, even if she couldn't quite name it. But every time she looked at Grace's sleeping form, healthy color returning to her cheeks, she found a reason to hope.

A nurse peeked in just after midnight to check vitals. Satisfied, she slipped away, leaving mother and daughter cocooned in rare calm. And so the hospital sank once more into its subdued nighttime hush, the wards humming with the perpetual cycle of care and caution.

Far below the surface, tension gathered like thunderclouds—unseen, but no less real. Yet in that quiet room, love and relief held firm, warding off the darkness for at least a little while longer.

The hush of the hospital at night had a different quality now—less foreboding than before, but still tinged with something unsettled. The lights at the nurses' station glowed softly against the muted walls. A handful of guards dozed on their feet, arms crossed, gazes drifting up and down the corridor in sporadic vigilance.

In Grace's room, Keesha woke just after one in the morning. The angle of her neck ached from having fallen asleep in the chair again, but she refused to leave her daughter's side. She glanced at Grace, who lay breathing quietly, the lines of worry on her young face softened in repose.

Outside, footsteps padded past. The shadow of a nurse flitted under the door, then disappeared. Keesha sighed, thinking how she used to find hospitals comforting—the crisp sheets, the promise of care. Now it felt as if every wall might be hiding eyes, every door concealing some new threat.

She rose, stiff-limbed, and moved to the small sink in the corner. Splashing cool water on her face, she caught her own reflection in the mirror. Dark circles framed her eyes, and her hair—once immaculately styled—hung in a messy half-ponytail. *We're almost there,* she told herself, summoning a fragile resolve. *Grace is coming home soon. You can do this.*

When she returned to the chair, she found Grace stirring. Her daughter's eyes fluttered open, flickering in the faint glow of the monitors. "Mom?" Grace mumbled, voice thick with sleep.

"Sorry," Keesha whispered, gently brushing a hand over Grace's hair. "Go back to sleep, sweetheart. Everything's fine."

For once, Grace nodded and let her eyelids drift shut again. Keesha listened to the steady beeping of the heart monitor until her own pulse matched its rhythm, gradually lulling her back into a restless doze.

By the time pale dawn light began filtering through the windows, word had spread among the hospital staff that today might be Grace's last round of major tests. In a few days, she could be discharged—an event that should have brought a collective sigh of relief. Instead, the atmosphere felt charged, as though everyone was waiting for the other shoe to drop.

Overnight, the chatter about Redwood Ridge had grown louder. A nurse in the cafeteria overheard two orderlies discussing a rumored break-in at another deserted property on the outskirts of town—possibly linked to the same group. The details were hazy, but it was enough to keep nerves on edge.

Dr. Flores arrived at Grace's room early, a determined set to her jaw. She still wore the brace on her shoulder and moved gingerly. "Morning," she greeted, giving Keesha a nod. "Ready for the big day?"

Keesha smiled weakly. "As ready as we'll ever be." She reached over to help Grace sit up, adjusting the pillows behind her. Grace's face was drawn with fatigue, but her eyes brightened at the mention of possibly going home.

Dr. Patel joined them soon after, carrying the portable EEG machine. "We'll do a quick scan now and another after lunch," he explained. "If both come back clean—meaning no abnormal spikes—then we can start the discharge process."

Grace exhaled, relief mingling with anxiety. "And... if there's a spike?" she asked softly.

Flores placed a reassuring hand on her arm. "Let's not dwell on worst-case scenarios. Your readings yesterday were completely normal. Chances are good you'll see the same result today."

With that, they attached the electrodes, and Grace closed her eyes, trying to calm her racing mind. Keesha hovered by the bed, carefully holding onto Grace's hand. For a few tense minutes, the only sound was the hum of the EEG device and Grace's measured breathing.

Finally, Patel smiled. "All clear."

A wave of relief washed over Keesha. Grace's lips parted in a tentative grin. "So... that means—"

Flores nodded. "You're still on track. One more test later, just to be sure." She offered a warm look. "We'll know by evening if we can sign the discharge papers."

Elsewhere in the hospital, Detective Rodriguez and Deputy Rhodes made their morning rounds. They paused in front of the ICU, where Darius's ten year old form lay motionless. Machines beeped a soft, methodical pattern—life persisting despite the soul-rending conflict that had preceded this coma.

Rodriguez peered through the small window set into the door. Darius's face was pale, tubes snaking across his mouth and nose. She had never gotten used to the dissonance of seeing that frail pre-teen body—a boy no older than Grace—tied so closely to such malevolence.

"He still stable?" Rhodes asked, though it was more a statement than a question.

"Stable, but no sign of improvement," Rodriguez replied, stepping back. "Flores says it's anyone's guess whether he'll ever wake up."

Rhodes gave a curt nod, lowering his voice. "Word is Redwood Ridge might be stirring. If they're planning something, it could be a rescue attempt—or worse."

She pursed her lips. "I know. I've asked for more officers, but it's not easy. We're short-staffed, and the FBI presence complicates jurisdiction." She paused, then glanced down the hall where Agent Weston had appeared the previous day. "Speaking of which, have you seen him this morning?"

Rhodes shook his head. "Not yet. My guess is he'll pop in when we least expect it. They always do."

Rodriguez sighed, adjusting the files in her arms. "Keep an eye out. Let's make sure no one gets near Darius without us knowing."

They parted ways, each consumed by the quiet worry that Redwood Ridge's next move might come at any moment.

Grace managed another walk before lunch, this one nearly double the length of yesterday's. Keesha walked beside her with a watchful hand near Grace's elbow, while a physical therapist offered tips for maintaining balance. The corridors bustled with the usual midday bustle—nurses directing visitors, a janitor mopping the tiled floor, trays of meals clattering.

As they finished, Grace leaned against the walker, breathing heavily. "I... I need a break," she managed.

Keesha guided her over to a bench tucked in a small alcove near a window. Sunlight streamed in, warming the sterile hallway. Grace settled onto the seat with a soft groan, pressing a hand to her heart as it hammered in her chest.

"Slow, steady breaths," the therapist reminded.

Grace nodded, following the instructions. After a moment, she glanced out the window and was startled to see Agent Weston standing in the parking lot below, staring up at the building. He looked odd in the bright daylight—like a crow among pigeons, dark suit and tidy hair almost anachronistic against the swirl of hospital traffic.

A sliver of unease slid down Grace's spine. She couldn't hear him or see his expression clearly, but his presence alone felt cold. He turned abruptly, heading toward a sleek, unmarked car. Then he was gone from her line of sight.

"Grace?" Keesha asked, noticing how tense she'd gone. "What is it?"

She tore her gaze from the window. "I saw Agent Weston outside," she murmured. "He was just... standing there, looking up."

Keesha followed her daughter's glance, but the lot was empty now except for a few passing vehicles. She laid a comforting hand on Grace's shoulder. "Probably just taking a call or something."

But the words didn't dispel Grace's unease. She forced a shaky smile. "I'm okay. Let's just... get back to the room."

Afternoon came, and the atmosphere grew heavier. Another rumor had trickled in—someone apparently spotted robed figures near the Redwood Ridge forest boundary. The credibility of the report was questionable, but it spread among the hospital staff like wildfire. By the time it reached the sealed ward, the story had morphed into an account of a dozen hooded cultists chanting in a circle, chanting *something* in an ancient tongue.

Detective Rodriguez tried to quell the hysteria, reminding everyone that the evidence was unverified. But the staff couldn't help recalling the strange events of the past weeks. They eyed the locked doors and the posted guards with fresh apprehension.

Keesha felt the tension the moment she stepped out to grab coffee. Conversations hushed when she walked by, and though she knew it was mostly concern for Grace, it only deepened her sense of dread. *This place feels like a pressure cooker,* she thought, *one spark away from an explosion.*

When she returned to Grace's room, she found Dr. Flores waiting with the portable EEG machine once more. "Time for the final test," Flores said. Her smile was calm, but her eyes revealed how desperately she wanted this to go well.

Grace sat with her hands folded in her lap, the lines of her face tight. "Let's get it over with," she murmured.

They attached the electrodes again. Patel, behind a small monitor stand, nodded for Grace to close her eyes. The hallway beyond the door felt too quiet, as if everyone was holding their breath.

Seconds ticked by. Keesha studied Grace's features—the slight pinch of her brow, the flicker beneath her eyelids. Was it discomfort, or just nerves?

Finally, Patel glanced up, his expression breaking into relief. "All clear," he announced, tapping a few keys to confirm the data. "No sign of abnormal spikes or tether activity. You're officially off high-level observation."

Grace's eyes fluttered open. A tear slipped down her cheek, unbidden. "So... I can really go?"

Flores nodded. "We'll finalize paperwork tonight. If all goes smoothly, you'll be on your way home tomorrow morning."

Keesha pressed her lips together, fighting back her own tears. She reached for Grace's hand, feeling her daughter squeeze back. "Thank you," she whispered to Flores and Patel, voice thick with gratitude.

Patel began removing the electrodes. "You'll still have regular follow-ups, Grace—weekly at first, then monthly. We're going to keep a close watch on your recovery."

Grace nodded, her gaze flicking to Keesha. "That's fine. As long as... I can be out of here."

Flores smiled gently. "You've earned it. I suspect your biggest challenge will be readjusting to ordinary life after... all this." She gestured vaguely, indicating the swirl of the last few weeks' traumas. "But you have a strong support system."

Keesha placed an arm around Grace's shoulders. "She does," she affirmed softly.

While Grace tasted the hope of freedom, the ICU remained a place of grim stillness. Armed officers rotated shifts at Darius's door, preventing any unauthorized entry. The hum of medical machines droned on as if mocking the tension swirling through the ward.

Rodriguez stood guard for a few minutes, watching the monitors track Darius's shallow vitals. Every so often, she found her gaze drawn to his face—a prepubescent face with no sign of the mind that had once violently hijacked Grace's body.

"Hey," came a low voice behind her. It was Quincy, carrying a tablet. "Just came from the station. Rumor has it Redwood Ridge might be planning something more concrete than random break-ins."

She arched an eyebrow. "You have a source?"

He nodded, grim. "Unofficial tipster in the local community. Says a small group's been seen meeting at an abandoned roadside motel. Cloaks, candles, the works. Could be unrelated weirdos, but... it fits the pattern."

Rodriguez exhaled slowly. "I'll send a patrol to check it out. But we're stretched so thin as it is. I hate that we're playing whack-a-mole with these rumors."

Quincy glanced at Darius through the glass. "We might not have a choice. If Redwood Ridge truly wants him back, they won't stop trying. And if they can't have him... they might try to destroy the evidence. Including Darius himself."

A chill wrapped around Rodriguez's spine. "All the more reason to keep a tight guard."

She turned on her heel and strode down the hallway, phone already in hand to dispatch another unit. Quincy lingered, eyes on the unconscious figure in the ICU. The lines on the heart monitor pulsed with excruciating calm, each beep a reminder that, for now, Darius was still alive... and still a threat, if he ever awoke.

Twilight brought a stillness that settled over the sealed ward, though tension shimmered in the corners like heat off a distant road. The nurses who knew Grace best stopped by her room, offering small congratulations or heartfelt hugs. Word spread quickly that she might be leaving in the morning.

Grace felt a swirl of emotions—joy, relief, apprehension. She had been so desperate to leave this place, but it had also become her fortress against Darius's menacing presence. With him still comatose just down the hall, part of her worried about stepping outside these guarded walls.

Keesha sensed her daughter's unease. After the last nurse left, she settled beside Grace on the bed, gently tucking a stray hair behind her ear. "You're not alone," Keesha murmured. "We have a home waiting for us, friends who'll watch over you. Detective Rodriguez won't let anything happen, and neither will I."

Grace looked down at her hands. They still felt thinner than they used to, skin paler. "I know, Mom," she said, voice soft. "It's just... every time I think about Redwood Ridge, about the cabin..." A shiver ran through her. "I feel like they're still watching me somehow."

Keesha's stomach twisted at the thought. "You were the one who beat Darius at his own game, honey. You're stronger than you realize." She squeezed Grace's hand. "He's not in your head anymore."

Grace managed a shaky nod. "Right," she whispered, as if convincing herself. "He's not."

Night closed in once more. The hospital dimmed its overhead lights, and the staff shifted into quieter routines. Keesha was helping Grace brush her hair—one of those small, ordinary gestures that felt miraculous after everything—when the door clicked open.

Detective Rodriguez stepped in, looking as if she'd just come off a long shift. Her hair was tied back in a haphazard ponytail, and worry shadows lined her eyes. "Sorry to bother you both," she began gently. "Just wanted to check on you."

Grace set the hairbrush down. "It's okay. Come in."

Rodriguez closed the door behind her, lingering near the foot of the bed. "How are you feeling, Grace?"

Grace mustered a half-smile. "Better. Eager to go home."

Rodriguez nodded. "I'm glad. You've come a long way." She shifted her weight, glancing at Keesha. "I also wanted to let you know: we're stepping up security around the hospital tonight. Nothing to be alarmed about—just a precaution."

Keesha frowned, feeling her heart give a lurch. "Did something happen?"

Rodriguez hesitated, choosing her words carefully. "We've had a couple of tips that Redwood Ridge members might be in the area. We don't have solid proof they intend to do anything here, but we're not taking chances. I don't want to scare you, but I do want you to be prepared. Just be alert."

Grace swallowed hard. "Can they even get this far into the ward?"

Rodriguez shook her head. "It'd be a tall order. We have armed officers at every critical entry point, and the lockdown protocols remain in place for Darius's ICU room. But Redwood Ridge isn't exactly known for playing by the rules." She offered a small, wry smile, trying to reassure them. "You two have been through too much already. We're not letting anyone near you."

Keesha exhaled shakily. "Thank you, Detective."

Rodriguez met her gaze with quiet determination. "It's my job." After a moment, she reached into her jacket pocket and pulled out a small, laminated card. "This is my personal contact number. If anything—*anything*—feels off, call me. Day or night."

Keesha accepted it, lips pressed into a determined line. "We will."

With that, Rodriguez gave them a parting nod and slipped out, leaving the door gently ajar. Grace and Keesha exchanged a glance, neither voicing their underlying fear: Redwood Ridge might be closer than anyone realized.

After Rodriguez left, the hospital settled into its nightly rhythms. In the corridor, a guard walked his round, passing by the windows that overlooked the parking lot. Through the glass, he could see only darkness—broken by the occasional flash of headlights or the glow of a distant streetlamp.

But somewhere miles away, within the hushed pines of Redwood Ridge, dim candlelight illuminated a cluster of figures. Their hooded robes shifted in the faint breeze. The forest floor was damp from recent rains, the air tinged with the scent of moss and decay. A slow chant rose among them—low, rhythmic, weaving through the trees like a living thing.

In the center of their circle stood a makeshift altar, carved with strange symbols that seemed to writhe under the wavering candle flames. A tall figure lifted a chalice skyward, murmuring words in an ancient dialect long lost to common ears. The others bowed their heads in unison, the chant growing in volume.

Though no one in the hospital could hear this haunting ceremony, a prickle of foreboding might have touched anyone sensitive enough to the unseen. It was a signal, perhaps—an invocation or a vow that Redwood Ridge would not simply fade away. They were gathering, waiting, planning.

And so the night wore on. Back in the sealed ward, Grace and Keesha fitfully drifted into slumber, the promise of morning and discharge overshadowed by the persistent question: what if Redwood Ridge's next move was already in motion?

When the first threads of gray light appeared in the sky, the hospital staff began their shift change. Nurses bustled, charts exchanged hands, and the smell of fresh coffee permeated the hallway. Word spread that Dr. Flores wanted to finalize Grace's discharge papers before noon.

Keesha was already up, quietly packing a small duffel bag with the few personal items they'd accumulated. A nurse wheeled in a fresh breakfast tray—scrambled eggs, toast, orange juice. Grace ate slowly, her stomach a twist of nerves and excitement.

Flores and Patel arrived with a discharge form on a clipboard. Both wore subdued smiles. "Everything's in order," Flores said, handing Keesha the pen. "You'll need to sign these, acknowledging Grace's outpatient care schedule and the follow-up appointments."

Keesha's heart fluttered. She scrawled her signature, then glanced at Grace. "Ready for freedom?"

Grace swallowed a sip of juice. "More than ready." Her voice trembled with a mix of joy and residual fear. She forced a small smile. "I never thought I'd be so happy to walk out of a hospital."

Patel returned her smile. "Just remember to take it easy. You're still rebuilding your strength. And if anything—physical or mental—feels off, call us immediately."

Grace nodded earnestly. "I will. Thank you, Dr. Patel. And you too, Dr. Flores. You saved my life."

Flores looked momentarily overcome, her professional composure cracking with quiet emotion. "We just did what we had to do. You fought like hell, Grace."

A tear slid down Grace's cheek, and she quickly wiped it away. "I had a lot of help."

Shortly after nine, a nurse wheeled a standard hospital wheelchair into the room, a customary protocol despite Grace being able to walk short distances. Grace looked at it with a mix of stubborn pride and resignation.

"You need to ride this down, honey," Keesha said gently, placing a hand on Grace's shoulder. "Hospital rules."

Grace sighed but nodded, settling into the chair while Keesha arranged her duffel in her lap. Dr. Flores and Dr. Patel stood by to say their final goodbyes, and a couple of the nurses who'd been most involved in Grace's care offered quick hugs.

The corridor leading to the elevators felt infinitely longer than Grace remembered. Every corner held a memory—of the day she'd been rolled in, confused and trapped in Darius's adult body; of the nights she'd woken in terror. And yet, with each push of the wheelchair, she felt a bit more of her fear slip away, replaced by cautious optimism.

They reached the elevator, and one of the nurses hit the button. The doors slid open with a hum. Keesha stepped inside first, making room for the wheelchair. Grace cast a final glance down the hallway that led to the ICU, where Darius still lingered in oblivion. Her stomach knotted. *Is this really over?*

Flores must have sensed her hesitation. She placed a gentle hand on Grace's shoulder. "We'll keep you updated on his condition," she said softly. "Don't worry about him. Just focus on healing."

Grace nodded, lips pressed together in a thin line. She remembered how it had felt to be trapped with Darius's mind—his rage, his cold cunning. A part of her would always fear that dark presence. But today... she was the one leaving. *He* remained bound to that hospital bed.

As the elevator doors slid closed, Grace let out a trembling breath. Keesha gave her hand a reassuring squeeze. The carriage descended, carrying them toward the main entrance—and a future they both desperately hoped would be their own.

They emerged into the ground-floor lobby, where sunlight spilled through wide glass doors. A security guard watched them pass, offering a polite nod. Outside, Keesha's car waited near the curb, courtesy of a helpful attendant.

Grace glanced around as the automatic doors whooshed open. The air smelled fresher than she remembered—tinged with the faint scent of dewy grass. For a moment, the vastness of the outside world felt overwhelming, the hospital's protective walls no longer shielding her from every threat.

Keesha helped her into the passenger seat, gently buckling her in. "There," Keesha murmured, leaning over to brush Grace's hair back. "Ready?"

Grace's heart pounded. "Yeah," she said, forcing a smile. "Ready."

Behind them, Dr. Flores and Dr. Patel stood at a distance, watching with a mixture of relief and worry. The nurse who'd wheeled Grace out stood by the entrance, arms folded. None of them waved a grand goodbye; it felt too solemn for that. Instead, they shared a mutual nod, as if saying *Be safe.*

Keesha started the engine, and the car pulled away from the curb. Grace turned in her seat to watch the hospital recede behind them, a mix of gratitude and lingering anxiety churning in her chest.

As they left the hospital grounds, the city stretched out before them—streets and shops, traffic lights blinking in orderly rhythms, people bustling about their day. To any outsider, it looked like the typical morning rush. But to Grace, every sign of normalcy was tinged with disbelief. *I'm free,* she thought, clasping her hands in her lap. *I'm really free.*

Keesha kept a careful eye on the road and on the rearview mirror. Part of her couldn't shake the notion that Redwood Ridge might appear out of nowhere—black robes in pursuit, or a mysterious sedan tailing them. But the roads were unremarkable, just the usual midweek flow of cars and commuters.

Up ahead, the skyline gave way to quieter suburban streets, lined with budding trees and neatly trimmed lawns. That was where home lay—a modest house that still bore signs of forced entry from Darius's earlier intrusion, though Keesha had hired a contractor to repair what they could.

For a moment, mother and daughter shared a subdued joy. There were no chants echoing in their ears, no hospital monitors beeping incessantly. Just the hum of the engine, the promise of stepping into their own living room, and maybe the scent of a home-cooked meal down the line.

Yet, as the city rolled by outside the window, an undercurrent of uncertainty remained. Redwood Ridge's faithful were out there, hidden in the forest or an abandoned motel, chanting in the shadows. Agent Weston prowled the periphery with his questions and his clipped, polite manner. And Darius... Darius lay comatose, but not necessarily gone.

Still, for this moment, Grace and Keesha let themselves believe in the victory they'd earned—a fragile respite from horrors that had nearly torn their world apart. If storms brewed on the horizon, they would face them as they always had: together.

With that unspoken vow, the car glided down the street toward a future both of them hoped might finally be their own.

Chapter 11: Return to the Nest

Morning light shimmered on damp pavement as Keesha guided the car into their familiar suburban neighborhood. For Grace, the tidy houses and carefully trimmed lawns looked almost surreal—remnants of a world she'd left behind when her own body became a battleground for Darius's twisted psychic power. Now, returning at last, she saw it all with heightened awareness: mailboxes standing like miniature sentinels, water droplets dancing off a sprinkler's arc, and a neighbor shuffling past with a sleepy-eyed dog. Every mundane detail reminded her how much she yearned for normalcy.

Keesha eased the car into their driveway, then let the engine idle for a moment. The hush felt thick with echoes of the night Darius broke into their home, his illusions and violence transforming the space that once sheltered mother and daughter. Grace glanced at the front door: a fresh deadbolt and mended wood, silent witnesses to the damage they'd repaired. Neither said a word, but the tension rippled between them—memory tightening its grip.

"You ready?" Keesha asked, her voice subdued yet warm.

Grace swallowed, a knot of anxiety twisting her stomach. "As I'll ever be," she replied, forcing a small, quivering smile. Her heart pounded with a dizzying mix of relief and trepidation.

They stepped out of the car, and Keesha moved around to help Grace to her feet. The cool breeze prickled her skin; it was either the chill of morning air or the lingering nerves from her recent ordeal.

She clung to the open car door for balance before leaning on the hospital-issued cane. Five steps, she told herself. Then ten. In the hospital, she'd practiced these tiny victories. Now she had to perform them in the real world.

A new security camera perched discreetly above the porch. Keesha unlocked the door, her shoulders tense, and nudged it open to let Grace pass. A faint smell of fresh paint and cleaning agents met them—reminders of bullet holes once lodged in the wall, of frantic patchwork done to hide the scars. Grace paused in the entryway, scanning the living room. There, the old couch with its threadbare armrest, family photos on the mantle, even her own artwork pinned to a corkboard. Everything looked familiar, yet felt fundamentally changed.

Keesha rested a hand on Grace's shoulder. "Come on in," she murmured.

Grace forced a breath, stepping inside. This was home. Hers—again.

Once they were inside, Keesha led Grace to the living room couch. "The doctor said you need to rest, but not stay put all day," she reminded, gently lowering Grace onto the cushions. "A little movement, a little caution."

Grace nodded. The cushions sank beneath her, and for a moment, she almost melted into them with relief—though her mind still raced, refusing to relax. She ran trembling fingers over the worn fabric, recalling nights she'd curled up to watch bad comedies, back when life was just life.

"You hungry?" Keesha asked. "Or maybe some tea?"

Grace hesitated, her appetite muted by lingering dread. "Tea, please—if we still have chamomile?"

"Absolutely." Keesha mustered a reassuring smile and headed to the kitchen.

Alone, Grace's eyes flitted to the front window. In the reflected glass, she saw a thinner, paler version of herself. The occupant in her skin had changed—she was free of Darius now—but the memory of him still clung like shadows. She shut her eyes. One step at a time.

Keesha returned with two steaming mugs. Sitting beside Grace, she offered one. "Welcome home," she said quietly.

Grace curled her hands around the warmth. "Thank you," she whispered. "It's—nice. Weird. But nice."

They sipped in silence, aware that Redwood Ridge's threat still loomed. Though neither spoke of it yet, each felt the weight of the past weeks pressing close.

While mother and daughter tried to reacclimate, Redwood Ridge was anything but still. Far off in a secluded pocket of forest, hooded figures gathered to reaffirm their cause. Their devotion to Darius—the man they believed capable of harnessing forbidden powers—hadn't waned simply because he was comatose. If anything, his incapacitation spurred them on.

At an abandoned roadside motel, a half-dozen robed worshippers lit candles and chanted in a guttural drone. They spilled lines of chalk and salt on the peeling floor, hoping to stir an old energy they swore still pulsed beneath Redwood Ridge. Many believed Darius's body was merely a vessel and that, so long as they performed the rites, his mind would awaken—stronger, more dangerous than ever.

Among these followers was Marta DeLeón, a tall, sharp-eyed woman who'd emerged as a de facto leader in Darius's absence. She spoke in low, fervent tones, rallying the faithful. "He sleeps, but the power remains. If we are worthy, Redwood Ridge shall rise—and with it, Darius's consciousness." By candlelight, her eyes flashed with something close to fanaticism.

The robed figures bowed their heads, murmuring their assent. The motel walls bore cryptic scrawl—symbols of older, darker traditions. In that decaying haven, Redwood Ridge's motives crystallized: awaken

Darius by any means, or harness the energies he once commanded, no matter the cost.

Grace and Keesha's reprieve was destined to be brief. Not only did Redwood Ridge gather in secret, but a new player had stepped into the spotlight: Agent Paul Weston, a federal investigator with a keen interest in all matters Redwood Ridge. He'd visited the hospital while Grace still lay recovering, questioning staff about Darius's sedation, Grace's medical scans, and even the strange illusions reported by eyewitnesses.

No one knew his exact mandate. He carried the official guise of an FBI agent investigating cult activity, yet he asked personal questions about Grace—her mental resilience, her recollections of Darius's psychic manipulations. More than one nurse felt uneasy under his calm, appraising stare. Detective Elena Rodriguez privately suspected he was fishing for something beyond a standard case report—something to leverage in a broader conflict that the Bureau might be planning.

Now, behind the scenes, Weston filed meticulous memos and sought clearance to interview Grace in depth. If Redwood Ridge represented a national threat, perhaps Grace was the key to understanding (or dismantling) it. The line between protecting a young victim and weaponizing her knowledge could blur dangerously.

Late afternoon found Keesha and Grace side by side on the couch, discussing the layout of the house to ensure Grace could move safely with her cane. The phone rang—a local number. Keesha picked up, half-dreading who might be on the other end.

It was Detective Rodriguez, her tone bracing. "How are you two holding up?"

Grace leaned forward to catch every word. "Okay. Just... adjusting."

"Glad to hear you're safe," Rodriguez said, relief evident. Then her voice dropped. "We've had fresh reports near Redwood Ridge—hooded figures, chanting, likely the same cult faction that once aided Darius. We're not certain they'll target you directly, but we can't rule it out. Patrol cars will circle your block periodically. Don't panic if you see them."

Keesha inhaled shakily. "Thank you, Detective. We appreciate everything."

Rodriguez hesitated. "One more thing—Agent Weston's been asking more questions about Grace's condition. He's cagey about his reasons. Keep me posted if he tries to contact you. He's supposed to go through official channels, but federal jurisdiction can get messy."

Grace felt her pulse pound. First Redwood Ridge, now the FBI. "We'll call you if anything comes up," she promised.

"Good," said Rodriguez. "You two hang in there."

When the call ended, they traded worried glances. Redwood Ridge's chanting, Agent Weston's inquiries, Darius comatose yet not fully beaten—it was all too close. The sense of normalcy wavered under the press of unseen forces.

After that unsettling news, Keesha insisted on a little movement for Grace's therapy. Cane in hand, Grace navigated the corridors of her own home—pausing in her old bedroom. The once-cozy sanctuary held stuffed animals, half-finished sketches, and a few lopsided trophies from school events. She touched a pencil drawing pinned to the wall: a self-portrait from an art class, back when life was simpler. The difference between that bright-eyed child and her current self struck her with aching clarity.

Keesha lingered by the doorway, concern etched on her face. "You okay?"

Grace's eyes roamed over the bed, the desk, the hamper still overflowing with clothes she outgrew before the fiasco. "Just trying to remember who I was... before all this."

Keesha moved closer, resting a gentle hand on her daughter's shoulder. "You're still Grace. A little changed, maybe, but still you."

Grace nodded, fighting tears. She wouldn't let Redwood Ridge or Darius define her. The air in her room felt charged with old hopes and new wounds. But she exhaled, letting a flicker of determination keep her steady. She had come home, and no cult or FBI agent would take that from her.

Evening settled over the neighborhood with a surprising hush, as if the entire block collectively held its breath. Headlights swept the street, occasionally pausing near Keesha's driveway—patrol cars, just as Rodriguez had promised. Grace found it both reassuring and nerve-wracking, worried that Redwood Ridge might be spurred to more secretive methods if open approach was impossible.

After a modest dinner, Grace felt a wave of exhaustion claim her. She let Keesha guide her to bed. The cane thumped lightly on the hallway floor, echoing in the stillness. In her room, she lowered herself onto the mattress, hugging an old pillow that smelled faintly of detergent. Despite her best efforts, the hush of night scratched at her nerves, conjuring images of robed figures chanting under moonlight.

Keesha stationed herself in the living room, unwilling to sleep until she was sure no unwelcome visitors would come knocking. She half-watched a news broadcast—another round of politics and economic updates—while her mind replayed Redwood Ridge's threat. Would they try to seize Darius from the hospital? Or target Grace again? Her maternal instincts roiled, but she forced herself to remain calm for Grace's sake.

Outside, the wind picked up, rattling the newly replaced front door. Keesha steadied her breath. They'd faced illusions and gunshots. A locked door and some chanting zealots wouldn't break them. She whispered a silent promise: we are not victims. Not anymore.

Elsewhere, Agent Weston sat in a dimly lit motel room—thankfully less decrepit than Redwood Ridge's hideout. Stacks of files and a laptop cluttered a small table. Weston studied a digital map pinpointing sightings of robed gatherings. Lines intersected in the Redwood Ridge area, forming a pattern that disturbed even his professional detachment.

He typed a terse email to his superiors:

> "Requesting additional clearance for deeper involvement. The subject, Grace Marshall, may have unique insights into Redwood Ridge's capabilities. Potential advantage if utilized properly. Will attempt to secure cooperation—warrant or not."

Weston paused, glancing at the police reports on Grace. A ten year old girl, forcibly possessed by a man with alleged psychic powers, yet strong enough to wrest control back. She intrigued him, not merely as a victim but as an asset in unraveling Redwood Ridge's ties to possible domestic extremism. The moral line between protecting her and exploiting her knowledge was one he might soon have to cross.

Closing the laptop, he rubbed his temples. If Redwood Ridge's members truly believed in resurrecting Darius, or if they sought to use the same unearthly powers, the threat might outstrip standard law-enforcement capabilities. He'd make sure the Bureau got what it needed—whatever that meant for Grace.

In the gloom of towering pines, the Redwood Ridge faithful held yet another vigil. Their numbers were small—perhaps a dozen total—but each wore devotion like a cloak. A ring of firelight cast flickering shadows on the ground, dancing over arcane symbols etched into the soil. The group's murmurings rose and fell, occasionally bursting into feverish incantations.

Standing at the center was Marta DeLeón, her gaze fierce. She stirred a small metal bowl filled with herbs and ashes, the scent curling through the night air. "He will rise," she proclaimed, voice charged. "And Redwood Ridge shall rise with him." The others bowed their heads, fueling each syllable with blind faith.

They had not forgotten Grace—the child who'd undermined Darius at his peak. A rumor whispered among them: that Grace's own psychic essence might be key to restoring him. Some whispered darkly about capturing her, forcing a ritual. Others suggested focusing on freeing Darius from the hospital, letting him reclaim his rightful place. Either path demanded cunning and stealth. Redwood Ridge waited, coiled like a serpent in the gloom.

Grace's first morning back brought a rattling knock at the door. This time, it wasn't a neighbor with a welcome casserole or a routine police check. The forceful rap jolted both Keesha and Grace from their uneasy sleep. Heart pounding, Keesha reached the peephole, only to find Detective Rodriguez outside again—earlier than expected, tension lining her face. The detective carried an envelope pressed against her side.

Keesha ushered her in. Grace, supporting herself on the cane, appeared in the hallway a moment later, wary eyes flicking between her mother and Rodriguez.

"I'm sorry to show up like this, but we need to talk," Rodriguez said, voice low. "Our patrols spotted more suspicious movement overnight—candles in the forest near Redwood Ridge, and we got intel that the group might be preparing an assault or kidnapping attempt. No confirmation yet, but we can't ignore it."

Grace's stomach twisted. She remembered all too well how Redwood Ridge had manipulated illusions to corner her once before. "Are they... coming here?" she managed, voice trembling.

Rodriguez looked grim. "We don't have direct evidence, but Redwood Ridge remains fixated on Darius—and possibly on you. We're doubling patrols and working to secure the hospital. I just wanted to warn you in person."

Keesha's heart thumped in her chest. "What about Agent Weston?"

Rodriguez hesitated. "He's pushing for a formal interview with Grace. My captain's holding him off, claiming Grace is still recovering.

But Weston's not backing down. I think he views Redwood Ridge as a domestic terror threat, and Grace... well, he thinks she could be crucial in stopping them."

A cold wave of unease rippled through Grace. She exchanged a glance with her mother. Another wave of fear battered her, but beneath it, a flicker of anger rose. "I just got my life back," she said, voice unsteady. "I'm not letting Redwood Ridge or the FBI turn it upside down again."

Rodriguez nodded, placing the envelope on a side table. "There's a list of extra security measures in there—emergency numbers, safehouse options if it comes to that." Her gaze swept over them, sympathetic but firm. "I know you want your normal life. Just be ready. Redwood Ridge is a cornered beast, and cornered beasts strike hard."

When Rodriguez departed, Keesha sank onto the couch, pressing shaky fingers to her temple. Grace limped after her, teeth clenched. The sense of returning to normal had never felt so fragile. Redwood Ridge might attempt a break-in, Agent Weston might pound on their door with official demands, and Darius's comatose form loomed over it all like a dark star.

Yet mother and daughter exchanged a determined glance. They'd fought illusions, body-swaps, bullet holes—somehow they were still here, breathing, living. Redwood Ridge could chant in the woods, and Weston could hound them with federal authority, but they wouldn't cower.

Grace gently touched Keesha's arm. "We have each other," she whispered. "No matter what they try, that's not changing."

Keesha exhaled, tears shining in her eyes. She looped an arm around Grace, cane and all, hugging her tight. "We stand together."

Outside, the sun's early rays cast faint patterns across the lawn, each patch of light interspersed with a deeper shadow. Redwood Ridge's gloom reached further than most realized; the FBI's scrutiny might become a new form of captivity. But for now, in this small suburban home with fresh paint still drying on the walls, mother and daughter found their resolve. They might be battered by the storms swirling at their doorstep—but they would face them, side by side, unbroken.

Even as Grace and Keesha settled into breakfast—scrambled eggs, toast, and an extra measure of vigilance—the Redwood Ridge faithful intensified their clandestine rites. In the hospital, Darius lay motionless in a guarded room, machines quietly marking time that might be running out. Agent Weston watched from the sidelines, orchestrating his next moves with careful calculation.

And in the dim corners of a forgotten motel, hooded figures plotted, chanting as if each syllable might reshape reality. The name "Grace Marshall" passed among them in hushed, urgent tones, a target for their twisted designs. If they could not restore Darius through direct means, perhaps the piece of him that once touched Grace's consciousness could be rekindled.

For now, Grace and Keesha cherished their fragile peace, aware it might shatter at any moment. The house was theirs, the day was theirs—but the shadows gathering beyond the threshold promised a reckoning that would test their courage all over again.

Chapter 12: Under the Watching Eyes

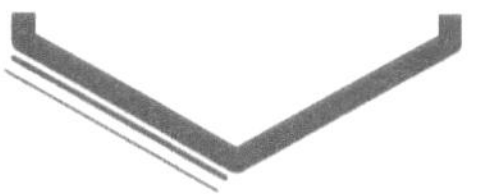

Late-morning sunlight filtered into Grace's bedroom, painting the walls in a muted gold. She blinked awake, momentarily unsettled by the comforting normalcy of her surroundings. So different from the sterile hum of hospital machines and the fluorescent glare that had been her reality for too many days. She lay there, letting her eyes roam over the ceiling fan—a fixture she'd once taken for granted but now welcomed like an old friend. Then came the dull ache in her limbs, a nagging reminder that she was far from fully recovered.

Yet she was home, and for a moment, that simple fact felt like a miracle. Until the memories crowded back in: Redwood Ridge, Darius, the FBI, and all the half-glimpsed threats that lurked just outside the safe glow of her suburban life. She let out a long breath. A single night in her own bed wasn't enough to banish those ghosts.

A gentle knock at the door roused her from her thoughts.

"Gracie?" Keesha's voice was soft, tinged with the caution of a mother who'd spent too long hovering by hospital bedsides. "You awake?"

"Yeah," Grace called, slowly propping herself up on her pillows. "Come in."

Keesha entered with a careful smile, balancing a tray laden with scrambled eggs, toast, and orange juice. "Figured you could use breakfast in bed. Save your energy."

Grace's stomach rumbled at the sight of real food—so different from hospital fare—but she also felt a knot of anxiety tighten in her chest. She gingerly pushed herself upright against the headboard, ignoring the twinge in her back. "Thanks, Mom."

Keesha placed the tray on her lap, then brushed a stray lock of hair from Grace's forehead. "How'd you sleep?"

Grace picked up her fork and poked at the eggs. "I slept," she said, voice subdued. "But I kept dreaming about Redwood Ridge... and these hooded figures in the woods."

Keesha's jaw tightened. She set a reassuring hand on Grace's leg. "I know you're scared, honey. But you're safe now. Detective Rodriguez has patrols circling the block. No one's getting near you without us knowing."

"I know," Grace murmured, but the words offered only partial relief. She couldn't shake the sensation of being watched—of Redwood Ridge's silent devotion thrumming just out of sight, waiting.

After breakfast, Grace insisted on practicing her walking routine. Though her body was weak and her joints stiff, she refused to remain bedridden, even if it meant leaning heavily on her cane. With Keesha hovering beside her, she shuffled down the hallway, each step a small victory over the lingering aches.

They reached the living room just as the phone rang.

Keesha answered, spotting the caller ID. "It's Dr. Flores," she said, pressing the speaker button. "Good morning, Doctor."

"Good morning, Keesha. Good morning, Grace," came the reassuringly familiar voice of Dr. Flores. Even through the phone, there was a note of concern. "How are you two holding up?"

Grace lowered herself onto the sofa, wincing as her legs protested. "I'm... okay," she managed. "Just trying to get used to being home again."

"That's natural," Dr. Flores replied. "Any headaches? Dizziness?"

Grace shook her head, forgetting momentarily that Flores couldn't see. "No major issues. Just... sore."

Flores's relief was palpable. "Excellent. We'll want to do another quick EEG and some scans tomorrow, just to be sure everything's normal. Ten o'clock?"

Keesha confirmed the time. Then Flores hesitated. "Have you heard from Detective Rodriguez about... security concerns?"

Grace and Keesha exchanged glances. "She mentioned Redwood Ridge might still be active," Grace said.

Flores sighed, the sound crackling through the line. "We're tightening security at the hospital. Everyone's on edge—this cult's unpredictability is worrying. If you see anything suspicious, call Detective Rodriguez or me immediately."

They promised to do so. When the call ended, a tense silence settled over the living room, heavy with the knowledge that Redwood Ridge wasn't done—and might never be, as long as Darius remained comatose but not gone.

By midday, a thin gray overcast rolled in, dulling the bright edges of the suburban landscape. Grace sat on the couch, flipping through an old sketchbook she'd unearthed from her bedroom. Pages of half-finished drawings—cartoon animals, fantasy landscapes—stared back at her, reminders of a life she'd once found so easy and carefree.

Keesha brought her a cup of tea, settling on the armrest beside her. "You used to fill sketchbooks every week," she said gently, watching Grace's fingers trace a half-finished castle. "Maybe picking up a pencil again will help."

Grace managed a small, rueful smile. "I want to. It's just... everything feels different."

Before Keesha could respond, movement outside caught Grace's eye. A police cruiser idled slowly down the street, the officer inside peering at each house. She felt a spike of adrenaline, half expecting Redwood Ridge to burst from behind a parked car in defiance. But no one appeared. The cruiser moved on.

"They're here to protect us," Keesha reminded her, voice deliberately calm.

"I know," Grace murmured. The rational part of her mind understood. But reason did little to soothe the persistent fear that Redwood Ridge—haunted by their twisted devotion—could strike in ways no patrol car could anticipate.

A sudden ping from Grace's phone made them both jump. She glanced at the screen: Detective Rodriguez's number.

Grace answered, breath catching. "Detective?"

Rodriguez's voice was brisk, edged with concern. "Heads up. We got a tip that hooded figures were spotted near the old train tracks on the west side of town—could be Redwood Ridge, or it could be another false alarm. We're sending units to investigate."

Keesha leaned in, eyes wide. "So what do we do?"

"For now, stay indoors," Rodriguez instructed. "Lock everything. If you go anywhere, let me know. We'll send a patrol car."

Grace's pulse thudded. "Understood."

Rodriguez paused, her tone softening. "I know this is hard, but we're doing everything we can to keep you safe. I promise."

The call ended, leaving mother and daughter staring at each other in a hush that felt ominous, as though Redwood Ridge's influence had stretched from the depths of the forest to their own front door.

The weight of enforced caution pressed on Grace's chest until she could hardly breathe. Needing a moment of open air, she convinced Keesha to let her step into the backyard. The yard was small—just a simple patch of grass, a weathered picnic table, and a few potted plants. Even so, it provided a semblance of freedom.

Grace leaned on her cane, the cool breeze carrying the scents of fresh grass and distant flowering trees. For a fleeting moment, she found solace in the rustle of leaves overhead. Keesha stood close, arms folded, eyes scanning the fences as if Redwood Ridge might be crouched behind every board.

After a few careful steps, Grace turned her face to the sky. An errant ray of sun broke through the cloud cover, warming her cheeks. She closed her eyes, letting that small warmth center her. "I'm alive," she whispered under her breath, a quiet mantra. "I'm me."

Keesha placed a hand lightly on her shoulder. "You're doing so well, Gracie. I'm proud of you."

A noise from the alley—just a stray cat knocking over a loose trash can—made them both jump. Grace's heart hammered in her chest. She caught Keesha's eye, saw the fear mirrored there, and swallowed.

"It's just a cat," Keesha said, breath shaky. "Let's go back inside."

Grace nodded, exhaling slowly. Reality crashed in again: Redwood Ridge was out there, somewhere, their motives as murky as the clouds gathering overhead.

They spent the afternoon under the watchful gaze of passing patrol cars, each slow roll down the street a reminder that the world saw them as targets. Over a quiet lunch of leftover pasta, Grace tried to muster the appetite for normalcy, but the dread killed her hunger.

"Have you thought about reaching out to your friends?" Keesha asked gently. "Just to let them know you're okay?"

A pang of longing hit Grace. She pictured her old circle—friends who had no idea of the horrors she'd endured. "Yes... but I don't know how to explain all this. They'd never believe me."

Keesha's gaze was empathetic. "You can tell them as much or as little as you're comfortable with. Maybe just a simple text: 'I'm back, recovering, missed you.'"

Grace fiddled with her phone, thumb hovering over the message app. "Maybe tomorrow," she hedged. Everything still felt too raw, too precarious.

Outside, the sunlight slanted lower, painting the living room in shades of dusky gold. A new tension gathered in the corners of the house, as if the fading daylight heralded the moment Redwood Ridge might emerge from the shadows. Keesha checked the locks on every door, a routine that had become almost ritual.

Meanwhile, in a run-down motel on the outskirts of town, Redwood Ridge gathered under flickering overhead lights. Maps of local roads and forest trails were spread across a battered table. Hooded figures moved like wraiths through the cramped space, murmuring in low, urgent voices.

"We must wait for the right moment," one of them insisted, tracing a line on a map that led directly to Grace Marshall's address. Her voice betrayed both fear and fervor. "The police are watching, and the FBI man is everywhere."

A tall, gaunt-faced man pushed back his hood. "Darius is not lost," he said, eyes gleaming with an unsettling devotion. "Even if comatose, he can be revived. We only need a chance to retrieve him."

A third figure, clad in a deeper black robe, stood at the table's head. Their posture spoke of authority, their voice a quiet hiss. "We will be patient. The slightest misstep will ruin our opportunity."

As if in agreement, a sudden gust of wind rattled the motel's thin walls, extinguishing the solitary lantern that lit their gathering. Darkness fell, but Redwood Ridge did not flinch. Darkness was their element.

Grace awoke early the next day to find Keesha already dressed, phone in hand. "I thought we could do a quick grocery run," she suggested, voice carefully upbeat. "Just to get a few supplies—and to show you the world still goes on."

The idea of leaving the house, of stepping out from under the shelter of locked doors and patrolling officers, sent a wave of nerves through Grace's stomach. But she also yearned to break the claustrophobia. "All right," she said finally. "Let's do it."

As promised, Detective Rodriguez dispatched a patrol car to discreetly follow them. Ten minutes later, Grace was settled in the passenger seat, cane balanced between her knees. She watched her own street roll by, each house strangely familiar and yet tinged with the fear of Redwood Ridge's possible lurking presence.

At the supermarket, Grace moved slowly through the aisles, leaning on her cane while Keesha guided the cart. Fluorescent lights buzzed overhead, and other shoppers bustled about, ignorant of the unspoken war Grace carried within her. She tried to focus on the mundane: picking apples, choosing cereal, examining expiration dates. Yet every overhead announcement made her start, every squeak of a shopping cart turned her head.

Keesha picked up on her tension. "We'll just get what we need and go," she whispered, placing a gentle hand on Grace's shoulder.

Grace nodded, swallowing hard. She wanted so badly to enjoy a simple errand—like she used to—but Redwood Ridge and its nightmares had stolen that innocent sense of safety.

They emerged from the store into a parking lot touched by midday sun, the sky still scattered with drifting clouds. Keesha loaded groceries into the trunk while Grace lingered by the car door, scanning the rows of vehicles as if Redwood Ridge might appear from behind tinted windows.

Her eyes landed on a man in a dark suit standing near the edge of the lot. He leaned against a sleek sedan, arms folded. Grace's heart clenched as she recognized Agent Weston—his gaze pinned directly on her. The half-wave he offered seemed more like an alert than a greeting.

Keesha followed Grace's line of sight, lips pressing into a grim line. "Get in," she muttered, guiding Grace into the passenger seat.

They drove off with deliberate haste, the patrol car following at a distance. In the rearview mirror, Grace watched Weston fade into the background. A thousand questions churned in her mind. Was he tailing them? Observing? Waiting for Redwood Ridge to make a move?

Keesha broke the taut silence. "I'll call Detective Rodriguez once we get home."

Grace nodded, voice thin. "I just want them all to leave us alone. Redwood Ridge, the FBI... all of it."

"I know," Keesha murmured, reaching over to give her hand a reassuring squeeze.

By the time they arrived home, the sky had darkened with an ominous bank of clouds. The wind picked up, blowing brittle leaves across the driveway. Grace stepped out of the car, cane tapping on the asphalt, her pulse thrumming with residual anxiety from the encounter with Weston.

Inside, the house felt strangely claustrophobic. Even though it was their refuge, it also reminded Grace that Redwood Ridge's shadow still loomed. She helped Keesha unload the groceries, setting cartons of milk and bags of produce on the countertop. A distant rumble of thunder underscored the tension clinging to every corner.

Keesha exhaled, glancing at the clock. "We should start dinner soon."

Grace nodded but said nothing. She felt like a balloon stretched to its limit, one pinprick away from bursting. "Mom," she finally whispered, setting down a box of pasta. "I'm scared."

Keesha turned, catching the tremor in her daughter's voice. Without hesitation, she opened her arms. Grace fell into them, resting her head against her mother's shoulder. In that moment, thunder rumbled again, closer, as if mirroring the emotional storm within them.

Night settled slowly, the rumble of distant thunder growing into the steady drumming of rain. They kept the lights low, blinds drawn, doors locked. Detective Rodriguez sent a text confirming extra patrols would sweep their street—more watchers for Redwood Ridge's watchers, a never-ending cycle of vigilance.

Grace sat in her room, the overhead lamp casting a warm halo. Her cane leaned against the wall. She thumbed through her sketchbook again, trying to recapture the solace she once found in drawing. But every time she put pencil to paper, her hand hesitated, stilled by the knowledge that Redwood Ridge was out there, plotting.

Finally, she closed the sketchbook with a soft sigh. Tomorrow she'd have to see Dr. Flores, get hooked to wires and machines again. Another reminder that normalcy was a fragile thing, still overshadowed by Redwood Ridge's madness and the FBI's suspicions.

Keesha appeared in the doorway, concern etched on her face. "Everything okay?"

Grace offered a shaky smile. "As okay as it can be."

With a tenderness born of sheer determination, Keesha crossed the room and wrapped an arm around Grace's shoulders. "We'll get through this," she whispered. "Step by step."

Outside, rain pelted the window, each drop a drumbeat of tension. Grace leaned her head against her mother's shoulder, letting herself draw strength from that simple contact. For now, they were safe, cocooned in the house's warm glow. But Redwood Ridge—and Agent Weston—lurked just beyond, tightening the invisible net.

And in that hush, Grace Marshall reminded herself: she had reclaimed her body from Darius once. She could face Redwood Ridge's threat. She could endure FBI scrutiny. She was tired—so bone-weary she thought she might break—but she was also alive, and determined not to let fear steal her life again.

However long the storm raged, she would hold fast to that promise.

Chapter 13: Under Currents and Over Watches

A pale, stormy twilight draped itself across the suburban street. The sky overhead churned with swollen clouds that allowed only thin streaks of gold and pink to filter down, painting the rooftops with an uneasy glow. All day, the humidity had been oppressive, as though the atmosphere itself anticipated a coming squall—one that mirrored the tension escalating within the Marshall household.

Inside, Grace perched on the living room couch, hugging a throw pillow close to her chest. A muted local news broadcast flickered on the television across from her, though neither she nor Keesha truly watched. Their attention skittered from the soft crackle of the TV to the windows and doors, haunted by the memory of Redwood Ridge's cultish devotion and Agent Weston's unsettling appearance at the grocery store.

Grace couldn't banish the image of Weston standing by his sedan, looking at her as though she were some pivotal piece in an unsolved puzzle. The knowledge that even the most mundane trips outside could spark new danger tightened her chest with dread. She'd always been a quiet, introspective girl—happiest while sketching in spiral-bound notebooks or losing herself in elaborate fantasy novels. Now, any step beyond the threshold felt like crossing a thin wire suspended above a yawning void, Redwood Ridge on one side and the FBI on the other.

Earlier that evening, Detective Rodriguez had texted Keesha to say that reported sightings of robed figures near the abandoned train tracks were "unsubstantiated." A term meant to reassure only served to heighten the tension. Grace understood how Redwood Ridge excelled at disappearing—if they wanted to evade detection, they would. She cast a glance at the curtained window, half-expecting the silhouette of a hooded figure to materialize or some eerie chant to waft on the air.

On the surface, the Marshalls' living room looked unchanged since before Darius tore through their world. The plush beige sofa still faced the TV, family photos still lined the walls. In one frame, a younger Grace grinned brightly, sparkly stickers smattered across her cheeks; in another, Keesha beamed at a middle-school art fair showcasing Grace's early drawings. But the atmosphere had changed. Tension crackled in the corners like static before a thunderstorm.

Keesha stood at the front window, arms crossed tightly, her shoulders rigid from hours of silent vigilance. Once known for her composure as a city clerk—balancing budgets and schedules with enviable ease—she now seemed wired by anxiety, checking door locks, rechecking security feeds, pacing. A faint bruise, barely visible under soft lighting, marred her left eye—a memento from the night Darius terrorized them both.

"You should sit," Grace offered gently, lowering the TV's volume. The hush between them made her voice seem louder than it was.

Keesha exhaled, her gaze still on the window. "I know, but I can't stop thinking. It's like my mind won't let me rest."

Reluctantly, she turned from the window and joined Grace on the couch, dropping into the cushions with a quiet sigh. Up close, the lines under Keesha's eyes were stark, telling stories of sleepless nights and unrelenting worry.

"What about you?" Keesha asked, placing a tentative hand on Grace's knee. "How are you feeling?"

Grace shrugged, carefully mindful of her still-healing muscles. After all the back-and-forth body-swapping with Darius, her own body felt foreign at times—tender in places, twitchy with lingering trauma.

"Physically, I'm okay. Sore, but getting better. It's the rest of it—knowing Redwood Ridge is out there, watching. That's the part that scares me."

Keesha's arm slipped around Grace's shoulders, pulling her close. "Me too, baby," she whispered. "But we have Detective Rodriguez's patrols, and Redwood Ridge hasn't shown itself in days. For now, at least, we're safe."

Grace leaned her head on her mother's shoulder, absorbing the fleeting comfort. On TV, a local reporter droned about a city council meeting—mundane issues like taxes and street cleaning. The triviality was, for a moment, a welcome distraction.

Just as they settled into that fragile calm, a gentle knock rattled the front door. Grace shot upright, heart thudding so violently she nearly dropped the remote. Keesha froze, tension flaring in her posture.

"Did Rodriguez say she'd be stopping by?" Grace whispered, eyes darting toward the hallway.

Keesha shook her head. "No. Could be one of her officers, though." Another knock echoed—firmer this time. Keesha offered Grace a silent warning to stay behind, then approached the door.

Peering through the peephole, she frowned. "It's a woman. Mid- to late-twenties, plain clothes. She's alone."

Grace rose cautiously, resting a hand on the couch to steady herself. Her cane leaned against the armrest. "Should we even open it?"

After a moment of hesitation, Keesha flicked the porch light on and cracked the door, keeping the security chain engaged. Standing on the porch was a visibly nervous woman with dark, loosely curled hair pinned at the nape of her neck. She wore a light sweater and jeans and clutched a small messenger bag, her anxious gaze flitting from the empty street to Keesha's face.

"Mrs. Marshall?" the stranger asked, her voice quivering. "I—I need to speak with you. It's about Redwood Ridge."

The name sent a ripple of dread through Keesha. "Who are you?" she demanded, gripping the door.

The woman took a shaky breath. "Corinne. Corinne Rook. I—" She swallowed. "I used to be part of Redwood Ridge. Please, let me in. It's not safe to talk out here."

Grace, now watching from behind Keesha, felt her stomach churn. A former Redwood Ridge member was the last thing she'd expected to see on her front step. But the urgency in Corinne's eyes spoke volumes.

With a final wary glance up and down the street, Keesha unlatched the chain. "Come in—slowly."

Corinne slipped inside, and Keesha slammed the door shut, flipping the locks. Silence stretched between them, charged with fear and mistrust.

Corinne lingered by the foyer, catching sight of Grace. Recognition flickered across her face, followed by a bleak sort of awe.

"You're... Grace," she breathed, voice trembling. "I—I saw you once at Redwood Ridge. Darius called you the key to something... bigger." Her words faltered, and she closed her eyes as though battling a memory.

Grace felt nausea clench her gut. She tightened her grip on the cane, remembering the swirling, torchlit rituals and Darius's smug confidence. "When?" she asked, voice tight. "When did you see me?"

Corinne's expression twisted with guilt. "Right before you escaped. I was there, watching from the edge of the circle. Darius bragged that you had 'gifts'—that if you just joined willingly, Redwood Ridge would become unstoppable." She shuddered, hugging her messenger bag to her chest. "After the fiasco in the hospital, a group of us left. But some remain loyal—and they think they can bring Darius back."

Keesha's eyes narrowed. "Bring him back? He's not dead—just comatose."

Corinne's gaze skittered to the floor. "They believe there's a ritual—something called the Reclamation Rite. They want to awaken

Darius by reconnecting him to the psychic currents they think he tapped into. And..." She trailed off, exhaling shakily.

Grace forced the rising panic down. "And what?"

"They believe you're still tied to him," Corinne whispered, eyes brimming with unease. "That even though you broke free, a tether remains. Redwood Ridge thinks if they can get hold of you—force you into another ceremony—it could spark Darius's consciousness back to life."

The living room felt suffocating, the air thick with dread. Keesha guided Corinne farther inside, gesturing toward a chair near the couch. "Sit. Explain everything."

Corinne perched on the edge of the seat, posture rigid. She spoke in halting sentences, describing the deeper levels of Redwood Ridge's belief system: their fixation on "hidden energies," the labyrinth of half-pagan, half-occult rites that had always seemed theatrical—until Darius's abilities proved there was something more.

"They think this last ritual is crucial," Corinne said, voice wavering. "With Darius in a coma, his mind's in... I don't know, some in-between state. They say you, Grace, have a unique psychic resonance with him."

Grace swallowed a lump of raw fear. "And you believe them? That I'm connected to him still?"

Corinne shook her head. "I only know what they believe. But if they're determined enough, they'll come for you—no matter how impossible it might seem."

Keesha's mouth pressed into a firm line. "Why are you telling us this now?"

"Because I realized how far they'd go," Corinne answered, eyes pleading. "And if they succeed, Darius... he won't stop at Redwood Ridge. He'll use his abilities to do so much worse." She hesitated, voice trembling. "I thought, if I warned you, maybe you'd stop him before they can complete the rite."

A thick hush followed Corinne's admission. Grace studied her face, searching for signs of duplicity but finding only raw desperation. Could Redwood Ridge send someone to trick them? Maybe. But Corinne's fear seemed too real to be faked.

"How do we know this isn't a setup?" Keesha's voice was steady but laced with steel. "Redwood Ridge could be using you to get to Grace."

Corinne visibly winced. "I know you have no reason to trust me. But if Redwood Ridge finds out I betrayed them, I'm as good as dead. I... I don't expect forgiveness, but I can't just stand by while they plot to hurt Grace again."

Grace's gaze dropped to her cane, remembering the harrowing journey it took to reclaim her body from Darius. She still woke with nightmares about Redwood Ridge's chanting, the swirl of unnatural energies she couldn't fully comprehend. "If there's even a chance you're telling the truth, we need to alert Detective Rodriguez," she said, mustering what confidence she could.

Corinne's eyes flicked toward the door, anxiety twisting her features. "The police? Redwood Ridge has people everywhere. If they see a squad car—"

Keesha's voice cut in, gentle but unyielding. "This is bigger than us. We can't fight Redwood Ridge alone. If they're really planning something, the only hope is law enforcement. Let us call Rodriguez. She can handle this discreetly."

After a tense pause, Corinne gave a shaky nod. "All right."

Keesha disappeared into the kitchen to text Detective Rodriguez. The tiles under her feet felt cold, a reminder of how many nights she'd paced these floors, haunted by what Darius had done. She composed a message rapidly:

Keesha (7:42 PM):

Urgent. Redwood Ridge insider here with info. Possibly in danger. Please come quietly—alone if you can.

The reply came swiftly:

Rodriguez (7:43 PM):

On my way. Don't let her leave. Will keep a low profile.

Keesha exhaled, shoulders drooping with relief. She glanced out the window, half-expecting shadowy figures to be lurking in the driveway. The street lay still, washed in the pink-gray haze of twilight.

When she returned to the living room, Corinne sat hunched, gripping the messenger bag as if it were a lifeline. Grace stood a few feet away, poised on her cane, wary but resolved.

"Detective Rodriguez is coming," Keesha announced. "She'll be discreet. Hang tight."

The three of them settled into an uneasy wait. Wind tapped against a loose shutter outside, filling the silence with a hollow rattle that made Grace's nerves prickle. She picked up the TV remote, muting the news altogether, as if even a murmur was too disruptive.

Corinne cast a haunted gaze around the living room—at family photos, at half-finished mugs of cold tea on the coffee table. "You have a nice home," she said softly, voice a little distant, perhaps remembering her own life before Redwood Ridge. "I'm sorry it came to this."

Grace's throat felt tight. What did you say to someone who'd been part of your worst nightmares—yet now claimed to be an ally? "I just want Redwood Ridge to leave us alone," she managed. "To leave me alone."

Corinne's expression flickered with regret. "I understand. Darius had this way of making us feel special, like we were chosen for something grand. But after I saw what happened to you—what he did—it opened my eyes."

Keesha, arms crossed, kept her focus on the window. "We'll sort it out when Rodriguez gets here."

At long last, the growl of an engine outside announced the detective's arrival. Headlights fanned across the curtains, and Keesha moved to the door. Checking the peephole, she confirmed it was Rodriguez—alone, dressed in her usual subdued attire.

Rodriguez slipped inside, scanning the room quickly, her posture tight with readiness. She fixed a firm yet curious gaze on Corinne. "Detective Elena Rodriguez," she introduced herself quietly. "So, you have intel on Redwood Ridge?"

Corinne nodded, cheeks flushed. "Corinne Rook. I... used to be part of it."

As Rodriguez listened, notebook in hand, Corinne recounted the rumors of the Reclamation Rite—the half-whispered plan to haul Grace back into Redwood Ridge's clutches and reawaken Darius. Grace stood by, arms folded, willing her racing heart to remain steady. None of this was new to her ears, but hearing it spelled out so blatantly made her shudder.

Rodriguez jotted notes, lips pressed in a grim line. "Any idea where they're meeting? We suspect an abandoned motel and maybe some cabins near Redwood Ridge's core territory."

Corinne looked away, shame flickering across her face. "I've heard talk of a motel, but the precise location of their main circle remains secret—even to most members. They protect it obsessively. But I know they're on the move, planning something soon."

Detective Rodriguez's eyes shifted to Keesha and Grace, who both wore identical expressions of exhausted vigilance. "We'll heighten patrols," she said decisively. Then she turned back to Corinne. "If you're willing, come to the station. Give an official statement. We can offer you protection if Redwood Ridge becomes a threat."

Fear and relief warred in Corinne's expression. She nodded, voice trembling. "Yes. I'll... I'll do whatever it takes to keep them from hurting anyone else."

A wave of cautious optimism washed over Grace. Corinne's warning felt like a dark prophecy, but at least they now had advanced notice. Rodriguez would intervene—maybe Redwood Ridge wouldn't catch them unprepared.

Rodriguez's phone buzzed, and she glanced at the screen. "My plainclothes backup is here," she told Corinne. "We'll leave out the back to avoid drawing attention. The fewer eyes on you, the better."

Corinne rose, gripping her messenger bag. "Thank you," she whispered. "I know I can't erase what I was part of, but... I want to make it right."

Grace found herself nodding, both wary and grateful. "Thank you," she echoed quietly.

Rodriguez ushered Corinne toward the kitchen's back exit, pausing only to shoot Keesha and Grace a look brimming with unspoken reassurance. "Keep the doors locked. We'll be in touch soon."

Keesha and Grace watched them slip into the dark yard, disappearing from view. A moment later, the sound of a car pulling away reached their ears. Then silence settled once more.

The house felt impossibly quiet. Grace collapsed onto the couch, cane clattering to the carpet. She pressed a hand to her chest, her breathing shallow. "Mom," she murmured, voice shaky, "they're serious about pulling me back into this... this nightmare. I thought it was over when I got out of his body. When I came home."

Keesha took a seat next to her, draping an arm around her shoulders. "We won't let them take you. We went through hell once with Darius—I'm not allowing it to happen again."

Grace exhaled, a tremor threading through her. "I'm scared. Even if Corinne's telling the truth, Redwood Ridge is so secretive. They could be anywhere."

Keesha's hand squeezed gently. "Detective Rodriguez is no pushover. She'll trace Corinne's leads, and we'll stay vigilant. Tomorrow, we're supposed to see Dr. Flores anyway. Maybe she and Dr. Patel can check if there's any sign of a lingering psychic link, or anything Redwood Ridge might exploit."

A distant rumble of thunder rolled across the sky, making the house lights flicker briefly. Grace's gaze flicked to the window, where dark clouds churned ominously, reflecting the chaos in her own mind.

Neither Grace nor Keesha slept well. The hours dragged, each one weighted by the knowledge that Redwood Ridge was regrouping, plotting, perhaps closer than they dared imagine. The wind picked up, rattling the windows, carrying with it a faint smell of rain.

Around midnight, Grace found herself flicking through TV channels aimlessly, every burst of commercial laughter or canned applause jarring against her raw nerves. Keesha stood guard by the window, phone in hand, occasionally glancing at the silent street.

"You can't stand there all night," Grace said softly, her voice cracking from exhaustion.

Keesha turned, offering a tired half-smile. "I can, and I probably will." Her features softened. "But if you want me to sit with you, I will."

Grace nodded, patting the spot beside her on the couch. Keesha settled in, and mother and daughter curled under a single blanket. Outside, rain finally began to fall, a steady patter that made the night feel both insular and exposed.

"Remember those weekend movie marathons?" Grace asked, voice tinged with nostalgia. "You'd make popcorn, and we'd watch silly comedies until we passed out?"

Keesha smiled, the memory briefly easing the tightness in her eyes. "Yeah. I miss those days."

Grace rested her head on her mother's shoulder, heart heavy with the realization that their lives might never return to that carefree simplicity. "We'll get through this, right?"

Keesha pressed a gentle kiss to her daughter's hair. "We survived Darius. We'll survive Redwood Ridge, too."

Thunder growled, and the house went dark for a flicker of a moment before the lights snapped back on. In that breath, Grace thought of Redwood Ridge's secret rites, of hooded figures chanting, of Darius—still comatose, yet so terrifyingly present in their lives. She inhaled slowly, resolved to keep moving forward, no matter what.

Outside, the downpour intensified, as though the universe itself sensed the storm of events converging on the Marshalls once more. Inside, mother and daughter huddled close, determined to face whatever came next side by side.

And as the late-night hours ticked away, Grace replayed Corinne's warning in her mind: Redwood Ridge believed she still held a thread connecting her to Darius. If that was true, she knew she had to sever it for good—or risk losing everything she'd fought so hard to reclaim.

Chapter 14: The Watchful Heart

Quincy Sloan rubbed the back of his neck, feeling the weight of too many sleepless nights press down between his shoulder blades. He stood on Keesha's front porch, leaning against the sturdy new railing he'd helped install months ago—back when they naively believed a few reinforcements could keep Darius's darkness at bay. The late-afternoon sky was a swirl of gray and gold, bathing the neighborhood in a somber glow. A police cruiser rolled by at its usual, unhurried pace, the officer inside pausing to nod in acknowledgment of Quincy. The unspoken message was clear: *We're here, but we can't do everything.*

Quincy returned the nod, letting his gaze drift toward the freshly painted door. He could still recall, with unnerving clarity, the night Darius had shattered the old frame, illusions snapping around them like forks of lightning. In the chaos, Quincy had been forced to face the brutal truth that he couldn't always protect the people he loved. That realization still wedged under his ribs, an ache that never quite went away.

He reached for the small notebook he kept in his coat pocket—an old habit from his time serving on security details years ago. Jotting down observations, license plate numbers, suspicious passersby... it was a small measure of control, a way to keep the swirling anxieties at bay. Flipping through pages of neat, utilitarian handwriting, he read entries from earlier:

- 7:15 AM: Patrol car circled once. No sign of suspicious vehicles.

- 9:30 AM: Keesha and Grace left for errands. Spotted Agent Weston in grocery lot.

- 2:10 PM: Delivery van across street—normal mail service, but documented anyway.

He sighed and snapped the notebook shut. No matter how many lines he filled, Redwood Ridge remained a phantom threat, creeping through the edges of suburban calm.

Stepping back inside, Quincy paused in the foyer—right where the bullet hole had once marred the wall. It was patched and painted now, nearly invisible. *Nearly*. He ran his fingertips over the smooth surface, recalling how his heart had thundered during that confrontation, Darius's mocking grin etched into his mind like a brand. That night, illusions had flickered, twisting the hallway into a nightmare. Gunfire echoed in his memory, along with Keesha's desperate scream and the terrifying realization that his training couldn't stop a psychic assault.

He shut his eyes, clenching his jaw against the rush of remorse. *All that experience, and I still couldn't protect them from illusions.* He remembered charging forward, tripping on invisible snags, his vision swarmed by flickering shadows. The frustration at feeling *helpless* still stung. *I should have been faster, stronger, better.* But illusions didn't care about skill—they preyed on fear.

His hand dropped to his side, breath hitching. That night, he'd sworn he would never let Keesha or Grace face such terror alone again. *Never*.

The memory triggered another recollection—one that both tormented and consoled him, because it was the night he and Keesha forged a bond deeper than either had thought possible.

It happened a week or so after Darius's first break-in. Grace was still recovering from psychic aftershocks—nightmares and sudden flashbacks—while Keesha tried to hold their world together with sheer willpower. One evening, Quincy had come over to patch up the broken windows and reinforce the back door, a practical chore that masked his deeper need: *to see if they were truly okay.*

He'd found Keesha in the living room, her posture hunched in the glow of a single lamp. She was holding a blanket so tightly her knuckles went white. On the couch lay Grace, tossing restlessly in a half-sleep haunted by illusions. Quincy's gut twisted at the sight. Keesha looked up, eyes brimming with tears she wouldn't let fall.

"Hey," he'd said, voice hushed. "I, uh—finished the door."

She'd nodded, lips parting to speak, but no words came. Then, as though a dam broke, her shoulders shook. Desperate to shield Grace from more distress, Keesha stifled her sobs, pressing a hand to her mouth. Quincy moved closer, crouching beside her. He'd never forget the trembling in her fingers when she finally let him pull her into a gentle embrace.

"I can't—" she'd choked out. "I keep hearing his voice in my head. Darius. I keep seeing that gun, that grin. I feel... powerless."

Quincy felt his own eyes burn. He wanted to say *you're not powerless,* wanted to promise that illusions meant nothing. But he knew what *helpless* felt like. So, instead, he murmured, "I'm here. You're not facing this alone." He stroked her hair, letting her tears soak into his shirt, guilt tangling with protectiveness inside him. For the first time since he'd begun helping them, he realized how truly frightened Keesha was behind her strong front.

They stayed like that for a long moment, breathing in sync, hearts pounding against each other—hers racing with terror, his with fierce resolve. When Grace whimpered in her sleep, Keesha pulled away, wiping her eyes quickly. But in that fleeting contact, Quincy had felt something shift. He sensed that his presence, his vow to stand guard, might be the one anchor in a storm she couldn't control.

Over the following days, they drew closer: hushed phone calls to check on each other, quiet cups of coffee at the kitchen table while Grace rested. Each step further from that harrowing night brought them an unspoken understanding: *they were in this together, and it wasn't just about duty—it was about love.* And though it scared Quincy to realize how deeply he cared for Keesha, it also fueled his determination to protect her and Grace from anything Darius might throw their way.

Snapping out of the reverie, Quincy eased open the living room door. Keesha stood by the couch, fiddling with the TV remote. She glanced up as he entered, and he caught the flicker of warmth in her eyes. Even exhausted, her presence steadied him. He sometimes marveled at how fiercely he wanted to keep her and Grace safe. After all they'd weathered, that initial bond—sealed by shared fear and quiet comfort—had only deepened.

"Hey," she greeted softly. "Any sign of trouble outside?"

Quincy shook his head. "Nothing. Patrols are on schedule. It's quiet."

"Quiet can be good," she said, lips curving in a near-smile, "or a bad omen."

He stepped closer, posture still carrying that soldier's alertness. The living room bore faint reminders of Redwood Ridge's lingering threats: a scarred patch of floor, the faint aroma of new paint overlaying old damage. "I've been thinking... maybe we add more cameras around back," he murmured. "That alley's too easy to slip through."

Her eyes softened. "If it helps you sleep at night, do it. I trust your instincts."

He dipped his head in thanks, though the truth was he hadn't had a decent night's sleep since Redwood Ridge came calling. At times, he caught the same weariness in Keesha's gaze: *When does this end?*

Grace's voice floated from down the hall, asking for help. Keesha went to her, and Quincy trailed partway, stopping at the bedroom doorway. Grace was perched on the edge of her bed, brow furrowed as she tried to slip on a shoe without straining her still-healing leg. She caught Quincy's reflection in the mirror, offering a small grin that belied her frustration.

"Hey," she said, cheeks flushing. "Could you help me tie the lace? I'm still clumsy with this cane."

Quincy's heart twisted at the reminder that Grace was a tween forced into adult battles. "Course," he said, crouching to tie her sneaker. "Let me know if it's snug enough."

She nodded, testing the fit before exhaling. "Thanks." A pause lingered. Then, softly: "You remember that night? The first time Darius broke in?"

His chest tightened. "I do."

"I keep thinking about it—how illusions trapped you, Mom, everyone. It's scary to realize how easily he twisted reality."

Quincy finished tying the shoe and rose, resting a reassuring hand on her shoulder. "We didn't see it coming," he admitted. "But we learned. Next time, Redwood Ridge won't catch us off guard."

Grace managed a shaky smile. "I hope so. I—I'm just tired of being afraid."

He gave her shoulder a gentle squeeze. "We'll take it day by day. You're stronger than you know, Grace."

Dusk deepened, and Quincy found himself in the backyard, scanning the perimeter. Rain threatened in the humid air, thunder mumbling in the distance. The world felt muffled, as though Redwood Ridge lurked beyond the fence. He paced a slow circuit, each footstep echoing his silent vow: *Never again.* Never again would illusions catch him helpless.

He paused at the chain-link fence, recalling the memory of patching up Keesha's windows after the first break-in, the hush in the living room as he'd crouched beside her trembling form. That was the moment he realized his feelings went far beyond duty. He *needed* them to be safe—needed it like air. A faint sheen of tears gathered now, quickly blinked away. *I'll stand guard all night if I must.*

A flicker of lightning lit the horizon. The air crackled, stirring Quincy's pulse. *Let Redwood Ridge come,* he thought with grim resolve. *They'll find I'm no longer the man tripped up by illusions.*

When the sky opened up with cold rain, Quincy stepped inside, dripping water on the kitchen tile. Keesha, rinsing dishes at the sink, arched an eyebrow and handed him a dishtowel. He accepted it with a grateful nod, patting at his shoulders.

"Did the weather take you by surprise?" she teased, half-smiling despite her fatigue.

He mustered a small grin. "I suspected it would rain. But the perimeter check seemed worth a little soaking."

She set down a plate and turned to face him fully. In the warm glow of the overhead light, he saw the etched lines of worry beneath her eyes—yet also the unwavering strength that had kept her and Grace going. "I know what you're doing," she said, voice gentle. "Keeping watch until Redwood Ridge stops haunting us."

"It's the only way I know how to be," he replied, an edge of apology in his tone. "Feels like I should never let my guard down."

Her gaze flickered, tender. "I remember a time you refused to go home until you fixed every shattered window and boarded up every hole," she said softly. "I was at my lowest, and you... you stayed anyway."

Quincy swallowed, memories rushing in—Keesha trembling in his arms, letting him see her vulnerability. "You needed someone," he murmured. "I needed you safe."

She took a step closer, bridging the space between them. The only sound was the soft patter of rain on the windows. "You never left," she repeated, voice thick. "Grace and I... we rely on you more than you know."

He gently reached out, fingers finding hers. "I'm not going anywhere."

Keesha let her free hand curl into his damp jacket, her eyes misting. "Thank you," she whispered, the words laden with love unspoken. For a breath, thunder rolled, and the old house seemed to cradle them in its battered walls.

They shared a quiet dinner in the living room—sandwiches and hot soup. Grace, drained from physical therapy and residual nightm

Outside, rain lashed the window, but inside, in the soft circle of lamplight, they found a fragile peace. Quincy's notebook lay on the coffee table, pages ready for more notes. But for now, he held Keesha, letting the storm rage beyond these walls. Their hearts beat in tandem, and though fear shadowed every corner of their lives, love bound them closer than any illusion could tear apart.

Chapter 15: Rain at the Threshold

Night settled over the Marshall household in fitful waves, its heavy silence broken only by the relentless, rhythmic drum of rain against the windows. The storm had intensified since dusk, mirroring the tangled web of anxieties that hummed within these walls. For Quincy, every fresh rumble of thunder wasn't just weather; it was a summons to duty—a jarring reminder that protecting Keesha and Grace was more than a promise made in a moment of crisis. It was a sinewy, absolute necessity.

He stayed awake long after Grace and Keesha had surrendered to what little sleep they could find. He moved through the house with a predator's quiet, pacing from window to window, checking the heavy deadbolts he'd installed, watching the rain-slicked alleyway out back. Each sweep of the flashlight across the swaying shadows of the yard reinforced his silent, ironclad vow: *Never again.* The memory of the illusions—the way Darius had made the very air warp and betray his eyes—still felt like a phantom limb, an itch he couldn't scratch.

At nearly three in the morning, a localized cell of the storm broke directly overhead. Thunder rolled with a violence that made the windowpanes rattle in their frames. Quincy paused in the hallway, his gaze shifting to the cracked family photos lining the wall. One particular frame caught the dim light: a bright-eyed Grace at eight years old, blue paint smudged on her cheeks as she proudly displayed a messy, vibrant watercolor. It was a relic from a time before Darius, before the "Psychic Seed" headlines, before Redwood Ridge had turned their lives into a fragmented nightmare.

He listened intently, his ears straining past the roar of the rain for any sign that Grace or Keesha had stirred. The house remained still, save for the hum of the refrigerator and the ticking of the clock. He told himself the sound outside was just the elements—not a hooded figure chanting in the wet grass, not a synchronized invocation from the Redwood Ridge faithful. He forced himself to believe that the shadows were just shadows, not illusions crafted by a comatose monster.

Eventually, the sheer weight of fatigue pressed him to rest. He sank onto the living room couch, his heart still beating a fast, vigilant cadence. With a soft, weary exhale, he flipped open the small, leather-bound notebook he used to document the mundane details of their defense: every patrol car that circled the block, every unfamiliar sedan parked two streets over, every flicker of motion at the neighbor's fence. He intended to jot down a final check for the night, a ritual to steady his mind.

But as he leaned forward, his gaze fell on the faint, jagged scar in the floorboards where a bullet had lodged months ago. It was a permanent mark of how Redwood Ridge's wrath had physically pierced their sanctuary. *We're not living in bullet holes and illusions anymore,* he reminded himself, gripping his pen so hard his knuckles whitened into stones. *We have each other now.* Letting the pen slip from his numb fingers, Quincy finally allowed himself a restless, shallow doze, his chin tilting forward until all he could hear was the endless, hypnotic patter of the rain.

Come dawn, a watery, anemic light filtered through the swollen clouds, casting the living room in shades of pale gray that did nothing to soften the jagged tension inside. Keesha woke first, her joints stiff from a night of bracing for impact. She found Quincy perched in a half-slumber on the couch, his hair tousled and the notebook still open in his lap like a shield. She approached him gently, her protective instincts flaring at the sight of his hunched, weary shoulders. There was a time, not long ago, when she'd borne the crushing burden of vigilance alone. Now, seeing Quincy so utterly consumed by their safety both comforted her and stung with a sharp, bitter guilt. She hated that their life was one that required a 24-hour sentry.

"Hey," she said, her voice scratchy and low from the night's humidity. "Did you get any rest at all?"

He blinked hard, rubbing his eyes like a man trying to physically scrub away a nightmare. Outside, the storm had softened to a persistent, gray drizzle. "Some," he muttered, straightening his back with a wince. "I'm fine, Keesha. I've got the perimeter."

Keesha's frown told him she knew he was lying, but she didn't push. She remembered the first time he'd insisted on sleeping in that armchair by the door—how she'd listened to him pacing the floorboards in the small hours, a man at war with his own perceived failures. "I'm making coffee," she murmured. "You look like you need it more than I do."

He gave a grateful nod, his gaze immediately drifting over her shoulder to the window. Water dripped from the eaves, tapping the porch with a hollow, metronomic rhythm. The day felt poised on a knife's edge, caught between the exhaustion of the storm and the hush of whatever Redwood Ridge was planning next. *We have to keep going,* he thought. Each morning was a minor miracle—another day they hadn't been pulled back into the gyre.

Grace stirred around eight, the rhythmic *tap-tap* of her cane echoing softly against the hallway walls. The oversized sweatshirt she wore seemed to swallow her still-slender frame, making her look younger and more fragile than she was. Her hair was pulled into a sleep-mussed ponytail, and her eyes carried the heavy weight of a child who had seen too much. Keesha was at her side in an instant, a hand hovering near her elbow to ensure she didn't slip on the humidity-slicked tiles.

"How's the leg?" Quincy asked, his voice softening as he watched her navigate to the kitchen table.

Grace shrugged, a shadow flickering behind her eyes. "It aches. But I can manage," she replied, forcing a small smile that didn't quite reach her gaze. Beneath the surface, her mind was a carousel of the same questions that had kept her awake. "I'm more worried about them. Redwood Ridge." The words dropped into the room like a lead weight, heavy and cold.

Keesha set a plate of eggs and toast in front of her, the domesticity of the act feeling like a thin veneer over a deep crack. "Eat," she said firmly, resting a hand on Grace's shoulder. "We need your strength. We're heading to Dr. Flores's office for the scans, and then we have to talk to Detective Rodriguez about what Corinne told us."

Grace's appetite vanished instantly. "Do you think they'll try something today?" Her voice trembled, reflecting the private terrors of her dreams—hooded figures gliding past the security cameras, chanting in a language that bypassed the ears and went straight to the bone.

"I don't know," Keesha admitted, her grip on Grace's shoulder tightening into a silent promise. "But I'm not taking chances. Not ever again."

The drive to the medical suite was a study in paranoia. Quincy gripped the steering wheel, his eyes constantly checking the side mirrors for any sign of a black sedan or a robed figure standing too still on a street corner. Grace sat in the passenger seat, pressing herself into the upholstery, watching the rain-slicked city roll by like a series of potential ambush points.

Dr. Flores's office was a sterile oasis of buzzing fluorescent lights and the scent of medicinal alcohol. The doctor emerged wearing a supportive brace—a grim reminder of the literal scars she bore from the Redwood Ridge confrontation at the cabin.

"Grace," she greeted, her voice a calm anchor in their sea of nerves. "Let's head back to the exam room."

Heart pounding, Grace followed her. The space was lined with cold, white equipment that seemed to watch her. Keesha and Quincy stayed close, their presence the only thing keeping her upright. A small EEG machine was already set up, its leads like tangled spiders. Flores guided Grace to a reclined seat, carefully attaching electrodes around her temples.

"Just like before," Flores said, her tone soothing as she checked the connections. "We'll take a quick look at your brain patterns. We're looking for any residue, Grace. Any sign of abnormal resonance."

Grace closed her eyes, the familiar hum of the EEG machine stirring a deep, cellular dread. She remembered being hooked up while trapped in Darius's body, the feeling of her soul being a broadcast on a frequency that wasn't hers. *No tether. I'm me. I'm Grace,* she chanted internally. She tried to picture the Redwood Ridge illusions, forcibly banishing the hooded figures to the back of her mind.

Minutes crawled by. The only sound was the scratching of the machine's internal printer. Flores studied the EEG lines, her expression inscrutable. Keesha hovered near the wall, her knuckles white. A fresh bolt of thunder rattled the windows, causing her to flinch. Outside, the storm's rumble lingered, sounding like a low, menacing chant.

At last, Flores exhaled, a genuine smile breaking through her professional mask. "Everything looks normal. No abnormal spikes, no wave patterns that suggest intrusion." She gently peeled off the electrodes, eyes meeting Grace's. "From a purely medical standpoint, Grace, your mind is clear. The link is gone."

Grace let out a shaky, hysterical laugh, tears pricking her eyes. "Good," she whispered. Free. The word rang in her thoughts, though she knew the psychological walls would take longer to rebuild than the neural ones.

Keesha stepped forward and hugged her daughter tightly. "You hear that?" she murmured against Grace's hair. "You're free."

Across the room, Quincy's tense posture relaxed, just a fraction. A weight lifted from his chest, though a kernel of worry remained: Redwood Ridge didn't care about medical proof. "So medically, we're in the clear," he said, voice measured. "But they won't believe that."

Flores nodded somberly. "They might try forcing a new link if they got hold of her. We can't let that happen."

The meeting with Detective Rodriguez at the precinct was no more comforting. The station was a cacophony of ringing phones and radio static. Rodriguez stood in a side corridor, her eyes bloodshot.

"Corinne gave us more details," she said, leading them into an interview room. "She confirmed Redwood Ridge is fixated on you, Grace. They want you alive because they believe your presence can spark Darius's mind back to consciousness. If that fails... they may turn to more violent means of 'reclamation.'"

Grace's stomach twisted. "So even without a tether, they'll try to make one?"

Rodriguez nodded. "That's the gist." She tapped a map on the table. "Corinne pointed out a handful of safe houses—an abandoned motel, a storage facility, plus some hidden cabins near the forest. We've got teams scouting, but they're masters of hiding in plain sight."

Keesha's expression hardened. "What do we do?"

Rodriguez hesitated. "Stay under watch. Consider relocating to a safehouse. Redwood Ridge is a cornered beast, and beasts strike hard when they're desperate."

Grace pressed her lips together, recalling her childhood room, her half-finished sketches, the smell of her home. "I don't want to run," she whispered. "We've barely reclaimed our life."

Quincy set a reassuring hand on her back. "Sometimes caution is the best call," he said, though the regret in his eyes spoke of how much he wished they could simply live unafraid.

By evening, they returned home under police escort. The sky had bruised to a deep, bruised purple. Once inside, they hovered near the entry, listening to the patrol car pull away. It should have felt safe—locked doors, new cameras—but the hush that settled felt more like a grim ceasefire than peace.

Dinner was a subdued affair of warm leftovers. Grace's mind drifted, replaying Redwood Ridge's chants like a memory that refused to fade. Keesha noticed the distant look in her daughter's eyes and gently offered to help her organize her art supplies. Grace agreed, wanting to ground herself in something she once loved.

She turned a pencil over in her hand at her desk. Her lines trembled, but with effort, she sketched a swirl of shapes across a blank page—nonsensical patterns, but each careful stroke felt like reclaiming a tiny piece of herself. Keesha watched from the doorway, pride and heartbreak warring on her features.

In the living room, Quincy checked the new camera feeds on his phone. The memory of the illusions cornering him burned like old scar tissue. Outside, thunder growled, urging him to stay vigilant. After a while, Grace emerged from her bedroom, cane tapping softly. She sank onto the couch beside him. "Any sign of them?" she asked.

He shook his head, turning his phone so she could see the silent feeds. "Not a flicker."

She managed a faint smile. "That's good. I guess."

Keesha joined them, and the three formed a circle, survivors in a lifeboat. "We should decide," Keesha said, her tone reflecting the tension of the day. "Detective Rodriguez suggested a safehouse. I'll do whatever keeps Grace safe."

Grace ran her thumb over the handle of her cane. "I'm torn," she admitted. "Part of me wants to hide. Another part wants them to see we're not scared. But... I *am* scared."

Quincy laid a steadying hand over hers. "Whatever we choose, we face it together. Redwood Ridge thrives on fear. We can't let them corner us."

Silence followed, broken only by the patter of fresh rain. In that hush, they weighed the cost of staying versus fleeing. Eventually, Keesha cleared her throat. "Maybe let's wait and see if Rodriguez's next raid yields any arrests. If they get cornered, maybe they'll give up." Her eyes flicked to Grace, hope mingling with sorrow. "And if they don't, we'll reconsider the safehouse."

No one voiced the darker possibility: if Redwood Ridge couldn't have Grace, they might lash out in ways no locked door could stop.

At last, night deepened. The rain tapped a lullaby on the roof as Grace, worn to the bone, returned to her room. Quincy resumed his vigilance, making a circuit of the hallway. Keesha lingered in the living room, watching him pass. She felt a surge of gratitude so powerful it stung.

"We'll rest eventually," she murmured, standing by the hallway lamp.

He nodded slowly. In the golden glow, their eyes met—a mingling of love, loyalty, and that persistent undercurrent of dread. Outside, the storm carried on, its restless susurration bearing witness to the fragile calm within. Grace drifted to sleep, sketchbook clutched to her chest, while Keesha looked out the rain-spattered window. Quincy stood at the window, fingers near the lock, phone in hand, his old vow resonating: *Never again.* Together, they awaited the dawn, spirits braced against a storm that was anything but over.

Chapter 16: Shifting Currents

A leaden dawn seeped through the windows of the Marshall home, the quiet broken only by the steady, rhythmic drip of the previous night's rain from the gutters. The storm had passed, yet its ominous weight lingered in the humid air, as though the skies themselves knew the danger was far from over. The faint gray light illuminated the living room with an unforgiving clarity, highlighting scuff marks on the hardwood—jagged reminders of the rushed exits and frantic, desperate movements that had defined their lives for far too long.

In the living room, Quincy stirred on the couch. He'd dozed off with one hand still clamped around his phone, the faint, dying glow of the security app illuminating his exhausted, stubbled features. A sharp crack of stiffness ran through his neck as he sat up slowly, blinking against the intrusive pale light. It took him a heartbeat to place the heavy hush that surrounded him. *Morning already.* He had intended to stay awake all night, a self-appointed sentinel, but at some point, the sheer gravity of fatigue had finally pulled him under.

As he shifted, he caught sight of Keesha. She was already awake, seated in the armchair near the window like a gargoyle carved from grief and resolve. Her arms were wrapped tightly around her knees, an empty mug perched precariously on the side table. She wore her usual expression of guarded composure, but the distant, hollow look in her eyes suggested she'd been lost in the labyrinth of her own worries for hours.

"Morning," Quincy murmured, his voice rough and gravelly with fatigue. He felt a sharp pang of guilt for having dozed; he'd promised himself he wouldn't let his guard down for even a second.

Keesha lifted her gaze, a small, flickering shadow of relief crossing her features. They had both been on a war footing for so long that a single unguarded moment felt like a dangerous luxury. She offered a tired smile that stalled long before it reached her eyes. "Morning," she echoed, her voice subdued and thin. She gestured vaguely to the mug. "Coffee's cold, but there's a fresh pot in the kitchen."

Quincy massaged the back of his neck, rising to his feet with a series of muffled groans from his joints. He noticed how the lines of stress were etched a bit deeper into Keesha's face today—dark semicircles beneath her eyes that spoke of a thousand-yard stare. *She's been through too much,* he thought, recalling the night he'd sworn to protect her and Grace at any cost. The house was eerily still: no sound of Grace stirring yet, no patrolling car passing by the front window. *Must be shift change,* he told himself. Even so, the quiet felt unnatural—a predatory hush that signaled Redwood Ridge might be repositioning their pieces on the board.

Before Quincy could make it to the kitchen, a soft, uneven shuffle in the hallway announced Grace's arrival. Her cane tapped against the carpet—*thump, slide, thump*—each step deliberate and heavy with effort. She appeared in the living room threshold, her hair a tousled mess and her eyes flicking warily around the space, as though half-expecting robed figures to materialize from the peeling wallpaper.

"Hey, Gracie," Keesha said gently, unfolding her arms to welcome her. "Sleep okay?"

Grace managed a non-committal shrug, her expression betraying the jagged, unsettled dreams that still haunted the edges of her mind. "Better than before, I guess. No illusions." She paused, her gaze landing on the cold, rain-blurred windows that looked out toward the tree line. "But I kept imagining them out there. All those hooded figures...

just standing in the dark. Chanting my name." Her voice caught for a moment—admitting the fear aloud made it a physical thing in the room.

Keesha rose to guide her to the couch, her touch light but firm. She remembered that same paralyzing fear from her own nightmares. "We're here," she reminded her daughter softly. "And the police are right outside. We won't be caught off guard again." A pang of fierce determination flickered in Keesha's chest. After watching Grace suffer through the horror of Darius's possession, she refused to let the cult claim another inch of their peace.

Quincy reappeared with two fresh cups of coffee, handing one to Keesha and offering Grace a glass of juice. He noticed how Grace's fingers trembled slightly around the glass, her knuckles whitening—a telltale sign of the internal battle she was fighting just to remain present. He recalled the first time he saw Grace attempt a simple task while her mind was still tangled in the aftermath of the swap; it had been bizarre and heartbreaking. Seeing her in her rightful form gave him hope, but it also served as a constant reminder of how fragile their victory truly was.

"Maybe we should get out for a little while," Grace said, her voice surprising them both. It trembled with a volatile mix of eagerness and terror. "Just for a drive, or a short walk in the park—something normal. Please." There was a raw plea in her eyes, a glimpse of the girl who once found joy in the smallest, sun-drenched outings.

Keesha hesitated, her eyes meeting Quincy's in a silent, worried dialogue. Even the idea of leaving the house felt loaded, like stepping onto a broader, unshielded battleground. "Are you sure, baby?" she asked quietly, her motherly instincts warring with the memory of the cult's cunning, psychological illusions.

Grace nodded, swallowing hard against the lump in her throat. "I'm tired of feeling like a prisoner in my own house." She tightened her grip on the cane, as though steeling herself for the very real possibility that Redwood Ridge might be lurking behind every oak tree in the city.

Something in her tone—a stubborn, jagged edge anchored by lingering trauma—made Keesha's heart twist. She understood the desperate desire to reclaim a fragment of an ordinary life. *We can't hide in the dark forever,* she thought, forcing down the bile of her own rising anxiety. "We can see how you feel after a quick outing," she offered gently. "But we'll text Rodriguez first. No exceptions."

Quincy set down his coffee, his jaw set. His protective instincts flared at the notion of letting Grace venture into the open, but he also saw the iron determination in her eyes. "I'll make sure the patrol car's aware of our route. Better safe than sorry."

They left late that morning, Grace insisting on walking from the porch to the car without leaning too heavily on Quincy's arm. The simple act carried a weight of significance that all three felt but didn't voice: Grace was standing on her own, reclaiming the physical space she'd nearly lost. A patrol car idled at the end of the block, its engine humming with a quiet, mechanical vigilance. Detective Rodriguez had texted back almost immediately:

> **Rodriguez (9:02 AM):** Understood. Let us know which park. We'll keep an unmarked unit nearby. Stay on the main paths.

Grace felt a pang of guilt at needing such suffocating supervision, but the fear of Redwood Ridge pressed at her more heavily than the police presence ever could. *I have to do this,* she thought, *or I'll never stop hiding.* She recalled the times she had cowered under Darius's illusions, the feeling of being buried alive in her own mind. Never again.

The short drive to the local park was tense, marked by a silence so thick it was hard to breathe. Grace stared out the window at rows of sleepy, suburban houses—children's bicycles left on porches, the occasional neighbor retrieving mail in their bathrobe. Everything looked startlingly, offensively normal, which only magnified her sense of profound unease. *How is it that the world can look so calm,* she wondered, *when mine has been turned inside out?*

When they arrived at the small, tree-lined park, Quincy parked as close to the entrance as possible. It was a modest space—a winding path, a duck pond, and a scattering of weathered wooden benches. A handful of joggers and dog-walkers passed by, entirely oblivious to the swirl of cult fanaticism and federal complications that had consumed the Marshalls.

Grace stepped out, her cane clicking against the asphalt as she inhaled the crisp, post-storm air. She could smell damp grass and the faint, sweet scent of blooming azaleas. For a fleeting moment, the tension in her shoulders eased. She remembered coming here with Keesha years ago, feeding breadcrumbs to the ducks and squealing with laughter when they flocked too close. The memory of her younger, untainted self stung her chest: *How much have I lost since then?*

Keesha kept pace beside her, her arms poised instinctively to catch her daughter if her leg gave out. Though the setting was peaceful, worry flashed across Keesha's features every time a stranger passed too close or a car slowed down near the curb. Meanwhile, Quincy trailed slightly behind, his eyes constantly scanning the perimeter like a radar. He was a silent protector, keeping a mental catalog of every face, matching each figure to the park's innocuous routine and looking for the one that didn't fit.

They managed a slow, grueling circuit around the pond, eventually pausing so Grace could sit on a wooden bench. Her breath came in shallow, ragged gasps—her muscles were still weak from the months of disuse—but a small, triumphant smile tugged at the corners of her lips. "We did it," she said softly, "and no Redwood Ridge in sight." Her eyes glistened with relief, but also the crushing weight of knowing this was only a single step in a very long journey.

Keesha brushed a stray hair from Grace's forehead. The gentle, maternal contact eased some of the lingering static in both of them. "Step by step," she murmured, echoing the mantra that had carried them through the worst of the body-swap nights. *We're healing. Even if they try to pull us back, we'll hold on to every victory.*

Yet even as Grace caught her breath, a chill prickled at the nape of Quincy's neck. He cast a surreptitious glance around the park. A woman jogged past with earbuds in; a man tossed a tennis ball for a lanky retriever. No black cloaks, no rhythmic chanting. But a single unmarked sedan sat near the curb—Rodriguez's people, presumably—watching from behind tinted glass, a grim reminder that this moment of calm was carefully, artificially orchestrated.

"Everything okay?" Keesha asked, noticing Quincy's scanning gaze. She recognized that specific tension; she'd seen it grow into a permanent part of him since the night the illusions nearly swallowed them whole.

He forced a half-smile that didn't reach his eyes. "Force of habit, Keesh." In truth, every shift of motion in the periphery made him want to check if a member of the Ridge lurked behind a tree. He couldn't banish the memory of his senses fracturing—he could still hear the ghost of Darius's mocking laughter vibrating in his ears.

After a few more minutes, Grace exhaled, her shoulders sagging with a sudden onset of fatigue. The outing, though brief, had taxed her more than she cared to admit. "I'm worn out. Maybe we should head back now."

Keesha helped her to her feet, her hand steady on Grace's back. Quincy kept watch, phone in hand, until they were settled back into the safety of the SUV. The drive home was marked by an odd, heavy stillness, as though they were all bracing for something to jump out from the mundane scenery. But they reached their street unchallenged, the patrol car still stationed discreetly nearby like a silent, mechanical sentinel.

Grace let out a breath she hadn't realized she was holding when they stepped back inside the house. "I know it was just a tiny outing," she said, leaning heavily on her cane, "but it felt huge." Her voice quivered with the exhausting conflict of relief and the residual terror that Redwood Ridge had hardwired into her.

Keesha smiled, gently guiding her back to the sanctuary of the couch. "It *is* huge," she said firmly. "This is your life, Grace. You get to do normal things—walk in the park, feed the ducks—without them looming over you. We won't let them take that away." *And I won't let them take you away again, either,* she promised silently, remembering the soul-deep despair of almost losing her daughter to a monster's mind.

Grace blinked back hot tears, overwhelmed by a surge of gratitude and the lingering, cold dread. "Thanks," she whispered. "Both of you." She looked from her mother to Quincy, sensing the staggering depth of the commitment they had made to shield her, even if it meant living in a state of permanent, exhausting vigilance.

Quincy set the grocery bag on the counter—he'd insisted on picking up some fresh produce on the way back—and joined them, his posture still taut and ready for a fight. "We're a team," he said quietly. "Always." He cast a quick, involuntary glance at the windows, half-expecting to see a black-robed silhouette against the glass. *Not today. Not ever again, if I have any say in it.*

They hadn't even had time to settle before the phone on the console rang. Keesha checked the caller ID: *Anonymous.* Her heart skipped a beat, a jolt of pure adrenaline shooting through her nervous system. She hesitated, her hand hovering over the receiver, then finally picked up.

"Hello?"

The line crackled with a sterile, high-frequency hiss. For a split second, she thought it might be the cult, calling with some cryptic, rhyming threat. Then a calm, terrifyingly level voice spoke. "Mrs. Marshall, this is Agent Weston. I need to speak with Grace."

Keesha's grip on the receiver tightened until her plastic groaned. Memories of the uneasy glances and veiled, bureaucratic comments from Weston replayed in her mind like a warning track. "Grace doesn't speak to anyone without going through Detective Rodriguez," she said, her tone ice-cold, maternal protectiveness flaring like a physical heat.

A faint, calculated pause. "I understand your caution, Mrs. Marshall. But there are developments with Redwood Ridge—and specifically 'Project Redwood'—that I believe she should be aware of. Matters that concern her immediate safety."

Keesha swallowed, her throat dry. She glanced at Grace, who was watching her intently, her face turning a ghostly shade of pale. "What developments?"

"I'd prefer not to discuss the specifics of a federal investigation over an unsecured line," Weston replied smoothly, his voice like silk over gravel. "May I come by? Or you can meet me at the local precinct, if that makes you feel more secure."

Her eyes flicked to Grace, who looked stricken by the thought of yet another clinical intrusion. Keesha's spine stiffened, a wave of cold indignation swelling in her gut. "No," she said, her voice like iron. "You can talk to Detective Rodriguez first. You're not cornering my daughter today."

Another pause—longer this time, dripping with unspoken pressure. "You realize we're all working toward the same goal: keeping the Ridge from harming anyone else. But if you insist on being difficult, I'll route the information through the detective. Just know that time is a luxury we don't have."

"Please do," Keesha replied, then hung up before he could argue or manipulate her further. She exhaled shakily, setting the phone down as if it were a live grenade. That one call had effortlessly undone every fragile sense of safety they had cultivated at the park.

"What was that?" Grace asked, her nerves taut as bowstrings, her hand gripping the couch cushion so hard the fabric bunched.

"Agent Weston," Keesha said, her face set in a grim mask. "He wants to speak to you directly about the cult. I told him no. He's not coming near you."

A heavy hush fell over the room. Quincy's jaw clenched so hard a muscle in his cheek began to twitch. *Weston just won't quit,* he thought, recalling the man's calculating, predatory stare. "He's not giving up," Quincy observed grimly. "He sees the Ridge as a threat, but I doubt he cares much about Grace's peace of mind. To him, she's just a variable in an equation."

Keesha nodded, a new kind of dread gnawing at her. "I need to call Rodriguez. Now. I need to warn her about Weston's persistence."

In a nondescript motel room a few miles away, Agent Weston ended the call, frustration simmering just beneath his measured, professional expression. He tapped a silver pen against his open notebook, scanning the scribbled notes about Redwood Ridge's known members, rumored hideouts, and the alleged psychic link they believed still existed between Grace and the comatose Darius King.

If Redwood Ridge is to be stopped, we need to understand the architecture of that link, he thought, and the ticking of the clock felt like a physical weight. *And time is running out.*

He typed another curt, encrypted message to a Bureau contact, requesting an immediate update on "Project Redwood." If the cult was preparing a more drastic move—and if Grace was indeed the crucial component—they might need to take her into protective custody, regardless of her family's objections. Weston frowned, conscious of how that approach could backfire and trigger a public relations disaster. But the intel suggested the Ridge's next ritual might be catastrophic. For him, the end always justified whatever means it took to neutralize a threat of this magnitude.

By late afternoon, another band of dark, heavy clouds rolled in from the west, rumbling low across the sky like distant artillery. The temperature dropped sharply, turning the air thick, damp, and restless. In the hidden glades of Redwood Ridge, Marta DeLeón surveyed her devoted followers in a ragged clearing lit by a ring of flickering, soot-stained lanterns.

"The time approaches," she intoned, her voice echoing in the eerie hush of the forest. "Darius sleeps in a cage of flesh, but our incantations stir his mind. Soon, we must retrieve him—or retrieve the piece of his divinity that still resides within Grace Marshall." Her tone dripped with a terrifying fervor, her eyes reflecting an obsession that had crossed the line into madness.

Her followers bowed low, murmuring prayers in the old, guttural tongues. One figure stepped forward, his voice trembling with a mix of awe and terror. "How will we reach her? The police watch her house like hawks. The perimeter is tight."

Marta's eyes gleamed with a predatory light in the lantern glow. "I have ways they cannot fathom. Patience," she hissed, an edge of sharp anger in her tone. "We will not fail him again. Not after all we have sacrificed." She recalled the night they lost Grace—Darius's most prized tether—and the way his fury had echoed in her own mind. Now, she would see that fury reignited by any means necessary.

Outside the ring of light, the wind stirred the ancient pines, carrying the faint, metallic tang of ozone. The faithful clenched their hands in fervent, desperate devotion, each breath a silent vow to see their master rise. All for Darius. All for the power the Ridge promised.

Back at the Marshall home, the lights flickered and dimmed in response to the gathering storm outside. Grace leaned against the back of the couch, her mind churning with the phone call from Weston, the ominous hints of the cult's new plan, and her own agonizing yearning for normalcy. She tried to banish the memory of the illusions—the robed men chasing her through a forest of her own making—and tried to focus on the mundane details of the living room: her worn sketchbook, the faint, comforting ticking of the clock. But the heaviness in her chest refused to lift.

Keesha ended a tense, whispered conversation with Rodriguez—who had promised to intercept any further attempts from Weston to corner Grace. "Rodriguez says she'll handle him," Keesha said, placing the phone aside with a definitive *clack*. "He can't just force an interrogation without a warrant or her presence." She tried to project a confidence she didn't entirely feel, though a knot of worry remained lodged in her throat.

Grace let out a long, shaky breath, her shoulders easing slightly. But something told her the cult would force the issue, even if the FBI didn't. "He still thinks I'm some... key," she muttered, recalling how Darius had once bragged about her "boundless potential" while he occupied her mind.

Quincy glanced at the new camera feed on his phone. "Still quiet outside," he said, though the tension never left his voice. "Let's hope the storm keeps them in their holes tonight." Hope felt like a very fragile shield against the Ridge's cunning.

It didn't.

Right around dusk, as the wind picked up and the rain began to lash against the siding again, a sharp flash of light caught Quincy's eye on the security app. He zoomed in on the backyard camera, his heart rate spiking. At first, it seemed like just a reflection of headlights passing in the alley. But the flicker came again—closer this time, dancing along the top of the fence line.

Keesha, noticing his sudden, statuesque stillness, moved to his side. "Quincy? What is it?"

His jaw clenched until it ached. He was reliving the memory of the illusions dancing across the perimeter months ago. "Not sure. Could be a lens flare." But the cold tightness in his tone betrayed the depth of his worry.

Grace, cane in hand, approached them, her eyes wide. "Redwood Ridge?" The words came out in a terrified hush, the sound of a child fearing the monster under the bed was finally climbing out.

He forced a calming breath, though his heart thudded against his ribs. "Could be a trick of the shadows and the rain. Let me check it out. Stay here." He refused to let a repeat of those illusions paralyze him.

Leaving Keesha and Grace in the living room, Quincy donned a rain jacket and stepped onto the back porch. The alley lay wet, black, and empty. The neighbor's yard was silent except for a single flickering floodlight that hummed with a failing ballast. His boots sank into the damp, muddy grass as he shone a high-powered flashlight into the corners of the yard. Nothing. Not even a stray cat.

Yet the uneasy feeling remained, a prickling along his skin like a static charge. Quincy scanned the fence line, recalling the cunning of the illusions that had once ensnared his senses. The memory still tightened his chest like a vice. "Just nerves," he muttered to himself, though he didn't believe it, as he returned inside.

Keesha and Grace were waiting, their faces etched with anxiety. "All clear," Quincy reported, though his expression was far from relaxed. "Might've been a weird reflection from the neighbor's light." He didn't mention the faint hum of tension vibrating under his skin—an animal instinct telling him that the Ridge was creeping closer, testing the boundaries.

Despite his reassurances, each of them sensed the looming weight—the feeling that Redwood Ridge was near, or that Agent Weston's meddling was about to escalate into something they couldn't stop. The hush that descended bore the echo of thunder beyond the windows, a threat that refused to dissipate with the morning sun.

Night fell, and the household locked down once more—curtains drawn tight, doors double-bolted, phones at the ready. Keesha made a pot of chamomile tea, hoping the ritual would soothe their rattled nerves. She remembered how, not long ago, sharing tea with Grace was a simple pleasure. Now it felt like a barrier, a desperate attempt to hold the encroaching chaos at bay.

Grace sipped hers slowly, each swallow a reminder she was alive and free in her own body. *I've come so far,* she reminded herself, clutching the warm mug. *I won't let them drag me back into the dark.* But a flicker of dread tugged at her whenever she imagined the chanting, or Agent Weston's quiet, calculated, and predatory questions.

The hours ticked past in a state of uneasy quiet, each occupant lost in the geography of their own thoughts. Quincy periodically circled the house, shining a flashlight across the windows, checking the app for motion alerts that never came. His footsteps echoed in the hallway—each step a defiant march against the shadows that had once bested him. Keesha busied herself tidying the kitchen—organizing the same stack of dishes three times—though her gaze drifted to the front door at every small, innocuous noise. Grace, drained from her earlier outing, lay on the couch with a thick blanket over her legs, her sketchbook nearby. She tried to draw a simple scene—the duck pond they'd visited—but her pencil lines felt shaky and haunted by glimpses of torchlit gatherings in the forest.

Eventually, Keesha sank onto the couch beside her daughter, pulling the blanket higher around Grace's shoulders. "Tomorrow, Dr. Flores again," she said softly, hoping the mention of something structured and clinical would help ground them. "We'll confirm you're healing well." She paused, an unspoken *and that the cult hasn't seized any secret hold on you* lingering behind her words.

Grace nodded, her eyes half-lidded with exhaustion. She thought about how Dr. Flores's tests had become oddly comforting—a scientific proof that she was truly herself. "Then maybe in a few days, I'll see my friends. Act like life's normal again." Her voice wavered on the last word—*normal* felt like a foreign language she was struggling to relearn.

Keesha smiled, brushing a gentle, trembling hand over Grace's forehead. "Exactly. Normal is coming back, Grace." She forced a warmth into her tone, praying the Ridge wouldn't shatter that hope before the sun rose.

Midnight approached, the neighborhood cloaked in a heavy, wet quiet once more. Quincy stationed himself by the living room window, phone in hand, his gaze fixed on the watery reflection of the streetlamps outside. The rain had started up again, tapping a muted, frantic rhythm against the glass. Behind him, Keesha dozed fitfully in the armchair, her arms crossed over her chest in a posture of weary, habitual defense. Grace had finally slipped into her room, wanting the privacy to wrestle her worries alone.

Lightning flickered in the distance, illuminating the yard for a jagged instant. Quincy peered outside—nothing moved, no hooded figures, no shadows out of place. The tension, however, lived in the walls, emanating from every battered, traumatic memory they shared.

He found his thoughts circling back to Corinne's warning: Redwood Ridge believed they could yank Grace into another ritual, rebind her to the monster in the hospital. *Not on my watch,* he vowed, his fingers tightening around the phone until his knuckles ached. *If they try to step onto this property tonight, they'll find me waiting, illusions be damned.*

As the hours wore on, no chanting swelled from the yard, and no illusions clawed at the windows. For the moment, Redwood Ridge seemed content to bide its time—or so Quincy told himself, uncertain which prospect was worse: an immediate, violent confrontation or this nerve-fraying, psychological limbo. He tried to remind himself that quiet could be a good thing. It could be, but deep down, he knew the Ridge was cunning enough to strike only when they felt the Marshalls were finally letting their guard down.

When Grace finally drifted into a troubled sleep in her bedroom, Keesha stirred from her light doze in the armchair. She joined Quincy at the window, her arms hugging her torso, her posture a testament to how many times she'd woken up to face the same old terrors.

"Think we'll ever have a normal day again?" she asked quietly, her voice carrying an ache that resonated deep in Quincy's chest. She recalled how, once upon a time, her biggest worry was paying the electric bill on time and making sure Grace finished her long division.

He glanced at her, the corners of his mouth lifting in a soft, bittersweet smile that didn't quite reach the shadows in his eyes. "We'll make one," he said, a quiet conviction burning in his tone. "For you, for Grace... for ourselves." He thought of how Keesha's trembling had softened in his arms once, and how the lines of fear on Grace's face had eased when she realized she was not alone. That memory fueled him now.

Outside, the storm eased into a slow, steady drizzle, each drop reflecting the streetlamp's amber glow like tiny sparks dancing in the gloom. Quincy gently looped an arm around Keesha's shoulders, and she let herself lean into him, comforted by his unwavering, solid presence. Together, they watched the rain trace jagged patterns down the glass—neither illusions nor intruders appearing, at least for this fleeting, stolen night.

At least for tonight, they had this fragile, hard-won calm. Tomorrow would bring new tests—questions from Agent Weston, possible sightings of the robed men, and the crushing weight of the unknown—but for the next few hours, they stood in quiet defiance against the fear that stalked them. Their hearts were steady, their eyes were open, waiting for the dawn and the promise that it might carry them one small step closer to reclaiming the life they had lost.

And in that heavy hush, as the rain beat a steady, ancient lullaby on the roof, the Marshall house remained vigilant, love holding firm against the next wave of shadows creeping ever nearer on the horizon. The three of them, weary but unbroken, ate slowly as the storm outside intensified, lightning flashing in the windows. Each flicker seemed to highlight the new paint that covered the old bullet holes, the replaced doors that had once splintered under Darius's assault. And yet in that same light, they looked like a family—worn, but holding tight to each other in the gloom.

As the evening wore on, Grace retired early, leaning on her cane for support. Quincy offered to help, but she insisted she could manage. Keesha lingered, clearing plates while thunder reverberated through the windows. Eventually, only the soft glow of a single lamp remained, illuminating Quincy's quiet vigil by the couch.

He watched Keesha sink onto the cushions, exhaustion etched into her posture. "You should rest," he said gently.

She gave him a weary, grateful smile. "You too. But I know you'll be up, checking locks all night."

Quincy let out a low chuckle. "You know me too well."

For a moment, they just looked at each other. In that hush, the depth of their connection thrummed—rooted in shared trauma, strengthened by mutual devotion. Gently, Quincy pulled Keesha into a warm embrace, feeling her exhale against his chest. "Sleep," he murmured. "I'll keep watch."

She nodded, her head tucked firmly under his chin. "I know."

About the Author

Landon Prosser is a North Carolina native who crafts gripping psychological thrillers and crime mysteries. Rooted in a love for family and life's everyday moments, Landon's writing explores the tension, twists, and human drama that arise when ordinary people face extraordinary threats. When not weaving suspenseful tales, he cherishes time with his loved ones, drawing inspiration from the bonds that make life both precious and worth defending.

www.ingramcontent.com/pod-product-compliance
Lightning Source LLC
LaVergne TN
LVHW090604110826
845146LV00001B/259